Julian Symons is primarily reme art of crime writing. However, ir produced an enormously varied k military history, biography and cri touched upon with remarkable success, and ne held a distinguished reputation in each field.

His novels were consistently highly individual and expertly crafted, raising him above other crime writers of his day. It is for this that he was awarded various prizes, and, in 1982, named as Grand Master of the Mystery Writers of America – an honour accorded to only three other English writers before him: Graham Greene, Eric Ambler and Daphne du Maurier. He succeeded Agatha Christie as the president of Britain's Detection Club, a position he held from 1976 to 1985, and in 1990 he was awarded the Cartier Diamond Dagger from the British Crime Writers for his lifetime's achievement in crime fiction.

Symons died in 1994.

The
Paper Chase

Julian Symons

HOUSE OF
STRATUS

Copyright © 1956, 2001 Julian Symons
Introduction Copyright © 2001 H R F Keating

This edition published in 2001 by House of Stratus, an imprint of
Stratus Holdings plc, 24c Old Burlington Street, London, W1X 1RL, UK.

www.houseofstratus.com

Typeset, printed and bound by House of Stratus.

A catalogue record for this book is available from the British Library.

ISBN 1-84232-918-9

INTRODUCTION

The French call a typewriter *une machine á ècrire*. It is a description that could well be applied to Julian Symons, except the writing he produced had nothing about it smelling of the mechanical. The greater part of his life was devoted to putting pen to paper. Appearing in 1938, his first book was a volume of poetry, *Confusions About X*. In 1996, after his death, there came his final crime novel, *A Sort of Virtue* (written even though he knew he was under sentence from an inoperable cancer) beautifully embodying the painful come-by lesson that it is possible to achieve at least a degree of good in life.

His crime fiction put him most noticeably into the public eye, but he wrote in many forms: biographies, a memorable piece of autobiography (*Notes from Another Country*), poetry, social history, literary criticism coupled with year-on-year reviewing and two volumes of military history, and one string thread runs through it all. Everywhere there is a hatred of hypocrisy, hatred even when it aroused the delighted fascination with which he chronicled the siren schemes of that notorious jingoist swindler, Horatio Bottomley, both in his biography of the man and fictionally in *The Paper Chase* and *The Killing of Francie Lake*.

That hatred, however, was not a spew but a well-spring. It lay behind what he wrote and gave it force, yet it was always tempered by a need to speak the truth. Whether he was writing about people as fiction or as fact, if he had a low opinion of them he simply told the truth as he saw it, no more and no less.

i

This adherence to truth fills his novels with images of the mask. Often it is the mask of hypocrisy. When, as in *Death's Darkest Face* or *Something Like a Love Affair*, he chose to use a plot of dazzling legerdemain, the masks of cunning are startlingly ripped away.

The masks he ripped off most effectively were perhaps those which people put on their true faces when sex was in the air or under the exterior. 'Lift the stone, and sex crawls out from under,' says a character in that relentless hunt for truth, *The Progress of a Crime*, a book that achieved the rare feat for a British author, winning Symons the US Edgar Allen Poe Award.

Julian was indeed something of a pioneer in the fifties and sixties bringing into the almost sexless world of the detective story the truths of sexual situations. 'To exclude realism of description and language from the crime novel' he writes in *Critical Occasions*, 'is almost to prevent its practitioners from attempting any serious work.' And then the need to unmask deep-hidden secrecies of every sort was almost as necessary at the end of his crime-writing life as it had been at the beginning. Not for nothing was his last book subtitled *A Political Thriller*.

H R F Keating
London, 2001

Chapter One

"What do you feel about boys?"

"I like them," Charles Applegate replied. He blushed. The reply seemed ambiguous, and he tried to clarify it. "I like girls too." His blush deepened.

"We are coeducational, of course." Curly, white hair fluffed up charmingly round Mr Pont's shining pink skull. His face was pink too, the skin beautifully clear, the expression cherubic. "And what is your attitude towards religion?"

"I keep an open mind," Applegate said cautiously.

"Splendid. How valuable it is, the open mind. We try to inculcate into all our pupils... " Applegate waited expectantly, but Mr Pont left the sentence, as it were, hanging. "Food," he said suddenly.

"What's that?"

"We use the Brooker-Timla Health Guide. I expect you know it."

"No. But I'm sure that will be all right."

"Qualifications we have already dealt with." Mr Pont drew a grubby sheet of paper from his pocket and ticked off items with a pencil stub. "Free expression, you understand, we insist on. Freedom is our rule, within the rule of law. Who said that now, John Stuart Mill? Or was it my wife? Janine is a very remarkable woman. Sheets, pillowcases, rehabilitation of the maladjusted in a new cultural environment, impact of the self upon the non-self. Yes, we seem to have covered everything. We look forward to seeing you next term at Bramley."

Applegate gulped. "Money."

Mr Pont's rosebud mouth pursed itself, his expression became for a moment less cherubic than pettish.

"Money is not everything. We must all be prepared to make sacrifices for our ideals. A teacher in… " He abandoned this sentence too, and went into details. The sacrifice demanded was greater than Applegate had expected, but finally he agreed to Pont's terms. It was true, as Pont said, that he was not an experienced teacher. He consoled himself also with the thought that he did not intend to adopt teaching as a career.

Chapter Two

Three years before his interview with Mr Pont, Charles Applegate was suddenly removed from his placid life as an Oxford undergraduate when his father came home one day to his desirable modern residence at Sanderstead, took a revolver from his pocket, shot his wife through the heart and then placed the revolver in his own mouth and pulled the trigger. Mr Applegate, a respectable accountant, had been moved to this impetuous action by the existence of a gap of several thousand pounds between the actual and theoretical bank balance of Bruce, Morgan and Applegate, a firm of industrial engineers in which he held the position of secretary. Within every really respectable man a gambler lurks, desiring excess and ruin. Mr Applegate's excess had been conventional and not very interesting. He had played the stock market, and had been a persistent bear in what proved an intolerably bullish time. Hence the unbridgeable gap, the revolver shots, and Charles Applegate's removal from the still waters of the University into the whirlpool of life.

Applegate senior had been essentially a serious man. He was a churchwarden, said grace on Sundays, and had once addressed the local Rotary Club. After his parents' death Applegate junior, their only child, became determinedly casual in his habits and relationships. He cut himself free as far as possible from all entanglements, financial and emotional alike. He refused the job on a provincial newspaper found for him by his Uncle Roger, and wrote a short note to a very nice girl at Sanderstead who had considered herself more or less engaged to him, saying that he thought there was no point in seeing her again. The very nice girl, the daughter of a bank manager, was justifiably annoyed because he had anticipated the almost exactly similar letter which she had intended to write to him. In matters of the heart it is always wise to act promptly.

Applegate also wrote a detective story. It was called *Where Dons Delight,* and was a story of University life. The book probably owed its success to the fact that the dons who were its principal characters were not, like the dons in many detective stories, merely mean, envious and cunning. Applegate's dons were lustful, perverse and violent. One concealed behind a false book-front labelled *The Lives of the Christian Martyrs* a pornographic library that would have been the envy of Lord Houghton; another imagined himself a vampire bat at the full moon and developed a considerable skill as a cat-burglar so that he was able to appear, with home-made membranic wings terrifyingly outspread, at the windows of selected bedrooms. The real villain was a don who was killing off his students with doses of a newly developed drug, in an attempt to prove that their brainpower was temporarily increased.

Where Dons Delight was well received in England. "Grips like cement," said one well-known reviewer. "Get stuck into it." It was in the United States, however, that the book had its real success, for there many critics praised it as an outspoken, although no doubt exaggerated, attack on the standards of modern English education.

Applegate published this book under the pseudonym of Henry James. He had taken a job at Bramley because he hoped to set his second detective story in a progressive school.

Chapter Three

At Ashford Applegate changed, with a thin sprinkling of other travellers, on to the branch line that runs through Romney Marsh. There was a wait of several minutes. He bought a *New Statesman* at the bookstall, settled himself in an antique railway carriage, and turned to the advertisements. One in particular caught his attention. No doubt he had, subconsciously, been looking for it.

> At Bramley Hall we welcome "difficult" children or, as we prefer to call them, maladjusted personalities. By modern methods the maladjusted become attuned to society. No authoritarian pressures but creative work, not instruction but co-operation. Expert staff. Particular attention diet, hygiene. Jeremy Pont, MA and Janine Pont, Bramley Hall, near Murdstone, Kent.

Perfect, Applegate thought. He gave a small sigh of pleasure and looked up to find that the other occupant of the carriage was staring at him. Applegate stared back. He saw a long, thin man wearing a neat dark suit with a pin stripe, not very new perhaps, but clean and carefully pressed. The man's Homburg hat, beside him on the seat, was well brushed. Above a snowy shirt and stiff white collar was a long, narrow face composed in vertical and horizontal lines. Two strokes for the cheeks, meeting at the bottom in a long, pointed chin. Another for the beaky, thin-nostrilled nose, two more for the deep-grooved cheeks. Then the horizontal lines, two across the forehead giving an expression of permanent worry, and another line serving for the almost colourless lips. One small red circle, a virulent pimple on the left cheek. And below the lips the long, tapering chin was blue. The total expression was one of caution, even anxiety. Not the kind of man to speak to a stranger in a railway carriage, you would have said, but now he was speaking to Applegate.

"These carriages are filthy. If you would like a newspaper I have one to spare."

Applegate saw with amusement that his companion was sitting on a protecting layer of carefully folded newspaper. "Thank you. I don't think I'll bother."

The thin lips became, if possible, thinner. "You are unwise. All public transport is filthy. You know the Marsh?"

"I've never been down here before."

"Beautiful country." The voice was as neat as the man's appearance.

Applegate looked out of the window. He saw fields and a great many sheep. The prospect seemed to him ineffably dreary. Since leaving Oxford he had found that simple candour often produces a devastating effect. "Is it?"

The stranger wriggled with embarrassment, but did not stop talking. "In this spring weather – "

"When the east wind whips the stunted trees?" Applegate asked politely.

"Perhaps when it's a little warmer," the stranger conceded. There was something obsequious about him, Applegate thought, something eminently dislikeable in his sinuous wrigglings. "Are you going far?" he asked now.

"Bramley."

"I go on to Murdstone myself." Applegate knew that Murdstone was a small town on the coast. About the man's next words there seemed something especially meaningful. They were uttered in the same precise, colourless voice, yet the effect of them was emphatic. "But I know Bramley too, of course."

Applegate stared. "Why of course?"

The man's fingers, long and white, moved with an effect of furtiveness to the pimpled cheek. "Everybody knows Bramley Hall. Progressive school, you know. And I used to go there long ago." He stood up abruptly, a telescope extending to full length, went out into the corridor and disappeared.

A square of white lay on the floor. Applegate picked it up and saw that it was a small snap showing two men together. One was the man of the train, several years younger, less furrowed, but perfectly recognisable. The other man was a head shorter, thick, square, round-headed, curly-haired. Something in the set of his shoulders and the way in which the head was thrown back seemed to show a natural arrogance, or at least a sense of self-importance. While Applegate looked at the photograph he had the feeling that he was being watched. In the corridor a small roly-poly dumpling of a man, red-faced, sports-jacketed, passed by. Had he been looking through the window?

A couple of minutes later the tall man came back, and Applegate gave him the photograph. He took it with a word of thanks, wiped it with a piece of newspaper, and put it back in a wallet which he drew from his breast pocket. Applegate idly wondered how the snap had dropped from the wallet to the floor.

The train, which had chugged slowly from Ham Street to Brookland, from Brookland to Lydd and on again, crawled into a station. It was Bramley. Applegate got up.

"Glad to have had this little chat with you, Mr Applegate," the tall man said. "I feel we have something in common. Look me up when you are in Murdstone. Jenks, Grand Marine Hotel, Murdstone 18345."

It was not until Applegate was on the platform that it occurred to him to wonder how the man knew his name. But no doubt the answer was simple. There was a label on his luggage. Mr Jenks was a luggage-label reader.

Chapter Four

One other passenger got off at Bramley. This was the roly-poly man who had looked through the window. Seen more closely he was not so young as he had appeared at first glance, and there were small purplish lines below the ruddiness of his cheeks. "Wonder if we're bound for the same place," he said as they gave up their tickets. "Bramley Hall, right?"

"Right."

"I'm a new boy there. New teacher, I mean. Name's Montague."

"I'm new too. Applegate."

They shook hands solemnly. "Transport all laid on to time, Daimler waiting no doubt," Montague said. They came out of the station to an open space of muddy earth and stood there for several minutes. The day was grey. A keen wind blew. "Transport definitely not laid on to time. Bad show."

The sun had been shining when Applegate left London, and he was wearing a thin overcoat. He felt cold and slightly miserable. "Perhaps we can walk it. How far is Bramley Hall?" he asked the gnarled porter who appeared to be also the stationmaster.

"Maybe three miles, little more, little less."

"Oh. Shall we split a taxi?"

"Good idea, old boy," said Montague enthusiastically. "Do things in style on our first day."

9

The porter had been listening with grim amusement.

"No taxi in Bramley. You want to get Ebbetts from Murdstone, it's four mile. Cost you a bit, I reckon, that's if you can get hold of Ebbetts now. Generally has a sleep in the afternoon, Ebbetts."

"Oh, my God," Applegate said.

"Would you be waiting for the car from Bramley Hall now?" Applegate said with restraint that they would. "You're the wrong side then," the porter said with satisfaction. "Car for Bramley Hall's the other side. Over the bridge."

They walked up the steps. When they had reached the top Montague whistled. "I say, old boy, do you see what I see? Transport *and* company laid on."

Looking down from the bridge Applegate saw a very old open car. A girl stood by its side looking at her wristwatch. Her hair was fair, and she was wearing a black jumper and red jeans.

"Tally-ho," said Montague. "Remember, I saw her first."

When they got to the car the girl said: "Eleven and a half minutes."

"What's that?" Applegate asked.

"The time it took you to realise that the car might be on the other side of the bridge. It's the first applied intelligence test, and frankly you don't come too well out of it."

"A damned silly test, if you ask me," Applegate said moodily. He had been wondering whether he would be able to endure the strain of life at Bramley Hall, but consideration of the girl cheered him up a little. Her face had the unremarkable prettiness of many blondes who pattern their looks upon those of the fashionable film star of the moment, but her blue eyes had a vacant wildness that interested him. These eyes seemed to glow for a moment as though a light had been switched on inside them, as she looked at the two men. Then the light was switched off, and they were vacant again.

"Let me see if I can tell which is which. You're Charles Applegate."

"Right."

"Applied intelligence, you see. And Frank Montague. Put your bags in the boot and get in. You don't mind having the top down?"

"A spot of fresh air never hurt anybody," Montague said.

Applegate, who did mind having the top down, said: "Won't you be rather cold?"

"I'm burning." She placed her hand on his for a moment. It was hot and dry. "You'd better get in front, it's not so windy. There's no point in putting the hood up anyway, it's full of holes. Here we go."

The car started with a jerk that flung Applegate back in his seat. Immediately below him, as it seemed, there was a noise like the clattering of saucepans. "What's that?"

"What?"

"That noise," he shouted.

"Just the engine. She doesn't like standing idle. Better in a minute." Like a rider urging her horse at a jump, she accelerated as they approached a gentle incline. A thunderous knock had developed by the time that they reached the brow of this slope. Then they were over. Applegate sighed with a relief that quickly changed to alarm as he saw a heavy lorry approaching them head on. The girl swerved to the left and missed it. "Pulls over to the right all the time. You have to be careful."

"I can see that. What's your name?"

"Hedda Pont. But call me Hedda. I'm the old man's niece."

"What do you do at the school?"

"I'm the matron."

"The *matron*."

"I was elected three months ago. Self-government. Elections every six months. You know the kind of thing. All the boys voted for me."

"I'm sure."

"What do you mean by that?" She turned to look at him.

"Look *out,*" Appleyard shouted. They had just turned a bend and he saw a stationary car a few yards ahead of them and another car coming the other way. He put his hands over his eyes and waited for the crash as he saw her pull on the hand brake. This time he was thrown forward against the windscreen. When he took his hands away from his eyes they were on a clear stretch of road, and the two cars had vanished.

From the back Montague shouted: "Good as the Big Dipper."

"You shouldn't drive like that."

"You should be more careful what you say to me. I'm a delinquent, you know. Or was, rather. Jeremy says I'm not any more, but I don't believe him. Sex has always been my trouble. If only there were no men in the world." She began to sing in a tuneless voice:

> " 'See the pretty lady up on the tree,
>   The higher up the sweeter she grows.
>   Picking fruit you've got to be
>   *Up on your toes.'*

How old are you?"

"Twenty-three."

"Isn't that odd, so am I. You don't look it."

"There's no point in trying to shock me. What's your uncle like?"

"Jeremy? He's a nice old boy. A bit cracked of course, and a bit of a fake. Anybody must be to run a school like Bramley. But really very nice. You've had no experience as a teacher, have you? Neither has Frank, back there. You won't stay, nobody ever stays. Except me. I've been here two years as delinquent, teacher, and now matron."

12

"How many pupils are there now?"

"Eighteen. Twenty-one last term. Four left and one has come."

"But the school must run at a loss."

"It always has done. Janine provides the cash, she's got quite a lot."

Applegate said no more, but concentrated on the drive through the winding Marsh roads. He noticed that Hedda's handling of the car was reckless but skilful. The scenery appeared to him a duplicate of the scenery he had seen from the train. If these were not exactly the same fields and sheep they were very good imitations.

"Here we are." Hedda turned right between two iron gates and went up a long, weedy drive. At the end of the drive was a large courtyard. With a screech of brakes she stopped the car, which steamed like a horse after a race. "Bramley Hall."

It was a remarkable structure. The middle of it must have been at one time a pleasant Georgian house of moderate size. The original doorway had been replaced by a much larger one in Victorian Gothic, with a pointed church-like door studded with bits of iron. On the moulding above it was carved: *JB 1937*. There were two additions to the original building. The first, on the left, was a variation on the Victorian Gothic theme. Built in Kentish ragstone it had mullioned windows. Above, the roof was castellated like a medieval castle. The addition on the right was aggressively modern, with a large expanse of glass window and a flat roof. The white paint used for this addition had flaked away in many places and was discoloured in others. The casement windows were rusty.

Applegate, who was not particularly sensitive to architectural detail, was appalled. "Did Mr Pont do this?"

13

Hedda laughed. "Oh, no, it was done well before Jeremy's time. The house had been empty for a year or two when he bought it."

Now the iron door swung open and Pont, pinkly benevolent, advanced upon them. "Welcome," he cried. "Welcome to Bramley Hall."

Chapter Five

Before Applegate sat down to supper that evening he had been all round the school, spoken to the ten boys and eight girls who were there, and had a long discussion with Pont. Against his will and belief he had been impressed by Pont's sincerity as the headmaster sat and talked to the new teachers in the sparsely-furnished room he called his office. This room overlooked the garden at the back of the house, with its weedy flowerbeds and neglected tennis court.

"Most of the boys and girls here are what society calls difficult or delinquent," he said. "Maureen Gardner has been a thief, Billy Mobbs is a bed-wetter, Arthur Hope-Hurry was sent here because he told lies. Some are merely thought difficult, said by their parents to be unresponsive to affection, or have been found stupid at ordinary schools. John Deverell, who is new this term like yourselves, has a father who lives in the Argentine. He wanted John to be educated in Europe and for the past two years he has been at a school in Switzerland. His father was worried by reports that he made no progress and was unco-operative, and decided to send him here.

"I mention these boys and girls to show partly that each is an individual case to be treated in a particular way, but also to show the contrary. There is one general answer to all their problems. The answer is love. It can never be punishment. That is not to say we allow unlimited freedom. If I find the boys and girls smoking I take their cigarettes away. If I find them drinking – that rarely happens – I take away the bottle." For a moment Mr Pont's pink face became pinker, then the flush receded. "These children have to live in society, and they must understand that society has certain restrictions which are called laws. I put it this way. *We allow children freedom in deciding what not to do.* Attendance at lessons is not compulsory. Work is not compulsory, except certain community duties like washing up. We provide a cultural environment and observe the reaction to it. We have our failures, but there are many more successes. Maureen Gardner no longer steals, Arthur Hope-Hurry is learning to be truthful within the proper limits of adolescent fantasy."

Applegate crossed to the window. "Do they look after the garden?"

"On a voluntary basis, yes. At the moment it is neglected. Is that what you were thinking?"

"The idea had crossed my mind."

"Three years ago that tennis court was made by boys and girls eager to play tennis," Mr Pont said warmly. "I wish you could have seen the work they put into it. They levelled the ground, returfed it in part, and saved their money to buy nets, posts, racquets and balls. These boys and girls have left us. Nobody today troubles about the tennis court. In another year or two there may be others who want to play."

"But – " Applegate stopped, unable to formulate all his objections.

"Did what's her name, Maureen Gardner, pinch things when she first came here?" Montague asked.

"She did. We found almost all of them. The impulse was a natural infantile one to gain attention from adults. When Maureen found that she was not punished, and that in fact little attention was paid to her petty thieving, she gave it up."

"Do you mean to say that if a kid pinches my wallet I'm not going to do anything about it?" Montague's chubby face expressed incredulity.

"I said nothing of the kind. I said that we should understand that the theft was an infantile reaction and treat it accordingly." Behind Pont's good humour Applegate sensed that invincible conviction of his own rightness from which martyrs and lunatics are made. "Now a personal word to you both. You are not experienced teachers. That is all to the good. The orthodox teacher is too hidebound for life here. In fact – I will not try to conceal it from you – few stay more than a couple of terms. They lack idealism. I hope you will bring fresh and unprejudiced minds to bear on the problems you meet. They will be *your* problems as well as those of our boys and girls. It is in solving them that you can find happiness, as I have done. Try to reach beyond the self to the not-self."

For a moment the intensity of his gaze held them. Then he ended, rather lamely: "Mrs Pont will be happy if you will drink coffee with her tonight. Now, shall we meet the boys and girls?"

They met the boys and girls. Fourteen-year-old Maureen Gardner was producing what she called thought-paintings composed of bands of vivid colour moving in waves across a sheet. "Liberate the instinct for creation," Pont said triumphantly. "And you see the result." Well, better thought-paintings than theft, Applegate said to himself.

Five boys were kicking a football about a meadow in a desultory way. Pont frowned a little at this. "Where did that ball come from?"

"I brought it back with me," said a boy with a squint. "Why shouldn't I? We're free to do as we like, aren't we?"

"Perfectly free, Arthur. If you would sooner kick a football about than do something constructive, that's up to you."

"We can't play a decent game. We've got no goal-posts."

"Build them, my dear boy. There is timber at the back of the woodshed."

"That stuff's no good. Too thin," said a long gangling boy.

"Adaptation, Derek, adaptation. I can't believe that human ingenuity would be unable to convert those pieces of timber into goalposts." They went on. "Arthur is still inclined to be a trouble-maker, I'm afraid. He leads the others on to play football, an infantile reaction again. Ah, here comes our new student, John, with Hedda."

They met on the neglected tennis court. "This is John Deverell, the newest inhabitant," Hedda said to Applegate and Montague. "John, here are two new teachers. You'll be expected to call them Charles and Frank."

John Deverell was brown-faced, slight and rather elegant, perhaps sixteen years old. He showed even white teeth in an unembarrassed smile. "That is a little different from my school in Geneva. We had a teacher there who rapped our knuckles hard – with a ruler – when we forgot to call him 'sir.'"

"Shocking," Pont commented briskly. Applegate expected him to add that rapping boys on the knuckles was an infantile reaction, but instead he went into his little talk about the cultural environment. Deverell listened with every appearance of attention. Hedda looked from one to the other of them with a frankly cynical expression.

"I'm sure I'm going to enjoy myself here," Deverell said composedly, and showed his teeth again.

"There's more to see." Hedda and Deverell walked away round the side of the house together.

Montague watched them with interest. "What do you do about the hydra-headed monster? Good old triple sec?"

"Triple sec?" Pont was baffled.

"Sex. What makes the world go round, you know. After all, Miss Pont – Hedda – is a pretty attractive matron. If I know anything about anything young Deverell was thinking she was just the type he'd like to tuck him up at night. Some of the other boys have reached the age of consent too, I should guess."

"It *is* a problem." Pont stood out in the neglected garden, a nipping wind ruffling the white curls round the edges of his pink head. "Speaking personally, I have no objection to any kind of youthful sex play. But we must be practical. I may not approve of the laws of this country, but I have to abide by them. There are limits to what the law will allow."

"You mean it's all right to advocate freedom as long as you don't practise it?" Applegate suggested.

"Something like that." Pont did not seem to detect any irony in the remark.

"Supposing there was some jiggery-pokery between a boy and a girl, would you get rid of them?" Montague asked.

"It happens very rarely," Pont said evasively. "At half-past eight, then, we shall look forward to seeing you for coffee."

Chapter Six

At seven o'clock a Brooker-Timla supper was served. It proved to be a hot meal of vegetarian food, all of which seemed to have been passed through a mincer. Oddly enough, the mixture was quite palatable; or perhaps the Marsh winds had made Applegate hungry. Boys, girls and staff ate together in a large hall in the Victorian Gothic addition. Pont sat beaming at the head of the table, and Hedda at the bottom. The meal was eaten with fair decorum, but just as it finished Applegate saw the boy next to him give a vicious pinch to a girl who sat on his other side. The girl yelped and then punched the boy in the stomach. Crockery clattered on the table, a glass of water went over. The girl was Maureen Gardner, the boy was the gangling Derek.

Applegate waited expectantly. Pont said mildly: "What was the reason for that?"

"He pinched me."

"She stole my knife."

"It's the kind of knife he's not supposed to have. Look." Maureen fumbled below her skirt and produced a short-handled knife with a long slender blade. "I found it in his locker."

"Take the knife, Charles, will you?" Applegate took it rather gingerly, and put it in his pocket. The point was extremely sharp.

"He's not supposed to have a sharp knife. He's violent," Maureen Gardner said, more to Applegate than to the others, who obviously did not regard this as news. Derek merely glared at her.

"He was not supposed to have it, nor you to take it," said Pont imperturbably. "You did the right thing for the wrong reasons. Let's say no more about it."

"Can I have my knife back?" Derek held out a large, grimy hand to Applegate.

"No."

"Why not? It belongs to me."

"It's a dangerous weapon." Applegate felt slightly absurd.

The grimy hand was bunched into a fist. "Supposing I took it? I can fight, you know, and no Queensberry rules either."

"I've been known to ignore them myself. But supposing you were able to take the knife away from me, what then? Everybody would know you'd taken it, and you'd just have to give it back again. Stupid."

The boy made no reply to this argument. He stood up, picked up his plate and dropped it on the floor, where it broke into four pieces.

"You look intelligent," Applegate said. "What made you do something so foolish? You'll simply have to pay for the plate."

"Liberty Hall," the boy snarled as he walked away from the table. Applegate felt a ridiculous sense of triumph, which was slightly marred when he saw the smugness with which Maureen Gardner was eating her treacle sponge.

The sense of triumph revived, however, when he presented himself at half past eight and was congratulated by Pont. "An awkward little episode, although of the kind we must expect. I thought you handled it perfectly. Derek Winterbottom is a difficult case. He came here a year ago with a record of sadistic activity applied to animals and other

21

children. He burnt another boy's hand with a poker. It was hushed up – his father is an important Civil Servant. Had it reached the courts he might have gone to an approved school. They sent him to Bramley instead, and we are doing what we can for him, but I fear it may be too late. His character was set when he arrived, and I am afraid I may have to ask his parents to take him away."

Pont looked genuinely distressed. They were talking in the square drawing-room of what appeared to be the Ponts' separate suite upstairs. It contained an old sofa and three or four armchairs covered with various materials, apparently indiscriminately chosen. There were a few books and an electric fire. The room was shabby without being comfortable. There was no sign of Mrs Pont, or of coffee.

There was a perfunctory knock, and then suddenly two doors opened at the same time, at opposite ends of the room. Through one of them came Montague, red-faced and perky. Through the other there entered slowly a large shapeless woman with beautifully waved silver hair, who walked with a stick.

Pont sprang up from his chair. "Janine, my dear, how are you feeling?"

"I have had a headache, but it is better now." With immense dignity she walked to one of the armchairs and sat down. It was an impressive entrance, and would have been more impressive still had not the chair springs creaked as she sat down.

"May I present my new assistants – Charles Applegate and Francis Montague. My wife has been more than a helpmeet, she has been an inspiration through the struggles of more than twenty years." Pont spoke the lines like a ham actor. The change from his assured manner in talking of Derek Winterbottom was remarkable.

Applegate and Montague advanced, took the limp hand that was offered to them, and murmured something. Mrs

Pont's great flat white face was turned up to them, apparently almost unseeing. She said slowly: "I am pleased to meet you. Jeremy, if you will bring the machine over here I will make coffee."

"Yes, my dear." The machine turned out to be a Cona and while Mrs Pont, with immense deliberation, lit the flame beneath it, her husband talked rapidly and nervously. "When I say an inspiration, that is no more than the literal truth. Through my struggles as an educationist, and the way of the pioneer is hard, it is a thick jungle of ignorance that we attack with our machetes, Janine has supported me. She has done more than that, she has made positive and very real suggestions about the nature and scope of education. No doubt you have read my little volume, *Education in an Ideal Society.* I think I may say that it was a forward-looking work, in ideas if not in expression. The ideas were Janine's, my task was merely to provide the clothing in which they were dressed. My dear – if you will excuse me… " He moved the methylated wick away from the bubbling coffee.

Mrs Pont, who had been staring straight ahead of her, said: "Will you take sugar and cream, Mr – ?"

"Applegate. Both, please."

She put in sugar and cream with the same slow-motion deliberation. "Jeremy is too modest. He has many admirers who have written about him. Bring me the album, Jeremy. From the cupboard by the window."

"My dear, please." Pont's cheeks were a little pinker than usual.

"I shall get it myself." Applegate and Montague watched in awestruck silence as she levered herself up in the armchair like some great ship slowly raised from the sea bed. Before she had finally risen Pont, with a murmured inaudible word, had darted across the room. He returned with a large green volume. Mrs Pont sank back in the chair, took the book in her white hands and began to read.

There ensued one of the most embarrassing half-hours of Applegate's life. The embarrassment came partly from the fact that she read badly, stumbling over words occasionally, and speaking with an almost total lack of expression. Partly he was embarrassed also by the nature of the material. There were many newspaper cuttings and a few letters. Most of the cuttings were ironical in tone, and perhaps half the letters had been written by people on the lunatic fringe of eccentricity.

"You will be interested to know that John shows a great talent for embroidery and that specimens of his work are to be entered in our local exhibition... Jennifer refuses to wear clothes even in bitter weather, she has such a *sense of freedom*... It is thanks to you that Lenore now identifies herself with un-Wordsworthian nature. Her book on fungoid and human growth is being published by... " This, or something like it, he had expected. The truly appalling thing was his sudden realisation that as she read on Mrs Pont was stumbling over words more frequently. He was thankful when she closed the album and gave it back to her husband.

"You see, Jeremy underestimates himself. His work is appreciated." Applegate and Montague nodded like mandarins. "And now I must leave you. I feel my headache coming back. Pray don't help me, Jeremy. I can manage perfectly well."

The levering process went on again, but this time she rose completely from the chair. The silver curls shifted a little to one side as she did so.

"Janine," Pont said despairingly.

"Perfectly well, thank you. We shall meet again, young men. I am always happy to greet disciples of the Master." She turned and made her way slowly out of the room.

Applegate and Montague left soon afterwards. "If I know anything about anything the old girl was potted," Montague said.

"Yes."

"Lovely head of hair that. Do you suppose any of it was her own?"

"I don't know." Applegate felt suddenly depressed. Pupils and staff were housed in cubicles in the Gothic addition, pupils on the first floor, staff on the second. They reached Applegate's cubicle. "I think I shall go to bed. Good night."

"Mind if I come in for a minute, old boy?" Montague was in before Applegate could say that he did not mind. He looked round at the iron bedstead, washbasin, utility wardrobe, deal chair and desk and skimpy rug, and shivered. "Just like mine. They don't spoil us with luxury, do they?"

"Plain living and high thinking," Applegate said absently.

"Cold enough in this spring weather, like an ice-box in the winter. But perhaps we shan't be here in the winter, eh?" Montague sat down on the bed.

"Why not?"

"You've got a job to do here, and so have I. That's true, isn't it? And when we've done it we go."

Applegate sat on the chair. "I don't know what you're talking about."

"Don't you? I suppose you'll tell me next that you're schoolmastering for the love of it. Let's face it, chum, let's have a little frankness. You and I only got jobs here because staff won't stay with Pont, and he'll take anybody. That's why we *got* jobs, but why did we take them, eh? Do I look the type to spend my life in a crackpot school?"

"No," Applegate said truthfully. Montague seemed to him like a Warren Street car salesman masquerading as a rugger tough.

"I'm being frank with you, but are you being frank with me? Hand on heart, old boy, scout's honour, are you?"

Applegate began to feel annoyed. "I don't see any reason why I should be frank with you, as you put it. What business is it of yours why I'm here?"

25

"Because your business is my business."

"Is it? I very much doubt that."

"Or put it this way, we're both here on Johnny's business, and we ought to join forces. Quarrelling won't do any good. Let's be frank. You know something I don't know, or you wouldn't be here. But two heads are better than one, and four hands are better than two. We're sensible men. We can come to an arrangement. There's enough in this for all of us."

Applegate began to warm to the scene, which seemed intrinsically more mystifying than the lurid adventures of his dons. "You're working on your own in this?"

"You know very well I'm not."

"Supposing I don't want to come to an arrangement."

"That will be just too bad. But you will. Think it over, old boy. Co-operation's a great thing." Montague got up.

"Not between us, I think." Applegate added politely: "I know you won't believe me, but the fact is I really don't know what you're talking about."

Chapter Seven

Applegate stepped on to the balcony outside his window, and noted idly that it ran right along this part of the house with no intervening railing, so that all the rooms opened on to it. Out here were odd night noises. A cow mooed somewhere nearby. The wind had dropped, but it was rawly cold. From his room a yellow shaft struck out into darkness. Farther along the balcony there was the spurt of a match. Then Hedda Pont's voice said by his side: "Have you got a light? The match blew out."

"In my room." She followed him in and stood smiling by the window while he looked for the matches. Then she took his wrist and held it steady, still smiling, while he lighted the cigarette.

"Come along now," Applegate said patiently. "Be your age. You're acting as badly as a heroine in a British film."

She let go. "Did you enjoy your coffee? And the conversation? Was Janine as usual?"

"I expect so."

"There's bound to be something wrong with anybody who runs a place like this. Janine's a soak. Sometimes she's better, sometimes worse, but on the whole, it gets worse. She stays in her room most days when it's bad, but occasionally she breaks out. A few weeks ago she walked down a corridor naked, shrieking out something about throwing off the trammels of civilisation. Another night she came down to the kitchens and said it was a scandal that we used salt in the cooking. She's been into a classroom before now, and taken over the teaching. She's nice, Janine, but she'd wreck any school."

"He's devoted to her."

She detached a piece of leaf from her cigarette, and looked at it critically. "She's got the money, you know. But I don't know what the hell makes me say that, or put it that way. He *is* devoted to her. Or he's devoted to his nutty school, and she makes it possible for him to carry on. Don't you think it's nutty?"

"In some ways, yes."

"I'm nutty too. But I come by it honestly. My father, Jeremy's brother Jacob, is in the bin. Has been since I was sixteen. And my mother ran away with another man when I was quite small. *I* ran away with a man, too. That was what sent my father finally round the bend." Applegate said nothing. "He was a boxer, used me as a punching bag. I left him and went to live with his best friend, then left him for a commercial artist named Piggy Lines. Do you know him? He's rather good. Used to give tea parties – marihuana. Everybody got very high and had a good time with everybody else. And so on, and so on. Living around. You don't want to hear about it all. Why am I telling you?"

"I wonder. Won't you sit down?"

Hedda sat on the bed and stared at the wall. Applegate took the deal chair again. "Jeremy and Janine took me out of all that, though it was against their principles really. I was living a free life, wasn't I? They fished me here out of the police court. It was all… Oh, silly. A party, that kind of thing, you know. I've been a prize convert. There shall be more joy in one delinquent converted than in ninety and nine – have I got it right? I can't remember. I've done a job here as teacher and as matron, really I have. And I'm grateful to them both. But there's something about it all that's wrong. Can't you smell it, how phony it all is?"

"Perhaps I can."

She lay back on the bed. It creaked under her.

"Well. Here we are."

"Here we are."

"Aren't you going to do something about it?"

"Not tonight. Since you're kind enough to ask me. I'm not in the mood."

She sat up. Her eyes, intensely blue, looked quite vacant. "I could make you be."

"Not at the moment. Or at least I doubt it. You see, I'm not sure there isn't something phony about you too. Have you ever heard of Johnny?"

"What do you mean, Johnny? Johnny who?"

"Montague was in here a few minutes before you. He talked what sounded to me like gibberish. He said we ought to be frank with each other and that we were both here on Johnny's business. He said I knew something he didn't know or I wouldn't be here. Do you know what he was talking about?"

"No. Perhaps he'd been drinking." Applegate shook his head. "I shouldn't worry. Bramley air makes people say odd things. You can put me down in your good books as a woman scorned but not indignant. Good night." She took Applegate's hand. For a moment her nails, small and sharp, pressed his palm. Then she stepped out again on to the balcony and was gone.

Applegate shut the balcony door, noting without surprise that there was no key to lock it, or to lock the door of his bedroom. He undressed and got into the bed, which creaked again in protest against his presence on it. There was something wrong about the way he took off his clothes, but he could not be bothered to discover what it was.

29

He switched off the light, but sleep seemed a long way away. He brooded over the events of the day, which seemed to have, from his point of view, a rather discouraging absurdity about them. The success of *Where Dons Delight* had been based partly on the fact that the sturdy respectability of most dons gave wide play to his sense of fantasy. But how could one write fantastically about Pont, Janine, and matron Hedda? To record their words and actions would be fantasy enough. Perhaps he should have tried for normality, a job in a State school. But then, of course, he would never have got one. His thoughts turned to Montague. What had he meant by saying that they were both at the school on Johnny's business? The lines of a poem came into his head:

> O last night I dreamed of you, Johnny, my lover,
> You'd the sun on one arm and the moon on the other,
> The sea it was blue and the grass it was green,
> Every star rattled a round tambourine;
> Ten thousand miles deep in a pit there I lay;
> But you frowned like thunder and you went away.

Montague frowned like thunder and Hedda went away, Jeremy burst asunder and Janine stood grand and grey. While Jove's planet rises yonder, silent over Africa. You had to say Mont*ag*ue to make it scan, Applegate thought, and then the tenses were wrong… He fell asleep.

Chapter Eight

What noiseless sound woke him, what jagged lightning flash of truth lit the arcades of sleep he never knew. Awake he was certainly, and panic-stricken, aware that something had happened and that action was demanded of him. Hand groped for light switch over bed. There was none.

For a moment place eluded him. Then he remembered, got out of bed, turned on the light, looked round the room. Nothing seemed changed. His watch said that the time was half past eleven. Annoyed with his own stupidity he put on a dressing gown, opened the balcony door and stared out into the night. An owl hooted. It was cold. He shut this door again, walked across the room, opened the door that led into the passage. Silence and darkness except for a line of light beneath the door opposite him. He remembered that Montague occupied this room. No doubt he was reading late, or writing a letter about Johnny's business. Yet something had woken Applegate up, and he wanted to find out what it was. He took three steps across the passage and, feeling slightly foolish, tapped gently at Montague's door.

There was no reply. As he waited Applegate felt more and more foolish. Yet at the same time he had a sleepwalker's determination to speak to Montague, to have it out with Montague as he put it to himself. "Are you there?" the sleepwalker asked. "Can I speak to you, Montague?"

Still no reply. He must be asleep. Without hesitation Applegate turned the handle of the door.

Montague lay on the bed on his back, fully dressed, one arm dangling. He was not asleep. From somewhere in the region of his heart there protruded the handle of a knife.

The effect of sudden death on the beholder is incalculable. It can leave him unmoved, make him exultant even (but that is generally when the beholder has been himself the agent of death), or induce feelings of dizziness and repulsion. In Applegate's case the effect of seeing Montague's body on the bed was to make him afraid. Whether this fear was associated with the deaths of his parents, which at the time he had treated so lightheartedly, is a matter of opinion. What he felt, however, was nothing exact. It was as though the activities of some terrible machine, which he had managed to avoid for years, had quite suddenly caught him up so that now he heard the gears grinding and at close range saw all the cogs involved with each other to some awful end. He sat down on the little hard chair feeling quite faint.

Slowly the faintness went away, to be succeeded by the stirrings of professional dignity and pride. He reflected that he was, after all, a writer of stories involving violent action. A certain duty was laid upon him to investigate the situation. Perhaps Montague might not even be dead.

Rather warily he approached the peaceful figure on the bed, put a hand near where he conceived the heart to be – but with care not to place this hand near the dark stain on Montague's pullover – felt for a pulse, lifted the eyelids with some distaste, even took down the bit of looking-glass on the wall and held it to nose and mouth. He felt no heartbeat and no pulse, and there was no shadow on the glass. All that was somehow satisfying. The man on the bed had no say in things any more, would not object to anything said or done, could be treated as a mere wax figure. Not quite wax, though, for he was still slightly warm. That meant he had not been dead very long, but just how long Applegate was not sure. Such problems had not faced the vampire bats and poisoners of *Where Dons Delight*. Memo, he said to himself, find out how long a body takes to cool. He noted provisionally that Montague must have been murdered, at most, half an hour ago.

He had been killed with a knife – a short-handled thin-bladed knife which Applegate was careful not to touch. As he looked closely at this knife, however, a frightful suspicion crossed his mind. He hurried back to his own room and felt in his jacket pockets. The suspicion was justified, and the feeling he had had when undressing explained. The knife he had taken from Derek Winterbottom at suppertime was no longer in his possession. That knife, or one exactly similar to it, had been stuck into Montague's chest.

Much shaken, he went back to Montague's room and stood staring down at the dead man. Without trying to think out the implications of the theft of the knife he felt action of some kind to be imperative. He resisted the idea that there might be unpleasant consequences of this action as he put his hand into Montague's pockets, now with no feeling of revulsion (was not Montague, after all, a wax figure?), and sifted the contents like a miner panning for gold.

Left-hand trouser pocket empty. Right-hand trouser pocket silver and copper. Hip pocket empty. Jacket pockets, two letters addressed to F Montague, Esq., Flat 277, Mattingley House, Edgware Road, W, a bunch of keys, a nail file. And now the wallet. Still with no feeling of revulsion he eased it out of the jacket. A shabby wallet, but bulky. The inner compartment contained a wad of pound notes, perhaps fifty. What else? Several old bus tickets, a book of stamps, another letter, a scrap of paper with an address on it. *HJ, Grand Marine Hotel, Murdstone 18345*. Applegate put the three letters and this scrap of paper into his own pocket, wiped with his handkerchief the wallet and everything else he could remember touching, and put them back. He felt perfectly calm, and was surprised to notice that his hands were trembling.

Back in his own room he looked at the things he had taken. One of the letters in Montague's pocket was a bill for whisky and gin. The other was from a girl. Applegate hastily skimmed the conventional phrases of love and came to something more interesting. *You have been acting so mysterious lately. What do you mean about something good coming up and only being away a few days? Have you got another girl, Frankie, because if you have I would sooner you told me. And sooner it was that than you were doing some job again. You told me you were going straight, Frankie, believe me it is the best policy, didn't you have enough trouble in the past through Johnny and Henry?* There were more conventional phrases. The letter was signed Edna.

He turned to the third letter, which had been in Montague's wallet. This proved not to be a letter at all, but a note typed on a piece of copy paper. With a shock he read his own name.

The agent must be Charles Applegate, arriving as new master at Bramley. Has no experience of teaching. Has written detective story under name of Henry James. Must be acting for ED.

There followed a reasonably accurate account of his history and of his parents' death, and a final instruction.

Try to find out what he knows. Offer to work with him. Get him to come in with us if possible. Point out that he has nothing to lose, ED is not reliable.

He read this piece of paper three times, and then tried to make sense of what had happened. Montague and the man in the train were engaged in some shady enterprise together. ED, whoever he was, must be a rival. The enterprise was in some way connected with Bramley Hall, and for some inexplicable reason they had identified Applegate as an agent working for ED.

He considered his own position. It seemed unfavourable. If he did as he had originally intended, and returned these letters to Montague's pockets he would be in for some intensive questioning by the police, questioning that would be made more uncomfortable by the fact that he really had no idea of what the note meant. Then there was the matter of the knife. When he took it away from Winterbottom he had put it in his pocket. Had it still been in his possession when they had coffee with the Ponts? Thinking back, he was bound to admit that he had not the slightest idea, and that the knife could have been taken at any time. Pont could have taken it easily, so could Hedda, and so could Montague himself. Or it might have been taken before he had left the dining-hall.

What should he do now? It seemed to Applegate that he would be acting with unnecessary foolishness by raising an alarm. It could make no difference to Montague whether he were discovered tonight or tomorrow. And it would be, surely, asking for trouble to return the letters. Tomorrow he would go and see Jenks in Murdstone and find out what this was all about. Tomorrow, after all, was another day. He became aware that he was very cold. He put the things he had taken from Montague's pockets into his own wallet, got into bed, and in five minutes was asleep.

Chapter Nine

In the morning things did not happen quite as he had
expected. He was wakened by a knock on the door. It
opened, and the face of Maureen Gardner peered round.
"Derek's murdered Mr Montague," she said.

Before falling asleep he had reminded himself that he must
simulate surprise. He found no difficulty in doing so.
"What?"

"Derek did it. Stuck him like a pig. With that knife you
took away from him, or another one like it. Have you still got
that knife?" She felt in his clothes. "It's gone. There you are."

"How do you know it was Derek?"

"He's gone. Run away. You'd better get up. I expect the
police will want to talk to you."

When she had gone he looked at his watch and saw that it
was half past eight. He washed, dressed, shaved, and went
downstairs to the empty dining-hall. He learned later that
Montague's body had been found just before eight o'clock
when one of the domestic staff took him some hot water, and
received no reply to her knocking. Applegate had slept
peacefully through the hysterics that immediately followed.
Subsequently disorder had spread like a rash through the
whole establishment. The central heating radiators were cold
and the toast was burnt. In the centre of the breakfast table
stood an enormous bowl of mush, which he took to be a
standard Brooker-Timla dish. He shudderingly avoided it

and tried to spread frozen butter on burnt toast. With this he drank lukewarm tea.

The dining-hall did not remain empty for long. Two boys and a girl, not known to Applegate by name, came in and stared at him. "Will there be classes today?"

"I don't know."

"Will you take them all, now the other one's dead?"

"I shouldn't think so. You'd better organise your own class if you want to work. I'll come and find you." Surprisingly they seemed to think this a good idea, and went away to do it.

A couple of minutes later Pont rushed in, his expression distraught. "There you are. I've been looking for you everywhere. How could you do it?"

"Do what?"

"Give Derek his knife back. You knew his record. You know what this means? Ruin." He sank into a chair at the table, spooned some Brooker-Timla food out of the bowl into a small dish and began to eat. "Ruin. After a lifetime of endeavour."

"I hope it's not as bad as that." He explained that he had not given Winterbottom the knife, and learnt that the boy had not slept in his bed.

"We should never have taken him." The rosebud mouth pouted. "I was against it, but Janine said we had a duty."

"Have you telephoned the police?"

"Oh, yes, yes."

"What do you want to do about classes today?"

"Whatever you think. Use your own judgement." All Pont's rosy elasticity had gone. He looked simply a bewildered old man as he got up and wandered away.

After Pont there was young Deverell, who said that he was feeling rather lost. After Deverell came Hedda, wearing this morning a bright green jumper with a roll neck, and tight black jeans.

"Hallo. What a clever thing you did when you took that knife away from Derek. What did you do afterwards, give it back and demonstrate the best place to stick it in? Poor Derek."

"What makes you think he did it?"

She stared. "Otherwise why did he run away?"

"That might be just because he didn't like it here." How much should he tell her? "You remember what I told you about my conversation with Montague last night."

"Oh, *that.* I shouldn't tell the police about that if I were you. They might think you were inventing. Let bad enough alone."

An hour or two later Applegate took her advice. He told a polite but critical Inspector with a large drooping ginger moustache that he had no idea when the knife had been taken out of his pocket. As far as he knew Winterbottom had nothing against Montague.

The Inspector, whose name was Murray, pulled his moustache. "He might have had something against you, Mr Applegate, eh? You took the knife away from him. He showed no sign that he knew this Montague? Ah, well, the lad had a bad record. But what would he have been doing in Montague's room now, eh, any idea of that? No? Well, we shall find out. Your room was opposite. You heard no sound, nothing that disturbed you?"

"No." That was pretty well the end of the interview. Applegate said nothing about Montague's visit to him, nor about the letters that were burning a hole in his pocket.

Little work was done during the day. Only four girls and two boys came to the Plastic Arts lesson, and although there were a few more for the Citizenship class their principal object was to extract information from Applegate.

"Will they hang Derek when they catch him?" asked the squinting Arthur Hope-Hurry.

"No. He's too young. And, anyway, there would be a trial. That's if they arrested him."

"They don't hang you until you're eighteen," Maureen Gardner said. "I'm against capital punishment. And against imprisonment too."

"You shut up, Maureen. If you hadn't pinched Derek's knife it would never have happened."

"I don't see why he didn't kill you first," Maureen Gardner said to Applegate. "He had a lust for blood. He once pinched my arm so hard it bled."

"That was for initiation into the order of Bramley Apples," said another boy named Levett. "Only you funked it."

"Maureen has a point though," said the brown-faced Deverell. "Why didn't he attack you, sir? Do you think he mistook the rooms?"

"We don't know what did happen and there's no point in guessing," Applegate said shortly.

"It's interesting, though," said Maureen Gardner. "It's the most interesting thing since Janine walked down the corridor with no clothes on."

"She was tight," another girl added.

"Citizenship," Applegate said rather hopelessly. "There is an ideal of good citizenship… "

Chapter Ten

At half past four that day he was walking down the weedy drive to catch the bus into Murdstone when Hedda ground to a stop beside him. "Off to the village? Give you a lift."

"Thanks. I'm going to Murdstone really. You aren't going there?"

"No, just shopping. Some of us have to work for a living. Tired of country life already? Or have you got a piece of skirt in Murdstone?"

"I've got to see somebody, but I wouldn't mind having a pair of jeans there. What about it? Meet me for dinner at seven-thirty?"

"Never been known to refuse an invitation. I'll see you in the American Bar of the Grand Marine. You can't miss it, pretty well the only hotel in the place." In a different voice she added: "You know, this is a hell of a thing to happen to Jeremy. I shouldn't be surprised if it broke him up. You don't care about that?"

"After all, he hasn't saved me from juvenile delinquency."

She stopped so abruptly that he bumped his head against the windscreen. Her face looked straight forward. "Here you are. Bus stop."

"What's the matter?"

"You don't take me seriously, do you? You think I was making it up last night. You can make all the smart cracks you like about Uncle Jeremy, but the fact is he's got more

40

humanity in his little finger than you have in your whole body." The car shot away down Bramley Village Street, belching smoke. Applegate was left reflecting that under the stress of emotion people almost always talk in clichés.

Five minutes later a green bus came along. In it he drove along curling country lanes. As they approached the sea the fields grew meaner, barer, slightly shaly. Wind whipped the small trees.

"Lovely country," said the conductor without apparent irony. Applegate weakly agreed. "Nothing to touch the Marsh sheep. Send 'em all over the world. Hardy they are, real hardy."

In the middle distance a square tower appeared, faintly reminiscent of the campanile of Westminster Cathedral. "What's that?"

"Murdstone water tower. Ain't been used as that for years. Someone living there now. Queer sort of home, but they say you can see for miles from the top. Here's Murdstone."

They went down a long avenue of pines which ended abruptly in a narrow street full of glossy-fronted, neon-lighted shops. "High Street," said the conductor. From the High Street they emerged into a decaying square. Through a gap slate-grey sea could be glimpsed. "Town Hall Square. Far as we go. You staying here?"

"Only an hour or two."

"One of the loveliest little places on the Kent coast. Ideal sands for children, golf walks – "

"And all the Marsh scenery."

"That's right. 'Course it's a bit nippy now, but healthy, mind you."

"Where's the Grand Marine?"

"Hundred yards along the front. Big grey place, you can't miss it. One of the best hotels in Kent."

41

"I'm sure." On the sea front he was met by a wind off the sea that stung his cheeks and seemed to cut right through him. His raincoat clung tightly to his body. He crossed over to the sea wall and watched grey-crested waves surge angrily up the beach. How intolerably untidy, how nearly vacuous, he thought, the operations of nature appear to the unbeliever.

The thought distressed him. "Really," he said aloud, "I must stop thinking like a character in *Where Dons Delight*. Eleventh rate Huxley just won't do. Pull yourself together, Applegate." He marched with a brisk, soldierly step, hampered a little by the fact that the wind blew him sideways, along to the Grand Marine Hotel, crossed the road, marched up its wide front steps and pushed open the swing doors.

His immediate impression was of emptiness. Nobody sat at the reception desk, there was nobody in the door to the left marked "Office," in the door to the right marked "Lounge" burned a feeble glimmer of fire like that of a deserted camp in a Western film. But where were the white men, in what quarter of this great Victorian grey elephant of a hotel prairie were they defending themselves against the assaults of Sioux chambermaids? Returning to the reception hall Applegate struck two imperious blows on the desk bell. The sound rang round the hall resultlessly. This cannot be a hotel, he said to himself, there is no smell of cooking.

He pushed determinedly on. Behind a door marked "Residents' Lounge" a stiff, dark figure sat in a large leather chair before an electric fire. At the sound of his entry the figure turned, revealing the long nose, blue chin and neat, dark clothes of Mr Jenks. At sight of him this figure expanded suddenly on scissor-like legs, became sinuous instead of stiff, extended a paper-thin hand.

"Mr Applegate. I am delighted to see you. Most kind of you to look me up."

42

"Nobody seems to answer bells here."

"They are understaffed. But then what can you expect? There are only three other people staying here. Do sit down." Jenks crouched in front of the fire and rubbed his hands together, making a sound like crackling paper. "Should I be right in thinking that you have decided after all that we have something in common?"

"I'm not sure about that." Deliberately he said: "Montague is dead."

"Dead. Is he dead? Poor Frankie. I loved him like a brother." Behind the unction of the words there seemed some genuine feeling. As Jenks picked at the red pimple on his cheek Applegate realised that it was fear. "How did he die?"

"He was stabbed."

"There was no need for that. Frankie was foolish in many ways but there was never any real harm in him." Applegate thought wonderingly: *He thinks I killed him,* and dimly he grasped that this thought was for Jenks a natural one. There was a note of reproach in the thin man's voice. "Frankie would have co-operated. I hate violence. It is never necessary."

"I thought we should have a talk. You suggested it in the train."

"Yes, that's the sensible thing. It would have been a good thing if we had talked before – "

"I had nothing to do with Montague's death."

"I never suggested it," the other said hastily. "I suppose the police have been called? That was inevitable, but still it is to be regretted. It should be a lesson to us all that nothing is gained by hasty action. That was something I often said to Johnny. Shall we talk here, then? We are in no danger of interruption."

Looking at the figure crouched before the electric fire Applegate wondered how to begin. "In Montague's wallet I found a piece of paper with your initials and this telephone number, and a typed note about me."

"You removed them, naturally."

"I removed them. I should say I haven't the faintest idea what the note means."

Jenks shook his narrow head. "I hope you will not persist in that attitude. But tell me first, what do the police think?"

"A boy named Winterbottom has run away from the school. They seem to suspect him."

"Well arranged, as I should have expected."

"If you mean that I arranged it you're wrong." He struck his hand gently on the cold arm of his leather chair. "I had nothing to do with Montague's death, I'm not an agent of any sort, and I've no idea who you mean by ED or by Johnny."

"Come now, Mr Applegate, we shan't get anywhere at all if we talk like this. You don't seriously want me to believe that you've never heard of Johnny Bogue."

Bogue, Bogue. The name woke an echo. "There does seem to be something – "

"Or that Johnny lived at Bramley Hall?"

Applegate snapped his fingers. "That's what the JB over the door stands for. But why should you think I'm there on Johnny's business? What stops Johnny attending to his own business?"

"What stops Johnny attending to his own business is that his plane was shot down during the war and he was killed. You're trying to tell me you didn't know that?"

"I'm telling you that I'd never heard of Johnny Bogue before this afternoon. Well, that's not quite right. I do seem to have heard the name, but I've no idea who he was." Applegate said this with a firm and, he hoped, convincing stare at the thin man.

Jenks did not meet this would-be compelling gaze, a mixture of Honest John and Medusa. He murmured apologetically: "Perhaps we'd better go upstairs then. I have something to show you."

They went out of the Residents' Lounge and up the stairs. In a passage on the first floor an old lady tottered along. She quavered a good afternoon at them. Otherwise there was no sign of habitation. Jenks stopped in front of a door, pushed a key in the lock, turned the handle and waved Applegate inside. He pulled a suitcase from a rack. "There's something in here I should have shown you before. Are you cold? Turn on the electric fire."

There was a subtle change in his manner, but Applegate did not bother himself to try and trace it to a cause. He turned round and switched on the inset electric fire. From behind him Jenks' voice was quaveringly determined: "Please put your hands above your head, Mr Applegate. Do not turn round."

He began to turn round. The voice repeated, with the quaver in it now ominously increased: "Do *not* turn round. I have a gun in my hand. I am nervous of firearms and if I have to use it I might hurt you seriously."

Could a threat of murder be more hesitantly put? Yet the very hesitancy called for respect. Applegate stepped away from the fire and put his hands slowly above his head.

"Stand against the wall please." He stood against the wall. Something hard was pressed into his back. He suffered the ticklish feeling of a hand moving over him, withdrawing wallet and papers. The pressure was withdrawn. He turned round. Jenks stood at the dressing table, rapidly turning over with one hand the things taken from his pockets. His other hand held a small revolver with a mother-of-pearl handle. Applegate took a step towards the dressing table. The revolver was immediately raised. "Please, Mr Applegate, do not compel me to fire. Believe me, I regret this as much as you do. It is most distasteful. Here are your things. I have taken only those that belong to me."

He walked quickly away from the dressing table and Applegate looked through his papers. The only things missing were the documents he had taken from Montague's body.

"I wish I could have spared you the humiliation of a search, but it was really essential that I should find out whether you were the innocent bystander you pretend to be. I hope you will accept my apologies."

"What about those papers of Montague's?"

"Poor Frankie was my business partner. I feel I have a moral right to them. Now, I propose to put away this hateful weapon and I hope we can have a talk. I have a great deal to tell you." Jenks' manner as he slipped the revolver into his hip pocket was almost skittish. "Let me begin by asking why you are at Bramley. Please be frank. It may be important to us both."

"I'm a detective story writer. You know that. I came to Bramley to get local colour."

"I don't understand you."

"Have you read *Where Dons Delight*?"

"I must regretfully say no."

"That was my first book. It is set in a University. I hope to use the setting of a progressive school for another book. That's why I came to Bramley."

Jenks took a few delicate, almost mincing steps up and down the room. "Unconvincing, Mr Applegate. But just for that reason I am inclined to think it may be true. I am going to trust you. I have a trusting nature. It has caused me a great deal of trouble in the past. I have been sadly deceived, betrayed you might say, through trusting others. Yet, isn't it better to be the deceived than the deceiver?" The question was rhetorical, Jenks' look almost lachrymose. "I'm going to suppose that your story is true. You know nothing about Johnny Bogue. Then I will tell you about him. You don't know who ED is. It's Eileen Delaney." Jenks' small anxious eyes looked shrewdly at Applegate. "Her name is also meaningless to you, no doubt. Eileen and I are – how shall I put it? – on opposite sides in a business matter. Frankie was my agent at Bramley. I have reason to believe that Eileen had also sent an agent there. I assumed you were that agent. I told Frankie to get in touch with you."

"Yes. I didn't know what he was talking about."

"I believe you. But Frankie was killed. He was killed, obviously, by Eileen's agent. Now, you can help me and help yourself. The agent is somebody at the school. Who is it?"

"I've no idea." Applegate felt a growing irritation. "And I'm bound to say that I still don't know what you're talking about. Why should you or Eileen Delaney, whoever she is, send agents to Bramley Hall?"

"Because of Johnny Bogue."

"But you said he died during the war."

"Yes. You say you've never heard of Johnny Bogue, but you've seen him." The thin man passed over a snapshot and Applegate looked again at the thickset curly-haired figure whose picture he had seen in the train. "That was dropped deliberately as you will have guessed, a little device to – ah, declare my own interest. That was Johnny Bogue in, let me see, nineteen twenty-nine, when I first knew him. At that time he was still an MP. Two years later, of course, he went to prison."

Something stirred deep in Applegate's mind, knowledge that he had never known he possessed. "Bogue was a politician, then. I seem to remember – no, I don't remember it, I was too young – I've read somewhere that he was mixed up with the Fascists."

"Socialists, Fascists, drink, dope, business deals – Johnny Bogue was mixed up with everything. And everything he did was crooked. Bogue was a rogue. I trusted him, to my misfortune." Jenks' hand moved furtively to the red spot on his cheek, and then quickly away again. "Would you care for

47

a drink, Charles? May I call you Charles? My own friends call me Henry. I must tell you about Bogue."

Applegate said that he would like a drink. From the drawer of a wardrobe Jenks produced a bottle of whisky and examined carefully a pencil mark on it. His trustfulness evidently did not extend to whisky. Two metal cups appeared, and were wiped with a clean white handkerchief. Whisky was poured, water added, cups raised.

"To our fruitful co-operation." Applegate drank with a feeling of discomfort. There was something ladylike about the way Jenks sipped his whisky. "I first met Johnny Bogue sometime in the autumn of nineteen twenty-nine, in a night club called the Hundreds and Thousands. I never cared much for such places, but I was married then, and Nora liked to go out. Night clubs were fashionable. You are so very young that it is all much before your time, but all sorts of people from royalty downwards used to go to Mrs Merrick's clubs, the 43 and the Silver Slipper, so that they could break the licensing laws. It thrilled them, can you believe it, to sit and drink after hours, and the fines were nothing compared with the profits. Mrs Merrick was called the Night Club Queen, but in the late twenties Eileen Delaney started up at the Hundreds and Thousands and one or two other places, and became almost as well known. There were always rumours that Mrs Merrick was backed by some financial group. Eileen was Bogue's mistress, and it was no secret that she was backed by Bogue. Or, of course, by people behind Bogue.

"At this time Johnny Bogue was only twenty-eight, but it was already said that he was making his mark. He got into Parliament at the 1923 election as Labour member for one of the Wandsworth constituencies. It was supposed to be a safe Conservative seat and he won it by a few hundred votes. In Parliament he used constantly to be asking the kind of questions that get into the papers. And at the same time he was on good terms with a lot of the right people in the City."

Jenks' voice was dreamy, his expression withdrawn. "This particular evening was the second time Nora and I had been to the Hundreds and Thousands. Soon after we'd got there Johnny came over to Nora and asked her to dance. Afterwards he came back to our table and introduced himself. I disliked him at once. You've seen what he looked like, you can imagine that he was full of Cockney conceit. Talked all the time about what he could do, in Parliament and out of it. And by no means a gentleman. On that first evening he waved his hand round, and said: 'You like this place? It's mine, I own it.' Then he ordered champagne and talked about the important people he knew and what the new Labour Government was going to do. It was all for Nora's benefit, not mine. That first evening he took hardly any notice of me. On Nora he made the kind of impression he intended. He had a way of looking at women – it was disgusting, really, but they seemed to like it. Nora liked it, anyway. She talked about nothing but Johnny Bogue after we got home, how clever he was, the great future he had ahead of him. She refused to believe that anybody as common as Eileen could be his mistress. I asked why not, since he was as common as dirt himself. Nora didn't like that."

"Are you still married to – ?"

"Nora's dead." Jenks' brown, anxious eyes seemed to look beyond Applegate. "The way she died… But I'd better go on with the story. A week after we went to the Hundreds and Thousands Bogue rang me up and reminded me that we'd met. 'You're the director of Jenks and Company, building contractors, aren't you?' he asked. I said that was right. 'You've got an estimate in for a new scheme of public works in North London. We ought to talk about it. Come and have lunch.'

"It was against my inclination, but I had lunch with him. It was in his flat off Buckingham Gate, and he set out to charm me. Up to a point he succeeded, but I was still suspicious of him. There were two telephone calls while we were having coffee. At one of them he gave instructions to buy a hundred thousand shares, at the end of the other he said, 'That was Jimmy Thomas.' You remember him, he was in the Cabinet of course. My word, I thought, you must take me for an innocent. Then something happened which convinced me that those telephone conversations were real. Bogue had said somebody was coming in to join us for coffee, and when the time came I recognised him at once. He was the First Commissioner for Works, George Lansbury. I'd seen photographs, and you couldn't mistake him. He greeted me briskly. 'So this is the friend of yours who wants to do some building for us, Johnny,' he began. 'Now, Mr Jenks, what I want to know is whether you've really got the organisation to carry out the work.' Well, I talked, and he listened to what I had to say, but it was his attitude to Bogue that impressed me. He was almost deferential to Bogue at times, asked his opinion on this point and on that. When he left after half an hour, he said to me that they would see what they could do. 'There are other people in for this contract,' he said. 'But anyone who comes with an introduction from Johnny has a head start.'

"After Lansbury had gone Bogue sank back in his chair and said: 'We put that over on the old bastard. Now let's get down to business. What's it worth to him and to me if you get the contract?'

"Do you know, when it was put like that it took my breath away for a moment. In England we've got so used to the idea of official incorruptibility that the idea of a police officer or a judge or a Minister of the Crown being open to bribery seems absolutely shocking. But after all, it's quite common in other countries, and why shouldn't it be so here? Bogue reminded me of the scandals about sales of honours a few years earlier. 'The trouble is, there are too many hypocrites in this country,' he said. 'They talk about the sanctity of public life and hold out their hand for a little of the ready at the same time. Now, I'm not a hypocrite. I'm saying straight out, what's it worth to you as a businessman? And remember, old Windbag has to be taken care of.'

"Put that way, I could see it was a matter of business. Bogue asked for two and a half per cent on the contract, I said we couldn't afford more than one and a half. We finally settled for two per cent." Jenks broke off suddenly. "What do you think of the story so far?"

"It's very interesting."

"You're shocked, I believe. You think I should have walked out of Bogue's flat."

"Not at all. I might have said that in nineteen twenty-nine. In the hydrogen bomb age commercial morality has no point."

"You're very lenient, Charles, to an old sinner. Have another drink." Whisky splashed into metal again. Applegate looked at his watch. The time was ten past six. "Before I left, Bogue warned me that there was a chance the contract might not come to me, that other pressures might be brought to bear on the Minister. In that case I should pay nothing. During the next fortnight Nora and I saw a good deal of him. We were his guests at the Hundreds and Thousands and at dinner one night, and he came to dinner with us. He made no secret of his admiration for Nora. He would say: 'This is a wonderful little woman you've got, Henry. Be careful I don't take her away from you,' but I took it as being all in joke. Then one day I received word that Jenks and Company had been awarded the contract. I telephoned Johnny to thank him. He took it coolly. 'What else did you expect?' A day or two afterwards I paid him twelve hundred pounds in pound notes." He sipped whisky.

"Corruption in high places."

"There was no corruption."

"You mean it wasn't corrupt for Lansbury to give you the contract?"

"I mean what I say. There was no corruption. We got the contract because ours was the lowest tender, Lansbury had nothing to do with it. Bogue had nothing to do with it. I paid him the twelve hundred pounds for nothing."

"I don't understand."

"Years afterwards Johnny told me the way it was worked. He found out that my firm was on a short list of four for this contract. Beyond that he had absolutely no influence. Lansbury – the man I thought was Lansbury – was an out of work actor hired for the day and coached in what to say. Johnny used half a dozen of them at different times. All Johnny risked was the actor's pay and a meal or two. He stood to gain twelve hundred pounds. Oh, Johnny was clever. Don't you agree he was clever?"

"Very."

"And after that, you see, I trusted Johnny. He'd shown his influence and I believed what he said. He was fascinating, you know, he could talk. And his smile was so boyish. Rather like yours." Jenks' long body wriggled, a white handkerchief wiped imaginary rheum from his little eye.

"After the affair of the contract I thought we should cultivate Johnny. I said so to Nora, and she agreed with me. I haven't told you about Nora, have I? She was ambitious, very. Always urging me to expand the business, take a house in town, give large parties, that sort of thing. After we got to know Johnny she wanted those things more and more. A nice house in Surbiton, a fur coat, anything she wanted in the way of clothes, you'd think that would satisfy a woman, wouldn't you? But Nora always wanted more than I could give her. More – I don't know if that's the right word. Something different, anyway.

"She always had a kind of contempt for me, Nora, and the better we knew Johnny the more she seemed to feel it. He used to take her out to lunch, the theatre, introduce her to important people, or at least she thought they were important. And she often went to the Hundreds and Thousands. What was going on between them I never asked. After all, Nora was my wife and Johnny was my friend. Wasn't I entitled to expect them to behave honourably? Yet people don't always behave honourably, do they, Charles? And I sometimes ask myself what were my own motives. The human mind is a dark forest. Would you like another little drink?"

"Thank you." The ritual was again enacted. Hunched now on the bed, his long legs drawn up like those of a jack-knife-diving swimmer, Jenks revived the past.

"The next scheme of Bogue's I was involved in came about through a slip he made when he'd been drinking. I wouldn't say he ever got drunk, but after a few glasses of champagne – he never drank anything but champagne – his tongue loosened and he'd talk about the people he knew, the New Radical Party he was going to form, the money he'd made and so on. One night when we were all at the Hundreds and Thousands in a party – somehow there was always a party when Johnny was in the club – he told a story about the way he'd used a piece of information to make a lot of money on some shares. I said that he sailed too close to the wind and that it was a good thing to look before you leap. One day, I said, he would land right in the ditch. Johnny didn't like that, he never could bear being criticised, and for the rest of the evening he called me Henry Caution. 'You're lucky to have a husband like Henry Caution, Nora,' he said. 'You may never be rich, but you'll never be poor either. Put Henry on a raft in the middle of the ocean and he wouldn't get his feet wet. Every quarter when he gets his bank statement Henry goes to the manager and asks to see the money. Henry Caution's the original man who wouldn't buy a pound note for sixpence when it was offered to him. He wouldn't waste his money like that, not Henry.'

" 'Oh, my God, Johnny,' Nora said. 'Is he really such a bore? I'm afraid he is.' They'd got into the habit of talking about me in that way in front of me, as if I wasn't there.

" 'Henry Caution's the original man who locked up his wife in a chastity belt while he was away and then gave the key to his best friend,' Johnny said. 'When he came back he said he hoped his friend had looked after it carefully and the friend said yes, he'd even put a drop of oil on because the key squeaked so much in the lock. And Henry thanked his friend for being so thoughtful.' Everyone laughed at that, including Nora. 'Never mind, Henry, you stick to Surbiton. Don't walk too near the riverbank, you might fall in.'

"I kept my temper. 'When you're in the river, Johnny, I'll stand by with a rope to pull you out.' I thought that was rather a good reply, but Nora said: 'God, Henry, you *are* stuffy. Johnny could have cut you in on something worth while, but – '

" 'Shut up, Nora,' Johnny said. She was quiet at once. She was never quiet like that when I said something to her. Not that I often did say anything. On the way home that evening, though, we had a terrible argument. I accused her of disloyalty. She shrieked at me about the thousands Johnny made every year, and said there was money ready to fall in my lap if I would take it. The trouble was I was too lily-livered to look at anything off the beaten track, although this thing was really right in my line. I asked her what kind of thing it was. She said she didn't know, but it was something in the building line. Johnny had mentioned it to her, but he said it would be no good approaching me, this was not my line of country.

"I might have left it at that, I don't know. But the next time I saw Johnny he was perfectly charming to me – and he had all the charm in the world when he wanted to use it. He said he'd had too much to drink, and that he was sorry. I asked him to tell me about the deal Nora had mentioned. At first he simply refused. 'This is not your kind of thing, Henry, and I don't want to get you into it.' It was half an hour before I got anything out of him, and then he wouldn't mention names.

"The scheme was very simple. A friend of his, A, had a paper mill for sale. It was worth perhaps ten thousand pounds, but a chartered accountant Johnny knew was prepared to value it at about fifty thousand. The mill was in need of certain improvements and alterations. The idea was that a building contractor, B, should buy the mill for fifty thousand. He would make these improvements, which would cost no more than a thousand or two. The mill would then be sold to another friend of Johnny's, C, who was looking for a paper mill on behalf of his firm, for round about a hundred thousand. A, B, C and Johnny would split the profit, some eighty-five thousand pounds, between them.

"Johnny told me this scheme in the cockiest, most impudent way in the world. When he'd finished I said, 'But that's dishonest.' He pretended to be surprised. 'Is that what you call it? You don't mind fiddling to get a contract and paying a bit of commission, but when it comes to big money you're frightened. Honest, dishonest, what's the difference? Who's going to suffer by this except the shareholders of C who'll pay through the nose for a paper mill. What the hell, they'll hardly notice eighty-odd thousand less off their profit. But I wasn't wrong, was I? You'll never get your feet wet.' At that I was stung into saying that he hadn't really told me anything. How could I say anything at all without knowing the names of the firms? He said he'd be a fool to tell me any names without knowing that I was prepared to come in on the deal. We talked round that for half an hour and then Johnny said he'd trust me. A was a man named Martin, who owned the Wrixford Paper Mill in Hertfordshire. I'd never heard of him. B could be me if I liked. But the vital name was C, the final purchaser. He was Sir Robert Rigby, the managing director of a big combine named Flitzens, which owned dozens of stationers' shops and libraries throughout the country. I suppose I should have felt incredulity when I heard his name, but my experience with the other business had hardened me against that."

The glance Jenks gave Applegate now was almost coy. "It really was not honest. You'll say I shouldn't have considered it. But I wanted to please Nora. And Johnny could be very – fascinating. And then it seemed to me he was quite right, nobody would suffer except the shareholders. In any case, I thought there could be no harm in having a look at the place. So Johnny and I went down to Wrixford and did just that. When I first caught sight of it I was surprised by the size of the place and its air of prosperity, then I realised I'd mistaken it for another factory, the Wrixford Printing and Binding Works. The Paper Mills were tucked away round a corner from the Printing and Binding Works, and they were nearly derelict. Ten thousand pounds seemed to me a high estimate of their value. To turn them into a profitable concern would have cost a good many more thousands than we were proposing to spend.

"When I said this to Johnny he just laughed, and said that was Rigby's headache. Then we argued about how the profit was to be split, and finally settled it should be forty per cent to Rigby, thirty each to Johnny and to me. Johnny suggested twenty for me and I fought him up to thirty, which would have meant just over twenty-five thousand pounds. It was like Johnny to fight about the percentages when there was no percentage in it for anybody except himself. The next week I met Rigby. Johnny warned me in advance to discuss things generally but not in detail, and particularly not to mention what we were each getting out of it. I had the strong impression that Johnny was getting a larger percentage than he'd told me. That was clever too, a good bit of camouflage."

"I suppose Rigby was another out-of-work actor."

"Of course not." Jenks sounded quite indignant. "Johnny never played the same trick twice on the same person. Rigby was absolutely genuine. We had lunch at one of Johnny's respectable clubs and talked about the plant at Wrixford. Johnny said I was a good friend of his, and that I would handle all the necessary improvements and extensions. He and I reckoned that when it was all done the total cost to Flitzens would be about a hundred thousand pounds. Without batting an eyelid Rigby said that a hundred thousand was a very fair sum on the figures Johnny had given him. I wanted to get things absolutely clear, and I told Rigby I should want to see something official from him before going ahead. Johnny looked annoyed, but said it should be possible to arrange it. A few days later he showed me a letter from Flitzens agreeing to buy the Wrixford Paper Mills from me at a figure of one hundred thousand pounds after certain improvements, which were put down in general terms, had been effected. 'Are you happy now?' Johnny asked. 'If you want to duck out there's still time.'

"I should have ducked out, or I should at least have insisted on holding that letter. But instead, we went ahead. I was seeing Johnny every day at that time, and so was Nora too, of course. I couldn't tell you all the MPs and businessmen I talked to. I let Johnny persuade me not to go to my bank manager for a loan to buy the mills, because the bank would ask too many awkward questions. I paid Martin a cheque for forty-seven thousand five hundred pounds, which I'd scraped together by putting Nora's and my own savings into the firm's account. It also included a sum of seven thousand five hundred borrowed from the bank with the deeds of the mill as security. As Johnny said, they didn't query a loan of that size, because it was just about what the mill was worth. Anyway, the loan would be only for a few weeks, until we got our money from Flitzens.

"The money was paid to Martin and as I learnt later, went straight into Johnny's account. Three days later I saw him at the Hundreds and Thousands and he gave me a little crooked smile. 'How does it feel to own a paper mill, Henry?' he asked. I said it would feel better to have sold one, and asked when that would be. 'Never, I should think,' he said casually. He took a piece of paper from his pocket, put a match to it and used the spill to light his cigarette. 'Shan't need this any more.' You can guess what the paper was."

"The letter from Rigby," said Applegate.

"Yes. It was a moment or two before I realised what he was doing. Then I jumped up to try to save it, but Johnny ran across the room and threw it in the fire. His face as he turned round to me was terrible – the lip curled up over his white teeth. 'What are you going to do about it?' he asked. What could I do? I'd paid nearly fifty thousand pounds for something which, when it came to be sold, proved to be worth seven."

"I still don't see how it was worked. You say Rigby was genuine, but he must have been in the plot."

"No. It was very simple." Applegate noticed again Jenks' reluctant pride. "The whole thing depended on a verbal trick. When I met Rigby at lunch we talked about the Wrixford plant. Johnny started off that way and we followed him. We never put an exact name to the plant, and we never discussed details. We were talking about different things. Rigby thought he was buying the Wrixford Printing and Binding Works. Johnny had started negotiations with the owners, and then got in touch with Rigby, but Rigby would have wanted to know much more before being seriously interested. The letter was typed by Johnny on a bit of the firm's paper which he'd got hold of."

"Couldn't you see Rigby?"

"What evidence had I got, without that forged letter? I couldn't have called Rigby without saying I thought I'd been his partner in a plan to get money – well – "

"By fraud."

"You are very harsh. I had trusted Johnny – and how was my trust repaid? He not only took my money, he took Nora. She was a true Eve, and he a serpent. When Nora learned what had happened, she left me. Johnny put her in a flat. I have often wondered how much she knew about the trick he played on me. When he went to prison in 1931 she waited for him. He came out eighteen months later, but by that time Johnny had done with her. I think the most important thing about her for him was that she belonged to somebody else. Johnny was like that. He really only had time for one woman, Eileen, and that was because she never bothered him. Eileen was there when Johnny finally told Nora he wanted nothing more to do with her. Nora went back to her fourth-floor flat, jumped out of the window and broke her back." Jenks wriggled, his fingers played ineffectively in the air.

"What did Bogue go to prison for?"

"He got money out of an old man named Keeble to start a lot of new night clubs, and then simply used the money. He spent a lot, Johnny, but he salted a lot more away."

Applegate put down his long-empty metal cup. "All very interesting. It doesn't tell me what Montague was doing down here, or what you're doing."

"You remember Martin, who was supposed to own the mill? He was Johnny's right-hand man, right up to the war. He helped with the New Radical Party, which Johnny founded when he came out. He organised the distribution of drugs – the party was used as a cover for that. During the war the New Radicals were stopped, but the dope ring still operated. Johnny was being used on all sorts of unofficial missions, and I don't know whether he still had any connection with the drug ring then. Johnny was on some hush-hush mission and his plane was shot down somewhere over Spain or Portugal. No survivors. Well, just a few weeks after Johnny died the drug ring was broken up and Martin got ten years in prison. I saw Martin while the case was still going on, and I asked what had happened to Johnny's money. 'That boy cached away a fortune,' he said. 'And you bet your sweet life I'm going to put my hands on it.' Now, listen to me, Charles. Martin came out of prison five weeks ago. Within a fortnight he had come down here."

From an envelope in his pocket Jenks extracted a newspaper cutting. Applegate took it and read about Tragic Death of ex-Convict at Kent Resort. Martin had come to stay at the Grand Marine Hotel. Two days after his disappearance from there his body had been washed up a few miles along the coast. He had been drowned, but bruises on his head had been caused by some hard object. Martin had last been seen near the village of Heartley, two miles from Murdstone, and it was suggested that he might have fallen off the slippery jetty at Heartley and struck his head in falling. The verdict was Death by Misadventure.

"You suggest that Martin was killed."

"I *know* Martin was killed." Jenks' manner now was furtive as that of a bad conjuror. "He had the secret, he knew where Johnny had hidden his fortune."

"Who killed him? And aren't you feeling a little nervous yourself?"

"I don't know who killed him. Johnny had a lot of associates. There was a Fascist tough named Barney Craigen, and a Eurasian named Max Degrine and O'Neill and Frankie Johnston the band leader. Then of course there was Eileen. You say you've never come across her. She's a remarkable woman."

"What do you hope to get out of this yourself?"

Jenks' voice rose to shrillness. "Forty thousand pounds. He robbed me of it, isn't that so? Forty thousand pounds, *plus interest.* I think I'm within my rights in asking for that, don't you, Charles?"

"Somebody evidently doesn't agree with you."

"I only want my rights," Jenks said, with no decrease in shrillness. "And now, my dear Charles, I don't want to hurry you, but I have an engagement. What do you say, are we to be partners? A co-operative enterprise."

"I don't know."

"You keep in touch with me, tell me anything you hear. On the word of Henry Jenks you won't be the loser by it." The white hand touched Applegate's, the bedroom door closed.

The hotel had evidently not been dead but hibernating. There were now distinct signs of life. A decrepit waiter stood at the door of the lounge, a snub-nosed girl sat in the office. There was a slight but distinct smell of food. Voices could be heard, distantly. A neon lighted sign showed an arrow pointing downwards and the words MERICAN AR. Applegate went down half a dozen stairs and found himself in a small and unexpectedly well-lighted bar. A man in a hacking-jacket sat on a barstool talking to the barman. Hedda Pont was at a table reading a Penguin thriller.

Applegate ordered two whisky sours and took them over to Hedda. "I feel bound to forestall the words I see on your lips by saying that I'm not late. I said seven-thirty and it's now twenty-five past."

"That's all right. I always get to places too soon. What's this drink?"

"Whisky sour."

"Never heard of it."

"Oh, come now, a girl like you who went to a reefer party every night." He saw a certain corrugation of her brow. "I'm not doubting your word in what you said about them of course."

"The trouble with you, Charles, is that you're too logical in a crackpot sort of way. That's a thing about men. You think because a girl hasn't heard of whisky sours it proves she can't have smoked reefers. Not so at all. It just shows that the kind of men I smoked reefers with didn't drink whisky sours."

"I see what you mean."

"Apply the same technique to you. How much did these drinks cost?"

"Three and six."

"Each?"

"Each."

"Right. Charles Applegate buys expensive drinks. Where does the money come from? Not from Bramley Hall, that's a cinch. Private income? Somehow I doubt it. Question: what is Charles Applegate doing at Bramley Hall? Answer: He's there under some kind of false pretence."

Applegate looked virtuously down his nose. "There is such a thing as a sense of vocation."

"But you haven't got it. I'm not really asking questions, though, just showing you the technique." She offered him a cigarette and lit one herself. "Three or four people seemed interested to know that you'd come in to Murdstone."

"Who were they?"

"The Inspector for one. Uncle Jeremy for another – he seemed to think it was rather like leaving your post under fire. And Maureen Gardner, who I think is getting a crush on you, and John Deverell who I hope isn't. In a school like ours it's important to keep things heterosexual. They're difficult enough in other ways."

Applegate sipped his drink, and wondered how much he should say to her. "Have you ever heard of a man named Johnny Bogue?"

"Wasn't he the man who owned Bramley before the war? Added the two wings and carved his initials over the front door. Is that the one?"

"That's the one."

"Had a pretty murky past, by all accounts, and died in the war."

"That's right." Applegate finished his drink, got two more, and decided that he was going to trust Hedda Pont. He felt like a man who has stepped through a looking glass and wishes to be assured, not of the reality of the world on the other side, but rather of his own reality. Applegate was a young man with what he would himself have called a strong sense of reality, meaning by this that he felt both indignant and disbelieving when confronted by aspects of life outside bourgeois convention. He had felt such indignation and disbelief; rather than grief, after the deaths of his mother and father, and he felt them now. He was gratified, but in a way irritated, to find that Hedda listened to his narrative with interest certainly, but without a trace of incredulity.

"I hope you're not going to the police," she said.

"The *police*." Applegate was quite disconcerted. "Do you know, that never occurred to me. I should have rather a lot of explaining to do."

"That's wonderful. Let's do some investigating on our own." Her blue eyes were bright as tinsel. Was it significant, Applegate wondered, that this should be the simile that occurred to him?

"What sort of investigation?"

She ticked off points on her fingers. "One, find out about Bogue. There must be something about him in old directories, *Who Was Who,* that sort of thing. Two, find somebody in Bramley who remembers him, and discover what they've got to say. I can easily do that." She hesitated. "Three – how much of what Jenks told you do you suppose was true?"

"I don't know. He sounded much more convincing about the past than about the present."

"Has it occurred to you that the logical place for Bogue's fortune to be hidden is at Bramley? Eileen Delaney sends an agent to Bramley, Jenks sends an agent to Bramley. Why? Because something's hidden there. The agent who killed Montague can't know where it is, or if he knows can't get at it for some reason."

"What kind of reason?"

She waved an impatient hand. "I don't know. Suppose there's a secret panel in the Ponts' bedroom. Aunt Janine hardly ever leaves those two rooms of theirs. Suppose the fortune is hidden in the cellars – nobody ever goes down there."

Applegate shook his head. "Too romantic. I'm not convinced that any fortune exists. I believe Jenks was making up all that part. My word, this place is looking up."

A man and a woman had come into the bar. The man was immensely tall, perhaps six feet five inches in height, and his body was thick. When he smiled he showed a mouthful of gold teeth. The woman was about fifty, and had a face like a parrot's. A beaky nose curved down to a mouth that was bent downwards in a bow. There was a multiplicity of wrinkles round her eyes. Her cheeks were bright with rouge. Above magenta hair was placed a plum-coloured hat decorated with a spray of flowers, and her coat also was plum-coloured.

"Here's mud in your eye, Eileen," said the man with the gold teeth. The parrot woman nodded. Applegate gave a brief cry of pain as his ankle was kicked under the table. Fortunately, it remained unheard at the bar. Hedda smiled at him sweetly.

"Need a drop of brandy to put some warmth into you," said the gold-toothed man. "Hell of a place, the Kent coast. Hell of a time of year too."

"Never mind, Barney, we won't go out on any picnics." The woman's voice sounded like a saw cutting wood.

"I got a job of work to do, I like to get right along and do it," said gold tooth. "Hanging about gives me the itch."

"You've been hanging about just four hours, Barney. And any time the fidgets get too bad, well, you can just go home."

"You got too sharp a tongue. You know Barney doesn't mean it." The man turned to the bar and Applegate saw the great roll of fat at the back of his neck.

Hedda had been fiddling frantically with her handbag. Now she pushed a scrap of paper across the table. Applegate read:

What are you waiting for? Get talking to them *somehow*, spill a drink over him or something.

He snorted, and took their glasses up to the bar, standing next to the man with gold teeth. Did he mean to knock over the man's drink or not? Afterwards he was never quite sure, but it was a fact that as he turned to take away his own drinks his elbow knocked the man's brandy glass off the counter to the floor.

"Why, you clumsy bastard," the man said. With horrified fascination Applegate watched the empurpled swelling of the brutish face, saw the great fists becoming knots. On a screeching parrot note the woman's voice said: "Barney."

The fists slowly unclenched. Applegate said rather squeakily: "Terribly sorry. Let me buy you another, what was it?"

"Brandy, large brandy." The man stared at Applegate while the latter ordered and paid for a large brandy.

"Nasty weather," he ventured inanely. The big man seemed not to have heard. "Here we are. Good luck."

65

"You're a gentleman," the woman said. "I can tell a gentleman when I see one. Have you mislaid your thank yous, Barney?"

"Thank you," the big man said. "Success to temperance."

"Success to temperance." Unable to think of anything else to say, Applegate went back to his table. "The cost of living's getting too high for me. He's drinking double brandies."

"You certainly missed your chance. If that had been me I'd be on the way to getting his life story by now. Your technique is… "

Applegate ceased to pay attention. The bar door had swung open to admit Jenks. With him was a young man who stood with his hands in his pockets. Jenks looked at the two standing at the bar, then murmured something to his companion and turned. But he had been seen, and the big man's voice boomed a greeting.

"Why, it's Henry. The Archbishop and his new choir boy. Don't be bashful, Henry, come on and have a drink."

Jenks hesitated, then advanced with his precise, slightly mincing step to the bar. "That's very kind of you, Barney. Just a little drop of whisky for me. Arthur drinks only tonic water."

"And how's my old chum Henry." The big man showed his gold teeth and gave Jenks a thump on the back. "What's Henry here for? Not for his health."

"Not for my health." Jenks sipped whisky.

"You'd be silly to come down here for your health. This isn't a health resort, eh, Eileen."

"Barney," Eileen Delaney said.

"Not at all, it isn't. No healthier than Earl's Court used to be for Ikeymoes."

"I am here on a little matter of business."

"I know your kind of business. You don't have to come down to Murdstone to do it."

Jenks said quite softly: "Oh, but I do, Barney."

66

The big man swayed a little on his feet. It occurred to Applegate that he was slightly drunk. "Not healthy to do business in Murdstone. Ask Eddie Martin."

There was suddenly silence in the shabby-smart bar. The barman stopped polishing a glass and looked thoughtfully at some point ahead of him. Hedda gasped and then put her handkerchief to her mouth. Eileen Delaney put down her glass on the counter with a sound somehow decisive. Jenks gave a slight, nervous snigger. Only the boy called Arthur sipped his tonic water, apparently unmoved.

Then the silence was broken. "Eddie Martin," the barman said. "Isn't he the one who was staying here and – "

Eileen Delaney said: "Let's go, Barney."

Jenks looked maliciously pleased.

"Now you must have the return drink with me, Barney. And you too, Eileen, for old times' sake."

Into the assurance of the big man's voice a whining note entered. "If I've said something out of line – shot my big mouth off – you know Barney never means – "

"Have the other half, Barney." There was the sound of a giggle in Jenks' voice.

The little woman gave Barney's sleeve a tug and walked towards the door. Reluctantly he shambled after her. The boy Arthur put his foot out and Barney stumbled. The boy laughed.

"Why, you little runt," Barney said. Then he stopped. The boy laughed again, a light, pleasant sound. The expression on his face was eager and even exultant. Something bright shone in his hand. Barney muttered something inaudible, turned and went out of the door. A couple of minutes later Jenks and Arthur followed them, Jenks giving Applegate a fluttery wave of the hand as he reached the door.

"Did you see what I saw in that boy's hand?" Hedda asked. "Was it a knife?"

"A knife or a razor."

Outside the hotel the old car was parked, but they did not get into it immediately, because Hedda suggested that they should go and look at the sea. In bright moonlight they watched waves coiling and uncoiling from the shore, very much as they had done an hour or two earlier. Hedda's lips parted as she watched. "Wonderful, isn't it? So sexy." She began to sing:

"When they dilute the bay gin, oh, oh, let them play,
   When the spire that was once a desire becomes a
         remember
 And our memories fade to the light of a lonely
         October,
 Then nobody knows the trouble I'm in
 When they dilute the bay gin."

The wind howled gently across the beach. Applegate shivered. "I'm cold. Let's go."

"Man, there's no romance in your heart." They stumbled up the pebbles to the promenade and then over to the car. It started with the usual jolt and pan-clattering sound, but fortunately this time there was no hill to climb. Wind shrieked through the tattered hood. While they bumped their way back to Bramley Applegate shouted his ideas about the scenes they had witnessed.

"That was Barney Craigen, the one Jenks said was a Fascist, and Eileen Delaney. What Jenks said about them seems to be true. Barney seems a fool, I wouldn't back him against that boy. Obviously they're two lots of cut-throats after the same thing."

Hedda had her head done up in a scarf. "What?"

"Two lots of cut-throats – "

"Yes, I heard that. What do you think they're after?"

68

"Bogue's fortune." He felt the lameness of the explanation. The car stopped with a sigh. "What's the matter?"

"I switched off the engine."

"Oh."

"Can't hear ourselves talk. That's a crackpot story about Bogue's fortune. Why should everyone be hurrying round just now to find it? It's something hidden at Bramley and connected with the people there, very likely. Do you suppose there are any nice rich skeletons in Uncle Jeremy's or Aunt Janine's cupboards that would be worth dragging out?"

"I shouldn't think so."

"Neither should I. And I thought you were going to buy me dinner."

"So I was. I forgot all about it."

"Doesn't matter." She leaned across, and he thought she was about to restart the car. Instead, a powerful arm coiled round his shoulders. Her face loomed before him, large as a cinema close-up. A mouth clamped itself upon his with the intensity of a rubber suction pad. His response to this forceful kiss was rendered less adequate by the fact that he had sunk down into the seat and some hard object was being pressed into his ribs. He wondered for a moment whether it could be her knee, and then realised that it was the gear lever. When he shifted in an attempt to get the lever out of his ribs her anaconda grip moved to his neck. He began to murmur inarticulately, afraid of being stifled. His feet frantically tapped the floor. Suddenly he was released and Hedda sat back on the other side of the gear lever adjusting her scarf. "You don't know how to kiss."

He felt his neck. "That's an extraordinarily powerful grip you've got."

"I told you I lived with a boxer who used me as a punching-bag. I had to develop some kind of resistance."

"You dug the gear lever into me."

69

"Sorry. Cars are never comfortable. What about it?"

"What about what?"

"It's a fine night. There's a rug in the back and an awful lot of grass out there."

"My dear girl." He was horrified. "You call this a fine night. We should be frozen stiff, very likely catch pneumonia."

"I shouldn't be frozen. Feel my hand." He touched her hot fingers. "I've got an electric generator inside me, but I see you haven't. Would you like the rug round your legs?"

"That's a good idea." He got the rug from the back of the car and wrapped it round his legs. They drove the rest of the way home in silence.

"Do you know what I think?" she said after they had put the car away. "I think you're one of those."

"You're wrong." He added primly: "There's a time and a place for everything. If I may say so it doesn't seem to me that your uncle's therapeutic measures have had much effect on you."

They stood by the studded iron door, beneath the moulding with the carved initials, "JB." She had taken off the scarf and stood looking at him with her fair hair tangled, her blue eyes vacant of expression. "I don't think you understand me. I'm really a one-man woman. Good night."

Later on Applegate looked at himself in the glass and saw a thin, dark head, eyebrows that almost met in the middle, a weakly, sensitive mouth, irregular teeth. "Can she possibly find me attractive with such teeth?" he asked aloud. He brushed the teeth, but still went to sleep with the taste of her lipstick in his mouth.

Chapter Eleven

The morning brought a return, not exactly to sanity, but to the familiar disorders of Bramley School as distinct from the more exotic ones of Murdstone. There remained in Applegate's mind a vision of the look on that young boy's face as the bright thing shone in his hand. He was perhaps no more frightened of violence than are most men. What terrified him about the bright thing in the boy's hand was that it seemed to represent a world where violence was not exceptional but natural. It was as though the polite stiff clothes of everyday wear had been removed to reveal a rotting body.

It was with a kind of pleasure, therefore, that he ate his burnt toast and drank his lukewarm tea. With pleasure, even, he looked at Maureen Gardner when she came up and whispered to him: "Old Ponty wants you in his room. Soon as you've finished."

"All right. What about classes?"

"Didn't say anything. Will you come and help me with my thought-paintings?"

"Later on perhaps." He found Pont in the drawing-room. Mrs Pont sat in the armchair looking grim. Her fingers moved as if she were knitting, although in fact there was no wool on her lap, no needles in her hands. As Applegate came in Pont strode forward and placed a hand upon his shoulder. "My boy, this is a crisis. Look at these."

They were six telegrams from parents, asking that their children should return home by the first possible train. "I suppose you had to expect them."

"Expect them. And why?" Pont exploded, like a small furious puffball. "I run a school – let us face it – for delinquent children. Social misfits with damaged personalities whom most people would call criminals. I try to recreate them as whole personalities. I am a man walking a tightrope, you understand, many of these damaged personalities are dangerous. They are young animals who do not like being caged. Through the years, how much trouble have I had? A few broken windows, one or two fights, a little promiscuity. Nothing at all. And now because, for the first time, something happens, how do these free, liberal, enlightened parents behave? They take their children away."

"After all, it is a matter of murder." Applegate forbore to mention that only yesterday morning Pont himself had said that the affair meant ruin for the school. Saying it, he realised, was one matter, having it said to you another.

With the air of an Old Testament prophet Pont brushed away the word. "An extreme expression of the anti-social instinct, yes. But I should have thought that those who consider themselves *enlightened* – those who are readers of the *intellectual weeklies…* "

Mrs Pont abandoned for a moment her imaginary knitting, and spoke. "It's no good, Jeremy. You may as well accept it. We're finished."

The words, although decisive, were gently spoken. Yet the effect they had on Pont was to make him crumple up almost visibly, so that he was transformed from an Old Testament prophet strong in indignation to a red-faced baby on the verge of tears. "Finished, my dear?"

This morning Mrs Pont did not stumble over words.

"I'm afraid so. We have to accept that it is all over. After all, you have done enough in your lifetime, you are entitled to rest. Other educationists will follow in your footsteps, respect your name. We have said so for years."

He listened with babyish pleasure. "I think my name may be remembered, yes."

"And what were you going to tell Mr Applegate?"

"Tell him? Oh, yes. The fact is – Janine thinks – with this collection of missives in my hand I am unable... " He dabbed at his eyes.

"Shall I explain, Jeremy?" Mrs Pont patted her beautiful silver hair. "Mr Applegate, these notices of withdrawal are almost certainly not the only ones we shall receive. The school will have to close down. There seems no prospect of giving you a full term's pay."

Applegate felt much embarrassed. "Naturally, I shouldn't expect it."

"Within the limits of our resources we shall – "

"No, no." Remembering guiltily the success of *Where Dons Delight* he raised his hand. "I couldn't accept anything at all. It has been an honour to come here."

"It is good of you to say that." Pont smiled warmly, sweetly, and turned to his wife. "In the very short time in which I have had the pleasure of association with him I have formed the most favourable impression of Charles. His presence of mind in dealing with Derek a couple of nights ago... " He stopped, evidently remembering the unhappy aftermath of Applegate's dinner table presence of mind.

"Is there any news of Derek?"

"None at all. I have had long telephone conversations with his father." From the look on Pont's face they had evidently not been agreeable. "I greatly fear the poor boy may have done himself some injury. It is not unusual in such cases for the ultimate hatred of society to be resolved by destruction of the ego."

"The police have no doubt that he did it?"

"I suppose not. Why should there be any doubt?"

"Do either of you know anything about a man named Bogue – Johnny Bogue?"

Applegate watched them both carefully as he asked this question. The watch was singularly unrewarding, for both of them nodded immediate agreement. "He owned this house," Pont said. "And there was a good deal of scandal connected with him at one time and another. I did not follow his career closely – and of course I should emphasise that I am far from an orthodox Freudian – but from what I remember I should say that he was a typical case of compulsive anal sadism." He beamed cherubically, pleased to have disposed of Bogue.

"You never met him."

Mrs Pont replied this time, hands working furiously over imaginary knitting. "Oh, no. He was killed in – 1943, was it? He died in debt, that kind of man is always in debt." She said this firmly, apparently forgetful of their own financial difficulties. "This house was taken over by the Army. They left it in a terrible state and we were able to buy it for a very low figure."

Pont had been chuckling away to himself, Applegate presumed in satisfaction at his definition of Bogue as a compulsive anal sadist. Now he said, "I'm wrong, my dear. I did meet Bogue once, in connection with my idea for Unispeka. You remember the universal language, based on psychologically live word-material? No – well, I suppose you are too young. We must have a talk about it some day. At that time, in the mid-twenties, I was an advocate of Unispeka. Later I came to think that a new language would be a mere palliative for the individual problems of human delinquency. Where was I?"

"Your meeting with Bogue."

"Oh, yes. I met him in connection with the APT – the Association of Progressive Teachers – who wanted to have Unispeka taught throughout all schools as a subsidiary language. He seemed a pleasant young man, I thought, with a great deal of ability, and he asked some questions about Unispeka in the House. Made quite a fuss about it, indeed. I remember that the APT got a great deal of publicity. But Bogue, I am afraid, used the idea as what I can only call a personal publicity device. Later on he dropped it."

"I see. I heard about him in Murdstone and wondered about his connection with this place." This explanation seemed to satisfy the Ponts. He left them, after promising to stay another few days.

"By that time," Mrs Pont said grimly, "a gallant experiment will have come to an end. Education has need of its martyrs."

He went downstairs to the great dining-hall, and saw nobody. He was going through into the Gothic addition when a voice said, "Here." He looked round, but saw nothing. "*Here*," the voice repeated, and Hedda stepped out from what he had supposed to be a cupboard at one end of the dining-hall. She was wearing her usual jumper and slacks, but this morning the jumper was blue-grey and the slacks nigger brown. From her hand dangled a large key. "Mission of exploration," she said. "Want to search the cellars? All sorts of junk down there – nobody goes down more than once a year. Come on."

They entered the cupboard, unlocked a door inside it, and went down a flight of curving stone steps. "No electric light here," Hedda whispered. The glow of her torch showed passages leading away in three directions from the bottom of the stairs. Applegate felt his hair entangled in something thick and clinging. A spider scuttled quickly over his face.

"Which way," he found himself whispering back.

"We'll take the left-hand passage, then we can come round into the middle and do the right-hand one last. They all join up." The left-hand passage took a sharp right turn and led into a storeroom. Here was an accumulation of dust-covered books and pamphlets. In the torch glow he read titles:

Patterns of Educational Life, Ego and Id in Childhood, Revolution and the Child. How many hundreds of thousands of earnest books and pamphlets gathered dust in cellars like these, he rhetorically wondered? In one corner of the room dust had been disturbed round some large object. Hedda shone her torch and Applegate saw that it was a hand printing press.

"Somebody's been looking at that."

She laughed. "Uncle Jeremy used to have a hand printing class – little poetry pamphlets, you know the kind of thing. Return to handcrafts. Then some little devil damaged half the type. Probably Jeremy came down to have a look at it one day, had the idea of reviving the printing class. He's like that... " She dropped the torch and gave a delicate, ladylike scream. A moment later she was in his arms. The circumstances, the place, and his feelings were all quite remote from those of the previous evening. The kiss he gave her was positively savage, some kind of recompense for a forgotten, secret humiliation. Did this kiss eradicate in some way the discovery he had made on that day at Sanderstead, or did it look further back still? He knew only that through it he experienced some kind of release, that he was glad to be holding the shoulders into which his fingers were firmly digging.

"A mouse ran over my foot," she whispered. Then she giggled. "Last night I wondered if you were a man or a mouse. Now I know. What's that?"

From somewhere beyond the storeroom came a scraping noise. It was repeated.

"A large rat." He dug his fingers more firmly into her shoulders.

"*Listen.*" The sounds continued. Something fell with a clatter. "There's somebody else in here. You go back the way we came. I'll cut him off this way. Better not use the torch."

In a moment she was gone, and he was left alone in the dense darkness. Blunderingly he felt a way along the passage, stumbling over books, until his hands came in contact with the wall. His ability to see in the dark was poor, but he counted paces. When he had counted fifty he guessed that he must be nearing the entrance point and felt around with his fingers, unsuccessfully. From one of the other corridors – was it the middle one? – a light advanced purposefully towards him. It could not be Hedda, since her last words had been that she would not use her torch. Applegate stayed quite still until the light was within a yard of him, then launched himself at it. He struck a hand and knocked the torch from it. Then there was a grunt, something hit him hard on the head and he fell over. Feet clattered on the stairs above him.

"Charles." In Hedda's voice there sounded a genuine anxiety. She was flashing her torch from side to side. "Are you hurt?"

"I shall live." He stood up. "I went for his torch and he was holding it away from him. I knocked it out of his hand, but he hit me on the side of the head. The torch should be around somewhere."

"Here it is." She illuminated a cycle lamp on the floor. "You said 'he.' Are you sure it was a man?"

"Yes, I think so, though I really haven't any convincing reason. Shall we go after him?"

"I don't see much point. Whoever it was must be well away by now. Nobody's got a key to this cellar except Uncle Jeremy and me."

"And Bogue."

"Bogue's dead."

"Yes, but I don't suppose the key has been changed since his time. Anyone who had a key then could get in now. Or it's easy enough to take an impression of the keyhole. The important thing is that we were right in thinking there's some kind of secret down here. Where did he come from?"

"I came back down the right-hand passage, he must have come down the middle. There's a store room in each passage. Let's have a look."

The store rooms, like the one they had seen already, were full of junk – bicycles with twisted spokes, a set of Indian clubs, two broken truckle beds, half a dozen damaged desks.

"A trap door?" Applegate poked about. He suddenly felt in very high spirits. "A secret passage? They're out of favour nowadays, but I should rather like to come across one. Generally rather smelly, I believe, and you have to crawl through them. Here's an iron ring fixed in the wall. That should have a purpose. If I pull at it... " He did so, without the slightest effect. "You'd better exercise that powerful grip of yours on it." She did so, with equal unsuccess. "Defeated. Not that I really care. Come here, Gabler." In the friendly darkness he kissed her again. "Were those stories you told me about delinquency and tea parties really true?"

"Yes." They began to climb the cellar steps.

"I don't mind. I've always said young men should marry girls with experience. Have you ever thought about marriage?"

"Marriage?" She laughed, and began to sing:

> "The man I marry has got to be
> As pure and white as a cemetery.
> The man I call my own
> Must be just as romantic as Franchot Tone... "

They reached the cellar door. Hedda carefully locked it behind her, and they stepped out of the cupboard to see the round face of Maureen Gardner. She surveyed them calmly.

"So that's what you've been doing. Towsing. That's what the Elizabethans called it, didn't they?"

"I believe they did." Applegate tried to suppress an unseemly simper.

"You look pretty much the worse for wear. All dusty." She began to beat at his clothes. "I thought you were coming to help me with my thought-paintings."

The brown-faced Deverell suddenly appeared and looked at them curiously. "What's happened to your head? There's a bump on it."

"I knocked it on something down there." Deverell looked at him quizzically and said nothing.

"Did either of you see somebody come up out of the cellar a couple of minutes ago? Somebody in a hurry?" Hedda asked. Maureen had just come downstairs and Deverell had been in the garden. Neither of them had seen anything.

"You look pale," Hedda said solicitously to Applegate. "A breath of air would do you good."

"I feel all right." She pressed his arm in a significant manner. They went out into the garden and walked round to the back of the house, by the disused tennis court.

"Did you notice?" she asked.

"Notice what?"

"Deverell said he had been out in the garden. He was wearing red slippers. It rained last night and the garden's muddy."

"All right. He likes walking in a muddy garden with slippers."

"But there was no mud on his slippers."

He was shaken, but not convinced. "That's odd, but I find it hard to believe that Deverell – after all, he's only a boy."

"So is Derek Winterbottom, but nobody has any doubt that he's capable of murder. Anyway, we're on to something, don't you agree? And it's something to do with Bogue and this house. There's a man in Bramley who can tell us things about Bogue, if anybody can. That's old Anscombe, who keeps the general store and post office. Let's go down and see him now."

Chapter Twelve

The village store of legend has a window in which gobstoppers, liquorice bootlaces and sherbet suckers nestle side by side with little bits of local pottery. There will be teapots made in the form of cottages and milk bowls with such mottoes as "He complains soon who complains of his porridge" or "Look before you leap." A bell tinkles when the door is opened. Inside the place is very poky but spotlessly clean, and the storekeeper is able to produce from some little box in an almost inaccessible cranny anything you want – as long as what you want is sufficiently quaint and unusual, like an ounce of snuff or a cut-throat razor.

The village store at Bramley was not very much like that. Its window had been filled with boxes of soapless detergent piled high in a pyramid. Some of these had fallen on their sides to reveal the words "Dummy Packet for Display" on them. The little bell was there, and tinkled when Hedda opened the door. Inside Applegate noted with approval gobstoppers and liquorice bootlaces, but a film of dirt seemed to rest over the whole interior. Two bad oranges were slowly corrupting the good ones in a bowl. Decorations and party hats unsold at Christmas stood at one end of the counter. At the other end a great neuter cat rested happily on some wrapped toffees, and regarded disdainfully an old, dull-looking piece of ham.

The girl who came from an inner room to serve them was lank-haired and sluttish. What a delicious little essay on the decay of the English countryside could be prompted by this village shop, Applegate reflected happily – and how many such essays had no doubt already been written. Hedda, he was amused to see, adopted a lady of the manor briskness in speaking to the girl, quite unlike her usual speech.

"Good morning, Jennifer." Jennifer, Applegate thought with a sense of outrage, her name should be Ellen. "Father in?"

"Yes, Miss Pont." The girl opened the door and shouted: "Dad." A little, red-faced, cheerful man came in, wiping his hands on his trousers. Like the bell and the gobstoppers, he appeared faithful to the legend. "Morning, Miss Pont. Terrible affair that up at the school. Have they found that young Winterbottom yet?"

"Not yet."

"Mark my words, Miss Pont, and I mean no disrespect to anyone by saying it, school is no place for young rascals like that. We talked about this very subject last week in the Murdstone and district discussion group." Oh, dear, Applegate thought, another segment of the legend dissolving. Discussion group, indeed. "The question was, are we too kind to our juvenile delinquents, and we had a very good speaker down, Mr Ormsby from the headquarters of the Kent Juvenile Welfare. He had a rough passage, I can tell you. I hope I'm as progressive as the next man, but spare the rod and spoil the child, you know, there's a lot in it."

Had the rod, Applegate wondered, been spared with Jennifer, who now stood listening to her father with her mouth slightly open? Hedda quite evidently took this kind of conversation in her stride. "We shan't agree about that," she said, with an air of finality. "What I wanted from you, Mr Anscombe, was a little information."

Anscombe had protuberant eyes, and at these words they seemed to stand out a little farther, so that the bulging, slightly watery eyeball was plainly discernible.

"About Johnny Bogue," Hedda said.

"Bogue." Was it Applegate's imagination, or was there a shade of restraint now in Anscombe's loquacity? "What do you want to know about him, Miss Pont?"

"Anything you can tell me." Hedda sat down on an upturned packing case.

"That's a tall order. Get off the toffees, cat." The cat turned amber eyes on him and leapt in a leisurely way to the floor. "Fact is, I got in a bit of trouble for talking about Johnny Bogue. During the war it was, when everyone said he was a German spy. I faced them out about it. Had some rare arguments. Nothing I enjoy more than a good argument."

"Didn't like it the night they ducked you in the pond," his daughter said.

"That wasn't argument, my girl, it was hooliganism. And who was proved right in the end? Wasn't he killed on a mission for his country?"

"And died owing you a hundred pounds you never saw."

"I got my share of the estate like everybody else. If Johnny had lived I'd have got the lot." The protuberant eyes glared angrily at her. "You go out back and help your mother. I'll tend to the shop."

She shrugged and went out, banging the door behind her. "They're prejudiced against him because of the money," Anscombe said. "But I think nothing of that. Do you know what Johnny – that's what I used to call him to his face *and* he liked it – would do? He'd always pay his bill in fivers, sometimes every month, sometimes not for six months, and he'd never take any change. If the bill was twenty-one pounds he'd give me five fivers. I'd offer him the change. 'Keep it, Bill,' he'd say. 'What is it, after all? It's only money.'"

Applegate felt it was time he said something. "You liked him," he remarked rather feebly.

"More than that, sir. I'm proud to have known him. I remember the first time he came in this shop. He put his arms on the counter and said: 'I'm Johnny Bogue. I've just come to Bramley Hall. Expect you've heard of me.' Of course the word had gone around that he was coming to live down here, and some were pleased and others weren't. 'I don't know *what* you've heard,' he said. 'But I'll tell you some facts. Once I was an MP and now I'm not. Once I was in prison and now I'm out. Don't think that means I'm a back number, or that you won't get your bills paid. You play straight by me and you won't be sorry.' And I never was sorry."

"That was some time in the thirties," Hedda said.

"When he started his New Radical Party, nineteen thirty-*four*. Wanted to make a clean sweep of everything, he did. No more Parliament. A government of businessmen was what he was after, with *a real man* at the top of it. He was that all right. He was for cutting down Income Tax by half, and do you know how he was going to do it? Through a State lottery and a tax on betting. You're an enlightened woman, Miss Pont, no doubt you're a progressive man, Mr – "

"Applegate."

"Applegate. Wasn't that sensible? But the politicians wouldn't do it, wouldn't have anything to do with his ideas though they didn't mind drinking his champagne at weekends. Look at these." From a box labelled "Cigarettes, various," he selected three from a batch of old photographs. They all showed the curly-headed, arrogant figure of Jenks' snap. Here he stood wearing an umpire's white jacket, a glass of beer in his hand, with the Bramley cricket team; here knelt laughing with one hand round a girl's ankle ("Judging the ankle competition at our local show," said Anscombe. "The girls loved him.") and here stood outside Bramley Hall in the middle of a group among whom he recognised Barney

Craigen and Eileen Delaney. Hedda's finger jabbed. "Who are those two?"

Anscombe put on horn-rimmed spectacles which gave him a surprisingly scholarly appearance. "That's Miss Delaney, she was what you might call his business partner. Being polite, you know. Johnny was always one for the ladies. The man, I've seen him often, but I don't know his name. But some of the real nobs used to come down – all political parties, *and* the aristocracy too. Pretty well every weekend they'd be down here eating his food and guzzling his drink, without giving him any more than a thank you. I'd tell him straight that he was wasting his money, if he ever thought he'd get anything out of them. But you know what he'd say? He'd put his finger to his nose and say, 'Trust Johnny, he's not such a fool after all.' That's why he had the Hall enlarged, you know, for parties and all that. Had one part done in what you might call the old style and the other very modern. What you'd call original." Applegate nodded in answer to his inquiring look. "Of course people used to talk, ask where the money came from, but then people always will talk."

Hedda shifted on her case. "What happened in the war?"

"*People*," the shopkeeper said with ineffable contempt. "Said he was too friendly with the Germans, ought to be interned."

"And he wasn't?"

"We-e-ll." Anscombe was cautious. "There were a lot of Germans used to come down here, business men who were over here, so it was said. But that all stopped when the war came. And it was then he told me what these Germans had really come for. Do you know what it was, and why Johnny used to see them? He was in a little group that was helping the Jews escape from the Nazis, arranging the ships and all that to get them out of the country. That's the sort of man Johnny Bogue was, and that's what he did. But you know what people are – ignorant. They got it in their heads Johnny was a Nazi himself. I told them different. I said he was a patriot. Stands to reason he was, else Churchill would never have employed him. You know he was on a mission, important mission, when he was killed."

"What sort of mission?"

"Ah, that I don't know. He never gave away Government secrets, Miss Pont. Johnny was *not* that kind of man."

"Did he say anything about money at that time? Did he say he was going to make a lot of money soon, or he'd just made a lot, or anything?"

"Miss Hedda. With all due respect, Miss Hedda, you don't understand that man. He wasn't interested in money. I told you what he said, 'It's only money.' "

"He liked having it, though," Applegate suggested.

"Which of us doesn't?" The shopkeeper roared with laughter as if this were a good joke. "But he did say a funny thing to me a couple of weeks before he died. He came down to the shop and put his arms on the counter the way he always did, and ordered some things to be sent up. Then he gave his smile, and said: 'Hear they ducked you in the pond on my account.' That was on account of a little argument I had with Bill Noakes and Jerry Thomas and some others in the pub, when they said Johnny Bogue ought to be shut up and I told them there was a name for people like them, and if they wanted to know what it was, R-A-T spelt rat. Do you know that Johnny had paid all the hospital expenses for Bill Noakes' wife when she was in six weeks with a broken hip, and that Jerry Thomas, who was our local builder then, must have done thousands of pounds worth of work for him? So one thing led to another and half a dozen of them said I was as bad as he was, and they put me in the pond. I've no hard feelings, though, I'm a natural philosopher. Where was I?"

"Something funny he said."

"Ah, yes. We chewed the fat about that for a bit, and Johnny said: 'That was a real friendly act, and I appreciate it.'

Then he gave his grin, and asked: 'Worried about getting paid?' There was only one answer to that, and I gave it. So then he said: 'Do you know, Bill, in a week or two's time I shall be the richest man in the world. And what does that mean? I'll tell you. Just nothing at all.' "

They waited expectantly. "Is that all?" Hedda asked.

"That's all. Funny thing to say though, or the way he said it was funny. Just about two weeks afterwards he died."

Two small boys came in. Anscombe served them with bull's-eyes and tinned herrings. Applegate raised his brows, and Hedda nodded. "We must be getting on."

They were at the door when Anscombe said: "There was somebody in yesterday asking questions about Johnny, and what he was saying and doing just before he died. Funny coincidence that."

"A tall, thin man, dressed in a dark suit," Applegate asked.

"No. This man was medium height. Nothing special about him. Ah, yes, there was one thing I remember. The lobe of his left ear was torn, missing almost, as if he'd been in a fight."

Chapter Thirteen

In the office of the *Murdstone and District Gazette a* blubber-faced girl dozed over a typewriter. Behind a glass panel a little bald man with glasses well down on his nose inspected galleys. The office was steamily warm. Applegate coughed and the girl woke with a start. "Pardon," she said thickly.

"Can I see the editor?"

"Did you wish to place an advertisement?"

"No, just to see the editor."

"Mr Fish is busy. Is it the list of prize-winners for the Benfold whist drive?"

"It is a private matter," Applegate said. "And urgent."

"I don't know whether Mr Fish can be disturbed. It's press day, you see." At this moment the little man, who had been observing this colloquy with increasing impatience, opened the door that separated him from the main office.

"What now, Miss Tranter? Am I to have no peace?"

"Gentleman says he wants to see you." The girl flapped hands helplessly.

"Press day. Very busy." He waved the galleys.

"I told him that, Mr Fish. Said it was urgent."

"Can't be done, Miss Tranter. Copy to the printer. Working against time." The glass door closed.

"There you are, you see." The girl looked nervously up at the clock. "He's working against time."

Applegate was not easily moved to annoyance, but he felt a certain indignation at the fact that his presence had been totally ignored during this conversation. He lifted the flap of the counter and began to walk through. The blubber-faced girl barred his way with an appearance of resolution until their knees touched. Then she backed away with an anguished scream and took refuge behind her typewriter. The glass door opened again and the little man popped out.

"This is an outrage, sir. An unwarrantable intrusion. Has the individual no rights today? Does lawlessness walk rampant?" He addressed the questions to the air.

"This won't take a minute."

"Last week the water jug broken at the Council meeting. Not by accident, mark you, but deliberately, in a fit of temper. Now this. Call the police, Miss Tranter. Let us see whether the law maintains its majesty."

Applegate moved to the telephone and placed his hand upon it. His forehead felt moist, whether from the steamy warmth or from anxiety he was unsure. He said pleadingly: "Look, this really is urgent. I simply want some information connected with a murder… "

The little man pushed the glasses up on his nose. He was magnificent. "Remove your hand, sir, from that telephone," he thundered.

" – and about a man named Bogue."

"Bogue." The little man pushed down the glasses again, looked at Applegate over them. "You have some connection with him?"

"Not exactly. I just want a little information – "

"Come in." He darted into his office, seized the galleys and pushed them into the hands of the blubber-faced girl. "Correct these, Miss Tranter. Correct and deliver. Be on your mental toes. Watch for literals. And remember, time is the essence of the contract." The blubber-faced girl grunted, and flashed Applegate a glance of pure hatred. The little man sat down in a swivel-chair, made a complete turn in it, and said: "You mentioned murder. Kindly explain."

Applegate explained, making what seemed to him judicious omissions. He told of Montague's murder, of his interview with Jenks and the scene in the hotel bar. He described the way in which he had been hit on the head in the cellar. Mr Fish punctuated his narrative with little exclamations and cries of excitement. At the end of it he said: "You really believe that there is a fortune hidden at Bramley Hall and that these – ah – rival gangs are after it?" Applegate said he did. "And what do you want of me, may I ask?"

"Miss Pont and I would like to know anything you can tell us about the Martin case. And I hoped to get some information about Bogue from the paper. I presume you had an obituary notice."

"We had. I wrote it myself. It was a fine piece of journalism." He stared at Applegate. "It's a tall story. Why not go to the police?"

"They wouldn't believe us."

"Neither do I. You're playing some game of your own, I don't doubt that. Suppose *I* telephone the police?"

"Then they won't believe you either. Do you think we could have that window open?"

"Open a window, let in a cold. However…" He opened it two inches. "Does that suit you?"

"Much better," Applegate said untruthfully. "You remember about this man Martin."

"Certainly. Perfectly straightforward case. Death by misadventure. No puzzle there. About Bogue now. You're barking up the wrong tree."

"How do you mean?"

"Miss Tranter," the little man cried. The blubber-faced girl came in. "Down to the printer, Miss Tranter. And within ten minutes. Time and tide, you know."

"I haven't finished correcting."

"To the devil with corrections. Let the presses roll." She sighed, took more proofs down from the wall, bundled them all together, and went out. "What were we saying?"

"You said I was barking up the wrong tree about Bogue."

"About his fortune, yes. He had no fortune when he died."

"How do you know that?"

"Ten days before his death he borrowed two hundred pounds from me. I never saw a penny of it back." There was a vague, soft look in Mr Fish's eyes. "You think I'm a fool. You never heard him talk."

"He talked you into it?"

"Nothing of the kind. But he was a wonderful talker. His voice could be soft and smooth like silk, and then again it could be cold as a knife blade. And enthusiasm, he had enthusiasm. When he talked about Britain's future and about democracy, and said the Royal Family should be the Radical leaders of a great radical people, he could bring the tears to your eyes."

"He was convincing."

"Certainly not."

"But you said – "

"I know what I said, young man. He was the finest talker I ever heard, but he wasn't convincing. You're too young to understand, but it isn't the same thing at all. There was always something wrong about Bogue. You could feel it. I always knew he was a scoundrel, but it made no difference. It made no difference about Nella, either."

"Who was Nella?"

"My daughter. Did somebody send you here, talk to you about her, eh? Is that the game you're playing?"

With as much earnestness as he could manage Applegate said: "I swear that I'd never heard of your daughter, and didn't even know your name, when I came in here."

For a long moment Mr Fish looked at Applegate. Then he nodded. "All right. I believe you. Nella was eighteen when she met Bogue. He took her up for a time, took us all up. Used to go to the Hall for dinner most Saturdays or Sundays, Nella and my wife and I. Bogue was going to start a new weekly paper, political paper, you know. Talked about it a lot. Some pretty important men down there, and they seemed to take him seriously. I did too. He was going to make me editor. Expect you think I was a fool to believe that."

"No."

"He was after Nella, she was all he wanted. But he was clever. He took much less notice of her than he did of my wife and me. And he played up to me. Knew what it was I'd always wanted. National journalism, a chance to make my voice heard. I would have made it heard, too, I'd have shaken them all. Don't suppose you believe it. All right, don't answer that. I took what he said as true, that's all that matters." He took off his spectacles, rubbed his eyes. They were weak old eyes, Applegate saw. Beneath the huffing and puffing he was a weak little man. His voice would never have been heard in national journalism, and probably he knew it. Tears formed in the weak eyes, he wiped them.

"What happened?" Applegate asked.

"We were fools, my wife and I. Never guessed what was going on until one day Nella went off to a so-called job in London. Fortnight later I went up and found she was living with him. That lasted for twelve months. Then she came back home. Never talked about what had happened, and we didn't ask questions. She was in a state of collapse when she came home, but we nursed her back to health."

"And then?"

"Then? Why, nothing. Never saw Bogue, of course, no invitations, nothing at all. Nella married a young chap down here who'd always been fond of her. Went off farming in New Zealand. Two years later they were both killed in a train crash. Then the war came. Bogue was very quiet at first, lying low. Rumours were that he was a spy, but I never believed them. Saw him sometimes, but never spoke, never acknowledged him, although he always smiled and nodded to me. Then he was supposed to be on these missions, some sort of secret work. Couldn't believe it when one day he pushed open the door here, walked in, said: 'Hallo, Fishy, still letting the presses roll?' Would you believe it, would you believe it possible a man would have the nerve to do that?" The question was rhetorical. "You think I should have shown him the door, I expect. So I should have done. But do you know what he said right away, very next words? He said: 'You won't have to let 'em roll much longer. Not here, anyway. You remember that little job I promised you. It's all fixed.' He talked and I listened. What do you think of that? What kind of a man was I to listen, after the way he'd treated Nella."

Applegate said nothing. There seemed nothing to say. Mr Fish blew his nose violently and put on his spectacles again.

"I believe he was the devil, Johnny Bogue. He knew your weakness, and knew just how to play on it. Knew what I wanted. You don't need to tell me I shall never get it now. Never would have done any good with it, I dare say is what you're thinking. Probably this is all I was fit for." He pushed over a copy of the *Murdstone and District Gazette* and Applegate looked at the headlines. "Scandalous Scene in Council Chamber." "Farmer's Licence endorsed. Break-Neck Speed, says Lorry Driver." "Marsh Farmers to visit Germany in late Spring." "Young Hooligans on Assault Charge."

"What I'm fitted for," Mr Fish repeated. "But Bogue knew what I wanted. The tale he told me was that he'd been asked to edit a series of official publications for the COI. All to do with the country's war effort, propaganda booklets. But written by our finest writers, something quite new. He was to be head of this special section, but he wouldn't have much time to give to the detail work. He'd asked for me as his

93

assistant. You think I was a fool to believe him, after all that had happened?"

"He must have had a lot of charm," Applegate said evasively.

"Charm, I don't know. You'd have believed him too. He had a lot of papers he showed me, letters from different people talking about the valuable work he was doing. And a letter from 10 Downing Street asking him to produce these booklets and pick his own staff."

"Forged," Applegate said. "He played a trick like that before."

"I don't know. Very likely. Then he sat on the edge of my desk, swinging his leg and humming. 'I'm hard up,' he said. 'Lend me five hundred pounds for a month, Fishy.' You think I'm a fool, but I'm not such a fool as that. I told him I hadn't got the money. He went on humming and said he thought I'd have done that much to oblige a friend. At that I fairly let him have it, you can guess, and told him how much of a friend I thought he was after the way he'd treated Nella. He stopped humming, then, and a sort of change came over his face.

" 'All right,' he said, 'I've tried to do it politely. Now I shall have to be rough. I thought Nella didn't tell you.' I asked him what he meant. 'Why, I'm not really asking for myself. I thought you'd be interested in your grandson's education. But I see this is a shock to you. I believe I've brought some papers.' He had a copy of the certificate, showing the birth of a boy named Geoffrey Bogue to himself and Nella. I asked him questions – oh, don't think I didn't ask questions. He said Nella had left him because she didn't like his ways of doing business. 'She's like you, Daddy Fish,' he said. 'At heart she's respectable.' I couldn't understand why Nella had left the child, or why she hadn't forced him to marry her. At that he burst out laughing. 'Nella made up her mind she didn't want to marry me. She found out that I'm not the marrying kind. She wanted Geoffrey, but I made up my mind to keep him. He's my son, you know. I wanted a son and now I've got one I mean to keep him. In the end she understood that I meant what I said. Here's a snap.' He gave me a snapshot of Nella and the baby. I've still got it."

The little man picked up from his desk a photograph in a small, leather frame. It showed a thin, intense-looking girl holding in her arms a small bundle of indistinguishable sex and appearance. " 'He's a bright-looking little chap now,' Bogue said. 'I've got him up in the north, but if you wanted him to pay you a visit that could be arranged'."

Fish had been staring at the photograph. Now he put it back on his desk. "Cut it short, cut it short," he said, with a momentary return to the impatience he had shown earlier. "I gave Bogue two hundred pounds. In return I got the address of a Cumberland farmhouse where he said the boy was living. He told me I should hear in a few days about the job as his assistant. Of course I heard nothing. That was the last time I saw him, and I think I saw him then for the first time as he really was. You know, he took a pleasure in telling me that story."

"And what happened?"

"I wrote to Mrs Averill, the woman who was supposed to be looking after Geoffrey at the farmhouse. The letter came back marked 'Gone away.' I went up there and found that there had been a woman staying at the farmhouse with a small boy. They had left, giving no address, after receiving a telephone call on the day that Bogue saw me. The farmer and his wife were a decent couple, but they couldn't help me. The little boy was named Geoffrey. They never heard his other name."

"What about Bogue?"

"It was a Wednesday when he came to see me. On Wednesday night I wrote to Cumberland, Saturday I got the letter back, Sunday I went up there. Most of the next week I spent in London trying to find Bogue. I went to his flat, saw people who knew him. Nobody could tell me where he was.

Friday of the next week he was killed in the plane. Whether it crashed or was shot down was never found out."

"So you didn't see Geoffrey?"

"I never saw Geoffrey. Never told my wife. Don't know why I should have told you. I wonder about him sometimes." Mr Fish took off his spectacles and rubbed his eyes. "But you see why I'm sure Bogue hadn't got a fortune when he died. You want to see that obituary? Tried to forget my feelings when I wrote it, just remembered that I was a journalist."

He took down a bound volume from the shelf behind him, blew the dust off it, and searched the pages.

"There."

The story occupied half one of the inside pages. Applegate sat down and read it.

TRAGIC DEATH OF PROMINENT LOCAL RESIDENT

Mr "Johnny" Bogue Killed In "Secret Mission" Air Crash

The Air Ministry announced this week that one of the passengers in the airplane presumed shot down by German fighters in the Mediterranean area was Bramley resident John Bogue. Thus the word "finis" has been written to the career of one of the stormiest petrels in modern English life. It is understood that Mr Bogue was flying on a special mission connected with propaganda work.

Mr Bogue first came to Kent as a resident when he purchased Bramley Hall several years ago. The property had been empty for some time before he bought it, and he effected many alterations and additions which, if they were not always entirely in harmony with the prevailing style of the building, were distinctive in their own manner.

96

The manifold demands of business and pleasure took him up to London a great deal, but if he was something of a "weekender" he was certainly one who imprinted his personality on local life. He was greatly interested in Bramley Cricket Club, and could always be relied upon for a generous contribution to any local cause. When the money subscribed for a bus shelter near the Hall fell short of expectation, Mr Bogue provided a cheque which made up the necessary sum. He was also the chief sponsor of a scheme for providing an airport at Murdstone. He believed that this would bring increased employment and prosperity to the area, but because of financial difficulties and objections from other local residents, the idea fell through.

In Kent we saw little of the stormy side of Mr Bogue's career. He first came into prominence in 1923, when he was elected MP for Wandsworth East, with a majority of 873 votes over the sitting member, Sir John Rolvenden. He retained this seat until 1931, when he was sentenced to eighteen months' imprisonment for obtaining money by false pretences from Mr Alexander Keeble. During the twenties he was associated with the night club craze, and played a prominent part in London social life.

Those who knew Mr Bogue in his activities here observed that he was a man of abounding energy. This was never proved more surely than by his action in founding the New Radical Party immediately on his release. The Party received considerable publicity at its foundation, but never made a great impact on English life. Six seats were contested at the 1935 election, but all the candidates except Mr Bogue himself lost their deposits. He stood again for Wandsworth East, but was defeated by some 3,000 votes.

Mr Bogue was a controversial figure, but his personal charm will be fully attested by all who were his guests at the lavish house parties held at Bramley Hall. At the outbreak of war he was much criticised for what was

97

thought to be the pro-German nature of his political activities. He always strongly denied that he was anything but a patriotic Briton, and his severest critics may now be silenced by the circumstances of his death. Perhaps it is true that too many of us see life and character in terms of black and white, forgetting that there is also such a colour as grey.

From the centre of the column Bogue's photograph looked up, curly-haired and insolent, smiling over its secret joke. He closed the volume.

Mr Fish looked up at him anxiously. "What did you think of it? As a piece of writing, I mean?"

"Excellent."

"And the last sentence? I spent a long time over it. Do you think I was right to put it in? There was a lot of criticism at the time."

"I don't know whether it was right. After your experience it was certainly generous."

"Foolish, perhaps." Applegate, deep in thought, did not reply. Mr Fish bristled slightly. "No more foolish, let me tell you, than your stuff about fortunes hidden at Bramley."

A door closed. Miss Tranter's blubber face appeared in the outer office. "You never saw or tried to trace the little boy, Geoffrey."

"The war was on. Nella was dead. What would have been the use?" Mr Fish, a little man hunched behind his desk, looked defeated and old. "You think I should have tried to find him."

"I didn't say that. Thank you for being so helpful." Applegate got up and put his hand on the door.

"If there's anything else I can do… " Now that the past had revived itself, Mr Fish was unwilling to let it go. With an obscure feeling of guilt Applegate backed out of the door and away.

Chapter Fourteen

In Murdstone there was always a wind. Applegate pushed his body against it, walked head down along the promenade into the wind. Stone steps led to the beach and he went down them, plunging through shingle down to firm sand. The tide was a long way out. Two ships, toylike, moved slowly along. Hands in pockets, he brooded over what he had learned – if indeed he had learned anything important. It seemed that the clues were dropped like the trail in a paper chase, but the invisible hare who had laid them was, he had to remember, long since dead. Behind the naïve phrases of Fish's obituary notice lay what realities? Financial frauds, drug running, every kind of trickery. It was the trickster, the man who took a positive pleasure in trapping such victims as Fish and Jenks, that Applegate saw in that photograph. Yet there had apparently been another Johnny Bogue, the man who had helped Jews to escape from Germany, the man who always paid his shop bills in fivers and never asked for change. What was it he had said to Anscombe? "In a week or two's time I shall be the richest man in the world. And what does that mean? Just nothing at all." How did that square with the fact that he was hard up for two hundred pounds? And what had those things to do with the death of a little man named Montague?

Applegate, walking along the sand, asked himself such questions and obtained no answers. A thin sun created his shadow, stretching out seawards along the sand – created also, oddly, another shadow, much bulkier, moving towards it. The sun was hidden behind cloud, shadows disappeared. Applegate looked up. Barney Craigen stood a few feet away, smiling at him with all his gold teeth. Applegate turned sharply. Behind him, at about the same distance, stood Jenks' bar companion, the boy called Arthur. His hands were in his pockets.

"All right, chum," Craigen said. "Let's go and have a talk."

Was it possible to run? The esplanade was some twenty yards away, and Craigen stood between him and it. Was it possible to fight? The boy took his right hand out of his pocket. Even under dull cloud the glint of steel showed.

Applegate cleared his throat. "It seems that I have no choice but to accept your joint invitation… "

The grin on Craigen's face broadened. "Certainly swallowed the dictionary, hasn't he, Arthur?"

" – Although I'm surprised that it came from both of you." He spoke to Arthur. "It was you that he called a little runt last night, wasn't it?"

The boy pursed his lips. Craigen said: "Are you coming quietly, or have we got to take you?"

Applegate's hero in *Where Dons Delight,* placed in similarly difficult circumstances (although his assailant had been the vampire bat don) had escaped by using the oldest deceptive tactic in the world. With little hope of success he essayed to use it now. He said in a conversational tone to a non-existent ally behind Craigen: "You can get him now. Round the neck."

The resemblance between life and sensational fiction was gratifyingly confirmed when Craigen turned his head. Applegate leapt forward and punched the big man forcefully in the stomach. Craigen staggered and sat down with a grunt. Then Applegate was past him and running along the sand with the slight feeling of exhilaration natural to those who have performed successfully some physical feat. He had run from sand on shingle, and was within a few feet of the esplanade, when something hit the back of his head. He did not fall but the blow, which one part of his mind registered as coming from a stone, caused him to stumble. A moment later his leg was violently jerked, and he slipped down on the shingle. He looked up to see the boy Arthur standing between him and safety, the razor held ready in its little pocket-knife casing.

Arthur spoke. His voice was thick, with a strong Cockney accent. "Don't try anything else or I'll cut you where it hurts."

Applegate sat up and watched the approach of Craigen, who came puffing up like a bull. His face was very red.

"You… " he said. "Come on."

They trudged up the shingle together. Applegate rubbed the back of his head, which ached slightly, and reflected that in the course of this investigation he was taking some hard, although not vitally injurious knocks. He reflected also that life did not resemble sensational fiction quite closely enough.

A car waited by the pavement. On the other side of the road walked a crocodile line of girls wearing green blazers and grey hats, mistresses marching self-consciously at head and tail. Would a loud halloo be efficacious? More likely it would provoke a shudder of distaste. Besides, he told himself, it seemed unlikely that serious harm was intended to him. A conscientious investigator should welcome the chance of penetrating a little nearer the heart of a mystery. He got into the car. Craigen sat in the driver's seat, the boy came with him in the back.

"You can put away that razor," Applegate said rather pettishly. "I'm coming for the little talk."

There was a click. The blade disappeared and the boy slipped it back into his pocket. The hand that came out was coarse and stubby, with nails bitten to the quick.

They turned left off the esplanade and then right past rows of semi-detached bay-windowed villas, then left again into a *cul-de-sac*. At the end of it stood the great red brick Victorian Gothic water tower which he had seen from the bus. It was approached through double gates, which led into a small forecourt. The water tower, seen thus closely, had evidently been converted into a number of square rooms, with windows on three sides. There seemed to be one room only on each floor, and the tower was six or seven storeys high.

Craigen opened a door in the side of the tower and Applegate followed him into a tiny lobby, which led into one of the square rooms he had seen from outside. The room was comfortably furnished, with two sofas, armchairs and small tables. In one corner a spiral staircase led upwards. There was no fireplace. Two people sat in the room drinking tea, and it was without surprise that he recognised them as Eileen Delaney and Henry Jenks.

Eileen Delaney wore a mauve woollen frock that contrasted oddly with her magenta hair. She stretched a claw-like hand with rings on it in greeting, and said in her rusty voice: "So glad that you could come. The crumpets are still hot."

"I didn't have much choice. Your friends extended a pressing invitation."

"I hope Barney didn't get into one of his moods. When he's in a mood you just can't do anything with him."

Deep in his throat Craigen said: "He tried to be funny."

"Arthur saved the day." Applegate looked at Jenks who sat nervously on a hard-backed chair, a cup of tea poised on one bony, striped-trousered knee.

"Sit down, all of you." There was something masterful about the little woman presiding over the tea trolley. "Milk or lemon? Sugar? Lift that lid and you'll find the crumpets."

Applegate took his cup of tea and his crumpet, and put both on the arm of a big, shabby armchair. Craigen sat on a sofa near the entrance door and patted the seat beside him with a slab-like hand. Arthur seemed not to notice. He remained standing while he sipped his tea, and there was no expression at all in his pale eyes.

"I thought it would clear the air if we had a little talk," Eileen Delaney said.

"Including an explanation, I hope." Applegate spoke with what he felt to be creditable self-possession.

Barney Craigen vented a disgusted exclamation. "Talk, explanation. Come down here to do a job and all we do is gab."

"You'll have something to do soon enough." Her beak was curved in his direction. "And you gab enough yourself. Too much. It was your gabbing in Earl's Court bars that brought Henry down here. Not that I'm anything but pleased to see him." She cackled.

"Now, Eileen – "

"So keep your mouth shut. Now, Mr Applegate. You say you want an explanation. I agree, I think you're entitled to one."

Applegate bit into his crumpet. "It will have to cover rather a lot of ground if it's going to satisfy me."

The wrinkled eyes were shrewd. "You're a young man of spirit. I like that. But don't let it lead you too far."

"One thing that really baffles me," Applegate said to Jenks, "is what you and boyfriend Arthur are doing in this galley. When I saw you last you said you were on the opposite side from Miss Delaney."

Jenks put his teacup back on the trolley and put one long leg over the other. His hand moved up and touched the red pimple. "We have come to an arrangement."

"You mean she'll see you get your cut?"

"We are – ah, at least temporarily – partners."

"You find Bogue's fortune first, and fight about it afterwards?"

"That's a very cynical way to put it," Jenks said reprovingly. "As partners Eileen and I contribute to the common pool of – ah – information and resources. And we have the kind of trust in each other that is essential to partners in any enterprise."

Eileen Delaney was collecting the tea things on the tray, Craigen lay on the sofa with his head back, Arthur had taken his knife out of his pocket and was clicking it. His best hope of learning anything useful, Applegate decided, was to play both ends against the middle.

"I don't want to be impolite, Henry – you remember we were on Christian name terms the last time we met – but I can't see what you've got to put into the pool. I doubt if it's any significant amount of cash. I feel sure it isn't information. I can only think of one thing, and that's what you might call a wasting asset."

"What?" Eileen Delaney croaked.

"Why, Arthur, of course. Miss Delaney doesn't love you for your own bright eyes, Henry, it's all for the sake of Arthur."

At the door Arthur straightened and said in his thick, whining voice: "Shall I shut him up?"

Jenks raised a slightly trembling hand. "No, this is funny. I want to hear it."

"Funny enough. Work it out for yourself, Henry. Yesterday neither Barney nor Miss Delaney was very polite to you. You might say Barney was downright rude, if that wasn't nature to him. They've only changed since they've discovered that you've provided yourself with a bodyguard. What's the answer? Just for a day or two they've got to play cautiously. They're waiting for something – I don't know what it is, perhaps you do. If you hadn't got Arthur to look after you, you'd have had an accident like Eddie Martin.

They don't want trouble at the moment. Afterwards, though – "

Jenks giggled. "I shall still have Arthur."

"I wouldn't be too sure of that. Remember Frankie Montague."

"Poor Frankie. But he couldn't really look after himself. Arthur can."

"But can you trust him? Won't Arthur sell himself and that razor-blade of his to the highest bidder? It's just as you said to me, Henry, you're too trusting."

Arthur moved. "I've had enough," he said. He had his knife out and he advanced on Applegate with his body slightly bent forward. Applegate picked up a chair and held it in front of him. He was much relieved to hear Eileen Delaney, from her position behind the tea trolley, shout: "Stop."

"I've had enough," Arthur repeated, but he stood uncertainly, the knife cased in his palm. Jenks said something soothing and inaudible to him. The boy shrugged his shoulders irritably.

"More than enough," the woman said emphatically. "I quite agree. Mr Applegate, you're simply trying to cause trouble. If that's your purpose, you'd better go. If not, put down that chair. And Arthur, I don't want to see any more of that knife. You and Barney can walk round the houses for half an hour. Or take a look at the concert party." She cackled suddenly.

Barney Craigen obediently lumbered to his feet. In the small square room he looked enormous. Arthur put the knife into his pocket. His pale eyes still looked at Applegate. He screwed up his mouth, and Applegate saw a patch of spittle on his jacket.

"Arthur," Jenks cried reprovingly, but the boy was gone.

Applegate wiped his jacket, put down the chair and sat on it. "Nice little pet."

Jenks was apologetic. "He's only a boy."

"If he's a boy, what's a rattlesnake?"

"*Stop it.*" Eileen Delaney rapped the tea trolley. "This is getting us nowhere. Mr Applegate, are you prepared to put your cards on the table if we do the same?"

"Certainly." His cards, Applegate reflected, were few and all of contemptibly low denominations.

"There are things we know that you don't know. And you may be able to help us." The little eyes considered him carefully. "Cards on the table. You want to ask questions?"

There could be no doubt of that. But what questions? He began rather lamely: "Do you own this place?"

"Matter of fact, I do. Johnny bought it. You know about Johnny?"

"I'm learning."

"Had the idea of turning Murdstone into a really popular resort, and doing something with this tower. Make it like the Blackpool Tower, say. Never came to anything, too many stuffed shirts round here. When Johnny died the tower went for almost nothing. But I had a fancy for something of his. There are six rooms in it. I come down and stay weekends in the summer. It's a bit of a change from what I was used to. Know about me?"

"Of course. The Hundreds and Thousands – and other night clubs." He tried to remember exactly what Jenks had said.

"Those were the days, say what you like about them. We had some wonderful times – you couldn't help having wonderful times with Johnny. There's never been anyone like Johnny." Between the wrinkled lids, into the tiny eyes, came genuine tears.

"Never anyone like Johnny," Jenks valiantly echoed. Applegate saw them suddenly, both of them, as harmless relics with no real existence apart from the legendary shyster upon whom they still brooded. His natural tendency to romanticism was checked when she wiped her eyes with a bright handkerchief and said sharply: "Well?"

"What are you looking for?"

"Johnny's fortune."

"Money?"

"It's money all right." Her cackle was blended with a little snigger from Jenks. "Money is what interests me."

"Where is it hidden?"

The magenta head was shaken emphatically. "No answer to that one."

"In the Bramley Hall cellars?"

"You searched them. If you find any fortune there, let me know."

"Someone else was there with me."

"I don't know about that."

"Why were Martin and Montague killed?"

She spoke carefully. "The verdict on Eddie Martin's death was misadventure. I'm not admitting anything else. But perhaps he was too greedy, would that explain it?"

"I expect so."

"It never pays to be greedy." She stared at Jenks and the tall man wriggled uncomfortably.

"And what about Montague?"

Just as carefully she said: "I should guess that Montague found out something he wasn't supposed to know."

"About this – agent of yours?"

"Perhaps. And perhaps the agent was a little hasty. Don't you think that's reasonable, Henry?"

"Oh, quite. I blame myself really. Frankie was not the man who should have been trusted with such a delicate matter."

"A small-time crook," Applegate supplemented. "He hardly carried enough weight."

Eileen Delaney looked at a wristwatch that was covered with jewels. "Three more questions."

"This is the thing that most puzzles me. You own this tower, you know where Bogue's money is. Why should you wait all these years before trying to lay hands on it?"

She waved one claw in the air. About the gesture there was something oddly theatrical and false. "We had to have Eddie. Put it this way. Johnny's money is in a secret place. A disused coal mine – there are some in the Marsh, did you know that? Eddie was the only one who knew just exactly where the money was hidden. He had the secret, but not the organisation to deal with it."

"Why do you need an organisation?"

"You just do." She lit a fresh cigarette from a dying butt. "Eddie comes to me. I still have a small organisation, I can be useful. We come to terms. But I told you the trouble with Eddie, he was too greedy."

There was silence. Both of them were looking at him. He did not doubt that in this story truth had been blended with lies. The truth would be what he already knew or could find out, the rest would be lies – perhaps not direct lies, but stories designed to lead him away from some point of vital importance. "One more question," the woman said.

"All right. What are you waiting for?"

"Something to happen."

"And when it does?"

"You'll know all about it. Now, I've answered your questions. Does that satisfy you?"

Applegate took a deep breath. "No."

Jenks wriggled triumphantly. "You see. I told you he'd be difficult."

The little woman stubbed out her cigarette. Dark eyes were hard above beaky nose, mouth was turned down at the corners. Good humour had dropped away from her. She looked dangerous.

"Let's get this straight. I wanted to talk to you because I thought if we put our cards on the table you'd stop poking your nose into things that don't concern you."

"I suspect you of having aces still hidden up your sleeve."

She did not respond to this facetiousness. "Henry says you write thrillers and that you're just curious. You told him that and he believes it. I don't care whether it's true or not. I simply want you and that girl you're running around with out of my way. A game like this is strictly for professionals. Understand?"

"But Henry said he was in it just to get back the money Bogue had stolen from him. Forty thousand pounds, wasn't it, Henry? Plus interest."

Jenks looked down his long nose in an embarrassed way.

She cackled. "Stolen from *him*. That's a good one. Anyone who could steal from Henry deserves a medal. Did Henry tell you how he pimped his wife to Johnny – so sure he was Johnny would make his fortune. And he thought Johnny wasn't smart enough to see it. My God!" She rocked back and forward a little with laughter.

"Now, Eileen," Jenks said. "We don't want to go into all that."

"I don't know what he's been telling you, but the fact is Henry threw his wife at Johnny's head. Then he was upset when he found she liked a man better than a cash register."

The thin man's cheeks were flushed now, but he still spoke with his usual finicky mildness. "You know Johnny didn't treat me properly."

"You tried to be too smart for Johnny, and nobody was ever that."

"Now, Eileen, you know that's not true."

"Shut up." Jenks subsided, muttering. "If Henry's the only person you've listened to, you may have got the wrong idea of Johnny. He wasn't a crook, don't think it. He did a lot of harm, Johnny, but he did more good. Did Henry tell you about his childhood, Johnny's? I thought not. His mother died before he was two years old and his father parked him out with a couple who beat him almost every day. He was with them three years, then his father got married again – he was a clerk in Leeds Corporation – and took him back. But his stepmother didn't like him, said he was dirty, and she beat him too. His father was mad about her and believed everything she said. When Johnny was six she got his father to have him put in a home for backward children. Backward, hell, there was nothing backward about Johnny. But I shouldn't like to tell you the kind of things they did to the children there. You know Johnny sponsored a bill trying to get all children's homes under much stricter supervision? You didn't? Of course it never had a chance. Ramsay MacDonald and Snowden hated Johnny's guts. But there you are, you see, that sort of thing never gets remembered, only the trouble. Selling drinks after hours, is that so very wicked?"

"Wasn't there some question of drugs?"

"That was Eddie Martin. It was never proved about Johnny's connection."

"He was too smart." Jenks sniggered.

She snapped at him. "It was never proved. And what about the Jews? Did you know Johnny used his contacts to get dozens of Jews out of Germany? My God, I've seen some of them weeping as they thanked him. That's the kind of scoundrel Johnny was, he risked his life to get Jews out of Germany."

"I see," Applegate said, although in fact he was far from seeing anything clearly. "What do you want from me?"

"The police. What are they doing about Montague?"

"A boy named Winterbottom has disappeared. They seem to think he did it."

She nodded. "The people who run that crazy school, the Ponts. What's happening to them?"

"They're going to close the school. I think most of the parents will want to take their children away."

"I should bloody well think so," she said indignantly. "A place like that – why, they never punish the kids for anything. How can you expect them to grow up anything but daft? This Pont and his wife must be a bit cracked."

Applegate was surprised to find himself speaking with warmth. "Not at all. They may have some queer ideas, but they've done a lot of valuable pioneering work. After what you've been saying about Bogue's childhood – "

"You talk like a book," she said, it seemed with approval. "I like you, kid. I wouldn't want to see you get hurt." He forbore to say that he had been hurt already, although only slightly. She asked abruptly: "How much longer do you reckon to stay? I mean to say, if everyone's going there won't be any classes, isn't that right?"

"I'm going in a few days." Deliberately he said: "I talked to a man today who's quite sure that Johnny Bogue didn't leave a fortune. This man lent Bogue a couple of hundred pounds a few days before he died. He says Bogue was on the rocks then. How does that square with what you've been telling me?"

She answered him, and although her voice could never be soft, it was less grating than he had heard it.

"Listen to me, kid. Keep your eyes closed and your nose clean. That way you won't get hurt. Henry here and me, we've got a little business to settle, and I've told you what it is without the word of a lie. On my honour as a Catholic," She suddenly fished out a small golden cross from the recesses of the mauve dress, and kissed it. "On my honour it's to do with money, and Johnny's money. I can't tell you more than that. But believe me, it's nobody's business but ours. Remember that, kiddo, and there'll be no trouble. Forget it and we'll have to play rough. Clear?"

"Quite clear." He stood up.

"And you can pass it on to your girlfriend." Jenks beamed at him benevolently. They were both smiling. The audience – which was how he now thought of it – might have ended upon this happy note, but for a last remark to which he was prompted by a sudden recollection. "About your little organisation... "

Two smiling faces looked expectant.

" – Does it contain a man with the lobe missing off his left ear?"

The smiles vanished from the two faces like lamps going out in a house. Jenks' hand pulled at his mouth. Eileen Delaney stood up behind the trolley and the voice in which she told him to get out had the anger of an animal's scream.

It is said that a persistent stare directed at the back of the neck can force the person stared at to turn round. When Applegate was a few yards away from the water tower some emotional pressure of this kind was exerted on him. There was no malign gaze, such as he had expected to see, directed upon him from a ground floor window. But at an upper window, on the third or fourth storey, he glimpsed a face. Almost in the moment he glimpsed it the face had gone, jerked away as though by a string, the pale face, it seemed, of a prisoner, nose pressed against glass.

Chapter Fifteen

He was walking back along the front when he was halted by a sign which said: "Barnacle Bill and his Limpets. Concert Party. Special Attraction, twice daily, 3 and 7 p.m." An arrow pointed round the corner and he followed it, speculating on the eccentricity that had led a concert party to Romney Marsh in April. A suicidal impulse it must have been, surely, that had brought them to this abomination of desolation rather than Bognor or Brighton, Falmouth or Folkestone, Littlehampton or Llandudno, Southport or Skegness. But Barnacle Bill and his Limpets had no doubt been unable to obtain engagements in any of those places. They had been forced down and down, through provincial engagements in dirty, empty, little halls. And now they had reached rock bottom.

A pleasing fancy, Applegate thought, but no doubt inaccurate. What did happen to concert parties in the wintertime? He paid a shilling at the door of the Rivoli Concert Hall and went in. To his surprise the glass-domed hall was half-full. Old women knitted or slept in the front rows, old men sat with their hands clasped round walking sticks, staring indignantly at the stage. Half a dozen bath chairs stood in various corners, their occupants swathed in rugs and shawls. It was evident to Applegate that he had underestimated the octogenarian population of Murdstone. How was it that the nipping winds failed to kill them off?

Conspicuous among the dodderers were Barney, who stared at the stage intently with his arms folded, and Arthur, who appeared to be playing a solitary version of cat's cradle. Heads turned to look at Applegate as he walked up the aisle. He glanced at his watch and realised that he was arriving ridiculously late, when the show was three-quarters over.

The concert party was like many other concert parties. A decayed-looking man played a slightly out of tune piano and the four performers, two of each sex, appeared in a variety of guises which gave them an excuse to sing comic or sentimental songs. A fat girl of forty, her legs pimpled with gooseflesh from the cold, sang "Knocked 'Em in the Old Kent Road." Barnacle Bill, a burly figure with his own dyed hair and a false handlebar moustache, engaged in a dialogue with his stooge, a melancholy-looking stunted figure with beautifully white false teeth. "Who was that wife I saw you with the other night?" asked the melancholy man and Barnacle Bill replied: "That was no wife. She's a lady." The knitting ladies in the front row looked up disapprovingly. One of the bath chair figures writhed with noiseless laughter – or was he perhaps coughing? Applegate could not be sure.

"I want you to lend me five pounds," shouted Barnacle Bill.

"Five pounds, what do you want five pounds for?" stooge shouted back.

"If you give me five pounds I'll turn it into fifty," Barnacle Bill roared, winking at the audience.

"Turn five pounds into fifty, how will you turn five pounds into fifty?"

Applegate sighed. The repartee between Barnacle Bill and stunted Limpet ended, and stunted Limpet reappeared as a kind of juvenile lead, accompanied by a stringy blonde with a look of invincible hostility to life. They sang "If You Were the Only Girl in the World" together. Then the decayed-looking man placed a rickety door in the centre of the stage and a pair of steps beside it. The stringy blonde, wearing a rather dirty nightdress, climbed the steps and mewed: " 'Who's that narkin at my dahr,' cried the fair young maiden?" Barnacle Bill staggered on from the other side of the stage waving a bottle and wearing a bulbous red nose. He knocked thunderously on the door, and croaked:

> " 'It's only me from over the sea,'
> Cried Barnacle Bill the sailor.
> 'I'm all lit up like a Christmas tree,'
> Cried Barnacle Bill the sailor.
> 'I'll laugh and swear and drink and smoke,
> But I can't swim a blooming stroke,'
> Cried Barnacle Bill the sailor."

The stringy blonde minced down the ladder, daintily lifting her nightdress. " 'I'll carm dahn and let you in, I'll carm dahn and let you in,' " she sang. " 'I'll carm dahn and let you in,' cried the fair young maiden."

Barnacle Bill stumped up and down, took a swig from the bottle, and croaked:

> " 'Then hurry before I bust in the door,'
> Cried Barnacle Bill the sailor."

Applegate closed his eyes. Words came through to him from a distance. "I'll drink your rum and eat your pies, I'll kiss the girls and black their eyes..." He opened his eyes again, it seemed no more than a moment later, to a thin spatter of applause. Barnacle Bill and the Limpets stood bowing and smiling, then Barnacle Bill stepped forward, his dyed patches very noticeable. "Thank you for a splendid reception, ladies and gentlemen. Don't let the fact that you've seen our show once stop you from seeing it again. We 'ave a considerable repertory of ever-fresh songs and jokes, and although we sometimes repeat a popular item, you never see the same show twice. Thanking you, ladies and gentlemen, says Barnacle Bill the sailor and his Limpets."

Barney and Arthur had gone. Evidently it was time for Applegate to go too. He came out, feeling gloomy, into a thick, misty rain.

Chapter Sixteen

He was standing at the bus stop from Bramley when he felt a tap on his shoulder. He turned to see the ginger moustache of Inspector Murray. "Mr Applegate," the Inspector said, "can you spare me a few minutes, eh?"

In spite of the interrogative *eh* he did not consider this really a question – or thought it at least a question permitting only one answer. There was, after all, a bus in another hour, it was raining, and after his encounter with Eileen and her organisation there was something comforting about the presence of a police official at his side. He wondered mildly where the Inspector would take him for their little chat. Did Murdstone boast a Lyons? Or would it be a slightly seedy Graham Greene-ish pub? If a pub, was Murray a bottled or draught beer man? He was a little disconcerted when the Inspector turned briskly into a dung-coloured brick building that said "Kent County Constabulary" on a lighted lamp outside. The sight of a sergeant sitting at a desk, and of constables who straightened up respectfully at sight of the Inspector was not after all as comforting as it might have been. Nor was the bristling of the Inspector's ginger moustache exactly reassuring, when they sat opposite each other in a little, bare room. As Applegate remembered, that moustache had formerly not bristled but drooped.

"I thought you'd like to know Winterbottom has been found." The Inspector seemed able to put a questioning note into the simplest remark. "At home," he continued. "It seems the knife was the last straw to him, as you might say. He felt his dignity was hurt, he'd had enough of life at Bramley, he wanted to go home. He hadn't money for fare, hitch-hiked his way back. His father doesn't intend to send him back to the school after what has happened. Can't say I blame him. Now, I've talked to the boy. I've checked his story and it seems all right. He's either a better actor than I've seen on the stage this year, or he had nothing to do with killing Montague."

It was unwise, a legal friend had once told Applegate, to say anything at all to the police, and it was almost fatal to offer statements. Nevertheless, there was something about the Inspector's interrogative air – his last sentence had ended on a characteristic upward inflection – that positively demanded answers. Fighting down an inclination to ask the number of actors the Inspector had in fact seen on the stage that year, Applegate asked instead whether any link had been traced between Winterbottom and Montague.

"None. I don't believe there is any link." Applegate was mute. "Eh?"

"Perhaps not."

"We may have been led up the garden, eh? So we come back to two questions. Who took the knife away from you, and when?"

"It might have been any time after I put it in my pocket," Applegate said lamely. "I thought nothing more of it."

"Careless, Mr Applegate. And who knew Montague before he came to the school. You didn't, eh?"

"Certainly not. I met him for the first time when we got out at the station and Miss Pont picked us up."

"Miss Pont, eh? That's a fine figure of a girl," the Inspector said irrelevantly. "So you had no contact with Montague beyond a little casual conversation, at suppertime and such." The way in which the Inspector's moustache bristled, and in which he almost said "leetle" for "little" alarmed Applegate. He shook his head.

"No little private conversation, never unbuttoned himself to you, said he wanted to get something off his chest, as you might put it in a manner of speaking." A rabbit conscious of impending doom, Applegate found nothing to do but shake his head again at this gingery fox.

"Then what were his fingerprints doing in three different places in your bedroom? By the light switch, on the wardrobe, and on the back of a chair?" Applegate gasped. Then, conscious of his open mouth, he smartly snapped it shut. He had remembered to remove the prints in Montague's room, but had entirely forgotten that Montague's prints were present in his own room. A fine detective story writer you are, he told himself gloomily. The Inspector had been waiting with an air of immense forbearance, but now he let loose a brisk "Eh?"

"No idea," Applegate mumbled. "Simply can't explain it."

"One very simple explanation. Montague came in to talk to you after you'd left the Ponts. Then you went over to his room, there was a quarrel, you stabbed him, took whatever it was you were quarrelling about. Simple, straightforward. What's wrong with it?"

This reconstruction was in some points so truthful that Applegate felt admittance of any part of it would be equivalent to admitting the whole. "Motive," he said, with a gulp. "What motive?"

The Inspector brushed up his ginger moustache. "Bit of a problem. But Montague wasn't a teacher by profession, you know that. He was a bit of a crook. Did a term in prison during the war. He was part of a drug distributing ring, and got caught. Always the little fellows who get caught. Smoke?"

Applegate accepted the tube, placed it in his mouth, and carefully lighted it. The Inspector stuffed tobacco into a curved pipe.

"Thing is he may have been going straight, but what did he want to take this kind of job for when he'd been selling cars in Warren Street?"

So he *was* a Warren Street car salesman, Applegate thought with a small feeling of self-congratulation. "Perhaps business was bad."

"Wasn't bad enough to make him choose school-mastering for a living. Tell you another thing. Ever heard of Eddie Martin, eh?"

The bigger the lie the better the chance. "No."

"He was the kingfish of the drug ring – biggest fish we caught anyway. He came down to Murdstone not long ago. Got drowned, accident. Coincidence, I suppose you'd call it."

"I suppose so. I don't see what it's got to do with me."

"Now, you're not a qualified teacher either. What are you supposed to be doing down here, eh?"

Here at last Applegate could give an answer that, however improbable it seemed, was true. "I'm a detective story writer, you've found that out."

The Inspector took out from the drawer of his desk a book, on the dust jacket of which donnish figures disported themselves like satyrs, with their goat feet dancing the antic hay. Applegate recognised *Where Dons Delight.*

"Have you read it?"

"Very clever," the Inspector said, without committing himself to a definite answer.

"I came down here to get local colour for my next book."

"And then you got mixed up with this, eh?" He walked up and down the room, puffing at the pipe and flinging out sentences between balloons of smoke. "Tell you something to make you laugh. I believe this story of yours, most of it. I'm just showing you the possibilities. Want you to understand one thing, though. You're in a mess, young man. You and that girl of yours. Up to the neck. Better tell me about it."

Had Applegate still possessed the letters and the note he had taken from Montague's wallet he would have felt strongly inclined to accept this suggestion. But he had not merely committed the offence of concealing material related to the crime, but had been stupid enough to lose it. He shook his head.

"I won't pretend to see my way through this," said the Inspector. Puff puff. "But I understand enough to know that you're in danger." Puff puff. "And Miss Pont, too, if that interests you." He took his pipe out of his mouth and stood staring at Applegate, suddenly foxily amiable. "Eh?"

Applegate felt a sudden resurgence of confidence. "Nothing to say, Inspector. About Montague's prints, has it occurred to you that he might have been in my room in the afternoon or evening, soon after we arrived?"

"Yes. But I don't fancy that's the way it was." Ginger eyebrows drew together with a slightly frightening effect. "All right. You can go."

"I'm not being detained?" Applegate asked jauntily.

"Why should I keep you in safety when you want to make a fool of yourself? But your blood's on your own head – or I fear it will be. I hope your head's a thick one."

Chapter Seventeen

He got back to Bramley Hall at suppertime, but there was no sign of supper. He went out to the kitchens, found them deserted, and carved off for himself a hunk of slightly dampish home-made bread and a piece of cheese. Bread and cheese in hand, he wandered out of the Gothic hall and sat down in one of the classrooms in the modern addition. On the blackboard was written in a slightly shaky hand that he recognised as Pont's, *Rats live on no evil star,* and beneath it *Palindrome.* Round the walls were a variety of paintings ranging from *collages* to linocuts. Among them was a motto, neatly lettered in sans serif capitals, *To learn freedom is to be on the threshold of a creative act.* Applegate sat at one of the rickety desks and ate his bread and cheese. Words were deeply carved into the desk: *Old Jerry Pont's a fool.* A creative act, Applegate wondered? He stuffed the last of the bread and cheese into his mouth.

The door opened behind him. Something hard pressed into his back. A voice said: "Stand up. Put your hands above your head."

He stood, and then suddenly whirled round, to be confronted by the fat face of Maureen Gardner. He looked furiously at her podgy, outstretched finger.

"Scared you," she said complacently. "I like you, you scare easily."

Perhaps it was a good thing that Applegate's mouth was full of bread and cheese. When he was able to speak he only said mildly: "Why do you do things like that? It would be much nicer if you didn't."

"I like to frighten people, it's fun. I used to steal things, but frightening people is more interesting. Less anti-social, too. I was going to put some beetles and things in your bed if Derek hadn't murdered Mr Montague."

"Derek didn't murder Mr Montague," Applegate said absently. "He just got tired of progressive education and went home."

"Almost all of them have done that. Gone home, I mean. There's only Jerry and Janine and Hedda left. And that boy who came the other day, Deverell. His father lives in South America or somewhere, and hasn't had time to hear about it."

"And you."

"Oh, well, of course my parents are... " She waved a beefy hand.

"Dead, you mean?"

"No. My mother's Rita Revere."

"Well." He was impressed. Rita Revere had been a Hollywood star for years, and she had even managed to graduate from her original celebrity as the "X" girl (a label devised by an enterprising publicity agent when she appeared in four successive "X" category films), all breasts and temperament, into a reasonable simulacrum of an actress. Yet even as an aspiring actress Rita Revere might well be embarrassed by a daughter of such an age, and of such formidable fatness. "What about your father? But of course, I suppose your father was – "

"Roger Gardner, yes."

"Well," Applegate said again, very inadequately. He was slightly horrified. The marriage of Roger Gardner and Rita Revere had been a three-days' wonder just before the war.

Gardner was a playboy and racing motorist, noted for his Fascist sympathies. The outbreak of war found him in Germany. He stayed there and made many broadcasts from Berlin, on the lines that the Germans were jolly good sportsmen and the Russians were not. Rita Revere divorced him. He was listed as a war criminal, but never came to trial. He had been seen in Berlin when that city was captured by the Russians, but his subsequent fate was unknown. Whether Roger Gardner was dead or alive did not seem very important, but Applegate could not resist sympathy for a child who had had Gardner for a father and Rita Revere for a mother.

"Roger's presumed dead, as you know," the girl said calmly. "And Rita doesn't want me any closer than a few thousand miles, she says I've got the seeds of Roger's degeneracy in me. Do you think that's so?"

"No."

"Neither does Hedda. She's smashing, isn't she? You'll find her upstairs if you want her."

"What's going to happen to you?"

"I shall go to the Anarchist Country Community. They'll take me in. I've been an Anarchist for two years now."

"The Anarchist Country Community," Applegate repeated feebly.

"Yes. They've got a hundred acres in Essex, rather inaccessible. And an old country house. Everything's communal, you know, all social activities. And no restrictions. Parents employ self-regulation for their children. Object of the community is to provide an example of living and also to release psychic energy. Generally we keep it bottled up." She jabbed Applegate in the stomach. "You keep it bottled up."

"I expect you're right. Does – ah – Jeremy know of your Anarchist sympathies?"

"Yes. Approves of them. Would be one himself if he had the guts."

"And will you go around the community frightening people?"

She looked at him with contempt. "Naturally not. I only indulge in anti-social behaviour under pressure of environment. But talking of anti-social behaviour, if Derek didn't kill that man Montague, who did?"

"Your guess is as good as mine."

"I might be able to help. I'm really very intelligent. I suppose it was something to do with you."

"What makes you think that?" Applegate asked, startled.

"I happened to see him come out of your room."

"What do you mean, happened? You're supposed to be on the first floor."

"I know, but I like to see what's going on. It gives me a feeling of power."

"I doubt if that will be encouraged in the Anarchist Country Community."

"I need reorientation," she said complacently. "But I can't get it here. I saw Montague coming out of your room."

"What about it?"

"Why should he have been talking to you if you didn't know each other?"

"It didn't occur to you that two new teachers might want to discuss their programme?"

"At a school like this, no. And that isn't all. A couple of minutes later I heard somebody else coming along the passage."

Applegate felt a certain tenseness. "Yes?"

"So I went downstairs. I knew there'd be trouble if I was found up there." She wagged a fat finger at him.

"But I went on up again. And I heard voices."

"Yes?"

"In your room. You had Hedda in there. I could hear her voice."

Applegate had a vision of Maureen Gardner, in her pyjamas, crouched outside his bedroom door. It was both comic and pathetic. "Is that all?"

"No. There was someone in Montague's room as well."

"A man or a woman?"

"A man. At least, I'm almost sure. You see, I was more interested in you and Hedda." Unhappily she added: "But I couldn't really hear even what you were saying."

"You're getting in some good training as a private inquiry agent," Applegate said sarcastically. "You'll improve in time. So what it really comes to is that you heard Montague talking to somebody, and feel almost sure it was a man. You didn't stay to see who came out of the room? And you don't know where he came from?"

She said slowly: "I think he was hiding somewhere on your floor while you were talking to Montague. I heard somebody move then. But I couldn't be sure."

"Industrious snooping could hardly have had less successful results. Have you told the police?"

She shook her head. "It's against my principles to help the police. But it means that whoever killed Montague came from inside the house."

"I don't think anyone's ever doubted that."

"They must have known all about him. Don't you see the obvious person, the one who certainly knew about Montague? Why, Jeremy."

"But he engaged Montague."

"Precisely. Why did he engage somebody obviously unsuitable? Because Montague had a hold over him. Then when he got down here Montague tried to turn the screw in some way, and Jeremy killed him."

"That's the silliest theory I've ever heard advanced by a girl who calls herself intelligent. The murder has ruined the

126

school, and if there's one thing Jeremy has at heart it's Bramley Hall and everything it stands for."

She stood up. Her blubbery face seemed to fold into creases. "You only laugh at me. Everybody's always laughed at me."

He was sorry for what he had said, or the way he had said it. "I wasn't laughing. I just don't think you're right. Hedda and I are working on another idea. Perhaps you can help. Shall we all have a council of war about it tomorrow?"

Her podgy hands were clasped tightly. "Oh, *yes.* What's your idea?"

"It's all to do with a man named Bogue."

"What, Johnny Bogue? The man who used to live here."

He was astonished. "How do you know anything about him? You were hardly born then."

"He was a friend of my father. I found out as much as I could about Roger, you know. And Johnny Bogue was one of his friends. Roger used to come down here for weekends. That's something I often think about. Would you like to see a picture of him?" She took out from a small, tartan bag two snapshots. One showed the platinum head of Rita Revere, the other a neat, dark, rather self-consciously handsome male profile. "Isn't he handsome? Just like Douglas Fairbanks. Nobody knows for certain what's happened to him. Perhaps one day he'll send for me. You know, like Maclean sent for Mrs Maclean. If he did I should go. I don't feel any allegiance to the Western democracies. Do you think I should?"

"I don't know. Did you hear anything else about Bogue?"

"Only that he kept in touch with Roger somehow during the war. Rita told me that once. Of course that was before she decided she didn't want me any more," she added in a matter-of-fact way. "I don't know how he kept in touch, but apparently Bogue had lots of friends in Germany, and he used to get messages through to Rita. But then she divorced

Roger, and Bogue was killed. I don't see how he can be mixed up in this. Do you mean there's a kind of secret about Bramley Hall?"

"Something like that. It's too late to talk about it tonight. Let's go to bed."

"I like you." They walked up the stairs together. "I wish I had a proper mother and father. It's a bore in many ways, but on the whole, I think it's a good thing to have them, don't you?"

"On the whole," Applegate agreed gravely. He left her on the first floor and went farther up. At the door of his cubicle he halted. From farther down the corridor he heard a tuneless, metallic voice singing:

"You've got that look, that look that makes me shriek,
   You with that lay me in the stable technique."

He went in pursuit of the voice, knocked on a bedroom door and went in when a voice called "Come." Hedda sat at her dressing table in a dark blue dressing gown, brushing her hair. She raised a hand. "Come and do this. I'm bored with it."

Applegate brushed the hair which crackled electrically under his touch, while he told her about the events of the day. She was inclined to treat his adventures with a light-heartedness of which he could not altogether approve. He had not yet understood that what happens to other people may seem to us tragic, pathetic or wonderful, but can never seem wholly real. We reserve rights in absolute reality for what happens to ourselves.

"What *do* you suppose they're after? And what *can* they be waiting for? I do feel you might have found that out. You don't seem to emerge from these trials of strength altogether triumphantly, do you?"

"I thought I'd done rather well. I certainly ploughed a deep furrow between Jenks and Eileen Delaney."

"Oh. That hurt." He had given her hair a vicious downward brush. "I know who they're waiting for. Geoffrey."

"Geoffrey?" He was momentarily confused.

"The son. Johnny gave him the key to the fortune, or left it for him in some way. They can't do anything without Geoffrey and the key, and they're waiting for him to turn up."

"You may be right." He put down the brush, pulled her head backwards and kissed her upside-down face. She responded in an absent-minded sort of way, and pushed him away.

"That's enough of that. The really baffling thing is, what can this treasure possibly be? Remember what Bogue said to old Anscombe, that he'd be the richest man in the world – and then he wanted the loan from Fish. I've got a feeling we ought to make something out of that. It's as though he were going to steal the Crown Jewels or something."

He stroked her hair thoughtfully. "It seems to be implied that whatever it was would be in some way a sort of a joke."

"Yes. He must have been a great charmer, that Johnny Bogue." She looked at him quizzically in the glass. He gave her hair a sharp tug. "Mustn't he now?"

"I think he was one of the nastiest characters I've heard of for a long time." Conscious that he must sound priggish, he told her about his conversation with Maureen. "Gardner was a nasty type too, even nastier than Bogue. Odd, isn't it, to think how this place is connected with it all, that it could tell us everything we want to know?"

She got up. "Don't be commonplace. I'm going to bed. I've had a frightful day. Parents calling for children, complaining about everything, as good as calling Jeremy a murderer. He took no notice of them, don't bother me with these trivial details, I'm worrying about the future of progressive education. You know the line. Janine's been soaking all day, glassy-eyed by the afternoon, wouldn't go and lie down, made the worst possible impression on the parents. Fortunately, the children themselves behaved pretty well. That boy Deverell was a help in a quiet way, and so was Maureen. It's a pity she's so fat."

"She thinks a lot of you."

"I admire her taste. And now, good night."

Rather unwillingly he moved to the door. "You don't seem very ardent tonight."

She slipped off the dressing gown, and he had a vision of round, white arms. Then she was in bed. "A girl just can't be ardent all the time. Will you turn out the light? Good night."

"Good night." He turned out the light.

"Do you know the most fascinating thing of all?" Her voice came from darkness.

"What's that?"

"The face peering from the tower. And the man with the lobe missing off his ear. Positively too John Buchan for words."

Chapter Eighteen

Applegate lay in bed and stared up into darkness. He closed his eyes and the darkness was full of luminous patterns. The patterns coalesced into a face, round headed and curly haired, the mouth set in a mocking smile. When the trail had been followed to the end, what kind of man did it reveal? A masterly opportunist, a crook no doubt, a man capable of the most vicious actions – but surely something more than that as well? The man who had been so brutal to poor little Fish was also the man who had saved Jews from the Nazis, the man who trafficked in drugs had also been engaged on some sort of official mission when he was killed.

What sort of mission? Was it linked with Bogue's boast that in a week or two he would be the richest man in the world? And if that was the case, wouldn't it be useful to know what the mission had been? Applegate suddenly spoke into the darkness. "Fazackerley," he said.

Edmund Fazackerley was a friend of Uncle Roger, a dapper little young-old kind of man who had a job in something which he simply called S. This really stood for ESS, or the Economic Statistical Section, which seemed to have some tenuous attachment to the Treasury. Fazackerley was the kind of man who is always anxious to display his knowledge, and he would certainly not admit defeat in a case like that of Johnny Bogue.

Fazackerley, then, must be telephoned in the morning. Applegate became aware that he was more than half-asleep.

He was suddenly startled into wakefulness by an appalling noise outside his door. There were shrieks, angry and excited voices, and there was a sound also as of a heavy body being dragged along the corridor. Applegate sprang out of bed, darted to the door, and opened it.

He recoiled from the sight that met his eyes in the ghostly light afforded by a blue night light in the corridor. Jeremy Pont, dressed in his pyjamas, his face furious with effort, was pulling a cardboard carton down the corridor. He was being hampered by his wife who with shrieks, pulls at his arm, everything short of actual blows, tried to restrain him. She wore a striped dressing gown tied together loosely enough to reveal that beneath it she had on nothing at all. By the side of Mrs Pont, with one hand upon her arm, was the youthful Deverell, who was attempting without success to persuade her to go back to her room.

She brushed off the hand he placed on her arm with the dramatic gesture of a third-rate Shakespearian actress. "I will not be stayed," she cried. "Jeremy, those are mine."

"If you'll just come back to bed, Mr Pont and I will… " Deverell's voice was low and deferential.

"I strove with none, for none was worth my strife," said Mrs Pont. A push from her brawny arm caught Deverell off balance and he staggered back against Hedda's door. At the same moment the door opened, so that Deverell fell back into Hedda's arms. Pont pulled the carton a little farther down the corridor. He looked up and saw Applegate.

"Stop her," he panted. "I've found her store of drink. She hides it, you know. In the – airing cupboard this time. Empty it down the sink. Keep her away."

Applegate moved in front of Mrs Pont, barring her way. "Now, now…"

Her eyes were wild. "He's taking it away. Let me pass."

"Taking what away?"

"Oil for the lamps of China. Grease for the axle wheel of progressive education. We must have more and more. Never enough. Let me pass."

"It's dark," Applegate said. "Too dark to grease any axle wheels tonight. Leave it until the morning and I'll help you." He gripped one arm firmly. Hedda came from her doorway and took hold of the other.

"Come along now," she said. "Come to bed, Aunt Janine."

"So that's your game, is it?" cried Mrs Pont. "Adventurers and defeatists all. I'll match you." She gave a great lunge forward. The arm Applegate held began to wriggle about as if with a life of its own. The arm held by Hedda got loose and flailed the air. Distantly, down the corridor, Pont could be seen trailing his carton of Haig and Johnny Walker.

"Janine," he called back. "Go to bed."

"Janine not me," cried his wife. "My strength is as the strength of ten because my heart is pure. Unhand me now, I say." Her roving arm struck the unfortunate Deverell, who was again sent staggering against the wall. It appeared for a moment that she might be successful in freeing herself, but her quite literal downfall was brought about by the grease for the axle wheels of progressive education. Her foot slipped on a bottle of Johnny Walker which must have come out of the carton. She skidded, and fell heavily to the floor. The dressing gown opened. Her silver hair was jerked aside to reveal a bald pate. She lay on the ground quietly moaning, and offered no resistance when Applegate, Deverell and Hedda hoisted her erect again. A weighty sack, she submitted as they propelled her across to the door of her room, and into bed. An odour of whisky surrounded her, she might have bathed in it.

"All right," Hedda said. "She'll be no trouble now. I can manage."

There was another outbreak of noise, thuds succeeded by crashes. Applegate and Deverell ran outside and down the

133

stairs to find Pont sitting at the bottom of the stairs, surrounded by whisky bottles, some empty, some broken and some full. The carton had been too much for him. They poured out the whisky from the full bottles and cleared up the others. "Do you suppose that's all she's got?" Applegate asked.

Pont made a hopeless gesture. "Possibly. She will find another hiding place. She always does. Janine, you know, is very highly strung. An emotional shock of this kind... " His voice trailed away.

"There may be more somewhere about?"

"I hope not." He gave them a wan good night.

At the door of his room Deverell said to Applegate: "I'm beginning to think it's a good thing I'm not staying here."

"Mr Pont hasn't been able to get in touch with your parents?"

"With Dad, no. He's a real grasshopper, never in the same place more than a few days at a time. Couple of weeks ago he was in Venezuela. Chances are he's in Lima now. He mentioned he might be going to Peru."

"Your mother's dead?"

"Dad divorced her when I was ten."

"If they can't get in touch with your father – "

Deverell laughed. "Don't worry. Dad keeps me well supplied with money, and I'm used to looking after myself. I'll just move into the local hotel and send cables until I get hold of him. Good night."

A very self-possessed youth, Applegate thought, taking drunken women as all in the evening's work. On his own mind the scene impressed itself as fantastic and gruesome. That great body flailing and writhing under the light of a blue moon, the discordant shreds of quotation, the odour of whisky everywhere, the silver wig falling off like a mask. Safely between sheets, he shuddered. It was a long time before he fell asleep.

Chapter Nineteen

"Bogue," Fazackerley said in a slightly insulted voice. "But naturally I remember Bogue. What's your interest in him?"

He was a little man with dark, wavy hair going grey at the sides and a handsome head which he held pushed up into the air to conceal an incipient double chin. The effort was rather as though his head was supported by an invisible high collar. His appearance was spoiled by his very short legs, and somehow he looked rather more like an assistant head waiter than like Sir Anthony Eden. Behind his desk in ESS, however, Fazackerley was quite reasonably impressive.

"Bogue died in 1943, when a plane in which he was flying was shot down by the Germans, or perhaps it just crashed. He was supposed to be engaged on a special mission at the time. I wanted to find out what that mission was."

"Yes, dear boy, but why?"

Applegate had his story ready. "A man has been killed in the school I'm working at, a place named Bramley Hall. The Hall used to belong to Bogue... "

Fazackerley nodded, with the merest trace of impatience. He did not like the implication that he was ignorant of any subject whatever.

"And I've become very interested in him. I wrote a detective story... "

This time the shadow of impatience on Fazackerley's brow was unmistakable.

"It seemed to me that Bogue would be an awfully good subject for a biography. An extraordinary life and a mysterious death. What do you think of it?"

Above the invisible high collar Fazackerley nodded again, sagely. "He sounds to me an excellent subject, as you say. I'm surprised nobody's dealt with him before."

"Delighted that you think so." He warmed to his work. "On the other hand, it may be that for reasons unknown to me it is impossible to tell Bogue's story. I asked myself who I should approach, and thought I really couldn't do better than come to the fountainhead."

It is rarely possible to spread the butter of flattery too thick. Fazackerley expanded before these words like a Japanese flower in water. He took a lip between thumb and finger and pulled at it. Then he consulted a file on his neat, glass-topped desk, talking as he ran through an alphabetical index.

"Strictly speaking, this kind of thing hasn't anything to do with ESS, or even with PED, which was the original department that was converted into ESS after the war, but we have our contacts, you know. There's Bosanquet now, moved from PED to some remote branch of the FO, now has a cosy little nook in J of L. No, hardly your man perhaps. Corliss, Mottingham, Peach, any of those *might* be able to help, but I think there may be somebody more – ah, yes, Tarboe. I really think Tarboe is your man."

"That's wonderful." Applegate simulated boyish enthusiasm. "Who *is* Tarboe exactly?"

"You haven't met him?" Fazackerley was delighted. "Well, Tarboe *does* operate behind the scenes, so I suppose that's natural. During the war he was in charge of one of those queer little organisations that were responsible for all kinds of things from sending out missions to Tibet to providing protection for distinguished visitors who weren't even supposed to be here, if you know what I mean. That was dak."

"Dak?" said Applegate foolishly. "I thought that was a trouser."

Fazackerley frowned disapproval of levity. "DAC was the Division for Administrative Co-operation. It has been merged with MOLE and WHY, but Tarboe is now with ENOS. Have you heard of ENOS?"

With some difficulty Applegate restrained the words that rose to his tongue.

"ENOS is really very hush-hush. Nobody knows just what it is concerned with as far as I know, except that it's got some sort of attachment to the Treasury."

"What do the letters stand for?"

"The letters?" Fazackerley echoed in surprise. "I'm really not sure – the European and National Operations Service, I believe. But that's not important."

"And Tarboe runs ENOS?"

"My dear boy, of course not. The chap who runs ENOS is – well, he's very hush-hush indeed. Tarboe is just an EO, Executive Officer."

"But why should ENOS have anything to do with Bogue?"

"Not ENOS, dear boy, but DAC. Anyway, you go and see Tarboe. I think you'll find he's your man. I'll just give him a tinkle." Fazackerley looked delicately at his watch. "Delighted to have put you on the track. Come along to the Club and have a drink when you're next in town. We'll talk about your book."

Chapter Twenty

"Why do you want to know about Bogue?" Tarboe asked. ENOS occupied two floors of a building in Soho Square, and on one of the floors Tarboe had a small, square box with a very tiny, square window. He was a lean, hard, wooden-faced man with grey hair, a grey toothbrush moustache, and one blind eye.

Applegate told his story. Tarboe made no direct comment, but he felt it had not been well received. "What do you expect me to tell you?"

"The end of Bogue's story. After all, he's been dead for years now. There can't be any reason for secrecy."

Tarboe raised eyebrows that were thin as pencil lines. "Can't there? Are you under the impression that all wartime secrets have been revealed because Sir Winston Churchill has published his memoirs and a version of the Yalta documents has appeared, and all sorts of agents have published stories in which they've told a little bit of the truth about how they tricked the Germans? Truth is like an iceberg. Nine-tenths of it remains always unrevealed. But you want to know the truth about Bogue. I warn you that you won't be able to use it."

About Tarboe's blind eye there was something mesmeric. Applegate said that he still wanted to know the truth.

"Very well. Fazackerley says that you are honest and discreet. Not that it matters much, because if you attempt to use anything I say in this conversation I shall simply deny it. I should say also that my only contact with Bogue was during the war. I have a file on his pre-war activities, but only one of them has any bearing on the story I am going to tell you. Bogue was not a member of the British Union of Fascists, but he had contacts with important members of the Nazi Party in Germany. You know that, I expect?"

"Yes."

Tarboe opened a manilla folder. "In January, 1940, Bogue approached a member of Neville Chamberlain's Government, and suggested that he might usefully be employed as an intermediary to negotiate peace terms with Germany. The offer was rejected. Later in the year – in August, when the period of the phony war was over – Bogue made another approach, saying that he had many German contacts but was a patriotic Briton, and offering his services in any connection in which they could be used.

"This time the offer was accepted. We were under no false impressions about Bogue, don't think that. We kept a close watch on his activities, and we were not impressed by his claim to patriotism. I was the security officer dealing with his case."

"And Fazackerley knew that?"

It was difficult for Tarboe's wooden face to express surprise, but he showed a trace of it now. "Naturally. That's why he sent you to me."

Applegate snorted. All Fazackerley's poking about among the files had been deliberate mystification. "Then DAC was – "

"Concerned with internal security," Tarboe said in a voice so severe that further questions seemed precluded. "Chief among Bogue's activities at this time was the running of a drug ring. The war had made it increasingly difficult for him to get supplies into this country. His organisation was busy building up contacts with merchant seamen, and he hoped by doing official work for the Government to obtain information which he could use to increase the amount of his supplies and the number of his agents. We knew all this. Nevertheless, we decided to employ him."

"Why didn't you clamp down on the drug ring?"

"Difficult to make someone like you understand. You look on drug selling as a purely moral problem. To us it's a practical one. Arrest the chief organisers of a drug ring, what happens? The addicts go to someone else. Arrest enough people and somebody obtains a monopoly, pushes up the price. Result, more suicides, more gangsterism, more blackmail pressure on addicts who must have their supplies of heroin or cocaine. What you can't do is to exterminate drug addiction by cutting off supplies. Witness the United States where the importation of heroin has been forbidden, but the market in it flourishes. There's a good case for keeping the cost of drugs as low as possible."

"You're not serious."

"Is that so?" Was it Tarboe's blind eye or the good one that imparted that boiled, ironic look? "Anyway, believe me, it's useful to know as much as you can about the details of a drug ring's operation in wartime. In Bogue's case we were able to trace through him dozens of important addicts, and we knew they were people particularly susceptible to blackmail by the cutting off of supplies. That information was potentially very valuable.

"I've said we decided to use Bogue. His contacts with the Nazis were mostly indirect, filtered through several European countries, or through the Argentine, Brazil or South Africa. He got through quite a lot of stuff to us about German progress with submarines and automatic weapons, most of it not very new but some undoubtedly useful. Occasionally we sent him abroad – he went with some sort of trade mission to Rio de Janeiro in April, 1941, as a special envoy to Buenos Aires in 1942, and on a mission to Lisbon in April, 1943. In Rio he managed to put pressure on an official in the German Embassy, von Sillert, who was a heroin addict. It was all done through intermediaries, you understand. Bogue and von Sillert never saw each other, but he got back the news that Germany intended to invade the Soviet Union. Unfortunately he got the month wrong – July instead of June – and also nobody here took much notice of it. Soon after Bogue left Rio von Sillert committed suicide. We never knew whether it was because his drug supplies had been temporarily cut off – we intended to renew them later – or because his leaks had been discovered. Bogue's Buenos Aires trip didn't have much result, but he came back from Lisbon with detailed information about the Italian military position, and about the number of divisions the Germans were taking away from the Eastern and Western fronts to try to contain the situation in Italy. Bogue got that information by making love to the wife of a second secretary in the Rumanian Legation at Lisbon. The second secretary himself was having an *affaire* with the wife of a third secretary in the Italian Legation, so there were quite a few sources of leakage."

Tarboe turned the pages of the folder. "That was April, 1943. I won't bother you with the details of Bogue's other jobs, most of which were handled in England through various agents. The results of them varied from good to indifferent, which is exactly what you'd have expected. We didn't flatter ourselves that the Germans were ignorant of what he was up to, or that Bogue himself wasn't perfectly aware that we knew of his drug-trafficking activities, and tolerated them because of his usefulness. It was in June, 1943, that we found that Bogue was acting as a double agent."

"How did you find that out?"

"In the simplest way. Bogue went to dinner one evening with a retired General, highly patriotic but renowned for his indiscretion. A story about the date of the opening of a Second Front had been planted on this General in some detail at a conference a couple of days earlier. The day after Bogue had dined with the General this information had been conveyed to a German agent here named Holmstetter."

"By Bogue?"

"No. By a creature of Bogue's named Jenks."

Applegate bit back the exclamation on his tongue. One of Tarboe's eyes stared at him, the other gazed across at the wall. "Fortunately we were fully aware of Holmstetter's activities, but we then looked more carefully at the information we had ourselves obtained through Bogue. The information about the attack on the Soviet Union, for instance. The fact that it was a month wrong rendered it really of very little use. And the information about troop movements in Italy – this had come from two other sources a few days before we had it from Bogue. At the time it seemed to be a valuable confirmation, but it was perfectly possible that the Germans, knowing a genuine leak had taken place, gave it to Bogue as well with instructions to pass it on. We reviewed all the information we'd had through Bogue, and decided that at the best it really didn't amount to very much.

"The case was talked about in all its aspects at a high level. Bogue's drug organisation, his notoriety at one time as a public figure, his potential usefulness as a means of planting false information. Finally, it was decided that he was more dangerous than useful." Tarboe closed the file and tapped it gently with two fingers. "It was decided that Bogue was expendable."

Applegate looked at Tarboe's wooden face, then away from him to the tiny square window that let in four slivers of light, then back again. It seemed now to be Tarboe's blind eye that was looking at him, but he had become confused. Whichever eye it was, the eye was wholly expressionless.

"I'm not sure that I understand."

"During July, 1943, we gradually tightened control over Bogue's drug ring, cutting off supplies and arresting some minor agents. He became very short of money, and complained about it obliquely. He was told that the police had apparently got onto the trail of his agents, and that he could not be protected beyond a certain point. Late in July we had word from the Germans that they were prepared to discuss the exchange of the '*Prominente*' for certain important Germans in our custody, in particular Rudolf Hess. You know about the '*Prominente*'?"

"Earl Haig and the Queen Mother's nephew, the Master of Elphinstone, and Churchill's nephew, Giles Romilly, and so on."

"Yes. Bogue was told about this proposition, and was asked to go to Madrid where a German envoy was coming to discuss the matter. On the 24th August Bogue set off for Madrid."

"And his plane was shot down by a German fighter." Tarboe said nothing. His face was expressionless.

"Wasn't it?"

"A security man named Shalson travelled with Bogue in the plane. The pilot and co-pilot were also security agents of ours. And by an odd chance they were also suspected of passing on information to the enemy. In fact, suspected is too mild a word. You hardly ever have absolute proof in these cases, but here the evidence was strong. We only have Shalson's story of what happened. According to him, the plane ran into some trouble in the air through a leaky fuel tank. They had to bale out some twenty miles inside Portugal. Shalson managed it safely. And the others jumped too."

"What happened to them?"

"Extraordinary thing." Tarboe looked straight at Applegate with the dead eye. The other wandered from wall to ceiling. "Awful lot of faulty equipment there was just about that time. None of their parachutes opened."

Applegate stayed silent, looking into the dead eye.

"We sent out another agent, but of course nothing happened. About the *Prominente*, I mean. They weren't freed until the end of the war. We clamped down finally on the drug ring, arrested Bogue's chief lieutenant, chap named Martin. No point in letting it go after Bogue was dead."

"And Shalson?"

"Shalson? He left the service when the war ended. Don't know what he's doing now. Growing flowers, I dare say. He was a great gardener. That's the end of the story."

Applegate shivered. "A hateful story."

A smile was carved for a moment on Tarboe's wooden face. "You are too romantic. There is no need to be sentimental about men like Bogue." Suddenly, dramatically, Tarboe put his hand up to his face and turned away from Applegate. When he turned back again his eye-socket was blank and he held a blue marble in his hand. "How do you suppose I lost this? Through a man like Bogue, one of our own agents who told the Germans where I was hiding. I have told you this story only so that you should understand that it is impossible to do anything about Bogue. In this department he has been forgotten. His file is permanently closed. You would be well advised to forget him also. Do you understand? Stick to your detective stories, Mr Applegate. Leave real life to those who know something about reality."

Chapter Twenty-one

Applegate had half-expected that he would be trailed up to London, was half-disappointed that he had seen no sign of a trailer. Wandering round the bookstalls at Charing Cross Station he looked again for Craigen or the boy Arthur. He found nothing to disturb him and turned again to the bookstalls. Men and women were snatching at evening papers and throwing down coppers and silver with frantic eagerness. What was the urgent need they felt to get home, he wondered, as he stayed on the edge of the crowd and placidly turned the pages of a woman's magazine? What were they returning to, the men with paunches and the chicken-necked women, the neat but spotty boys and the girls lacquered with smartness? An hour in the garden and the evening paper, leftover supper and a cold bed-sitter, a cinema ticket or a motor-bike ride. Something that grotesquely parodied what they heard on radio or saw on TV or read in such magazines as the one whose pages he was turning now. The fantasy life of the mass, Applegate said to himself with delicious sententious superciliousness, the snob's desire to move one step up the social scale. It is not art, but the *Tatler,* that life really mirrors.

He was reflecting that there was something wrong with this epigram, beside the fact that it was borrowed from Oscar Wilde, when a voice said, "Quite done with that, sir?" Unable to confront the assistant's yellowly bilious gaze he hurriedly put down *Woman's Home Life,* bought the *New Statesman,* the *Spectator* and *Tribune,* and scuttled away to the platform where the Ashford train was waiting. So long had he brooded at the bookstall that he had hardly more than a minute to spare.

With mild self-congratulation Applegate told himself that this was an astute move. He was scrutinising with particular care the three passengers who had passed through the barrier behind him when a green flag was waved and a whistle blown. He pulled open a carriage door and scrambled in just as the train was beginning to move. Poking his head out of the window he saw that in fact nobody had boarded the train after him. The three people he had been looking at all stood waiting placidly for a train on the other side of the platform. He had outwitted his possibly non-existent pursuer. The train was fairly full, but he found a seat in the dining car opposite a dowdy, middle-aged woman, and ordered dinner. He knew better than to expect a meal at Bramley Hall.

He was thinking about Bogue when he changed on to the Romney Marsh line at Ashford. Some of the things that had puzzled him were cleared up by Tarboe's story. Bogue had been short of money because his income from the drug traffic had been cut off, and the mystery of his employment on official missions was cleared up. But he had learned nothing from Tarboe that explained the mystery of Bogue's legendary fortune or told him why crooks should be gathered round Murdstone like wasps round jam. By this time, also, Applegate had in fact become fascinated by Bogue's character, and his biographical interest was more than a pretence. We like to think that there is a centre to every man and woman, a central coil of motive from which their actions spring, but in Bogue there seemed to be no such central coil, but merely a persuasive voice and various disgraceful actions. He had reached this point in meditation when a voice said: "Had a good day?"

There was only one other person in the carriage, and Applegate had summed him up as a local man who had gone to Ashford for the day or the afternoon. Not a farmer, but someone connected with the land. He had a homely air, although there was nothing particularly rural about his pepper-and-salt suit, rather shiny at the elbows. A man of fifty perhaps, cheeks slightly ruddy, thinning hair neatly brushed, and a certain warm solidity about him.

"Pretty good, yes." The answer was involuntary, but one quick glance revealed the reassuring fact that both his companion's ears were fully equipped with lobes.

"Mind if I smoke?" The stranger took out a pipe and began stuffing it with square, capable fingers. "I suppose you saw Tarboe?"

"How do you know that?"

"Been following you most of the day." The stranger, Applegate saw, managed to be both markedly an individual, and yet inconspicuous. You would not look at him twice in a crowd, yet if you did look at him you could not fail to be impressed by the face's placid forcefulness. "Saw you go into ESS and then into ENOS. It was a fair bet you'd seen Tarboe. Get anything from him?"

"What's that got to do with you?"

"I might be of some use to you, that's all, if I knew how much Tarboe had told you." Smoke rose from the pipe. "Depends how much that was. Did he mention me? My name's Shalson, or at least that's the name I used then."

Applegate had thought himself proof against surprise, but the fact that he was face to face with the man who had accompanied Johnny Bogue on his last journey surprised and delighted him.

"Tarboe said he thought you might be growing flowers."

Shalson laughed. "I ran a market garden for a couple of years but couldn't make a go of it. You need capital, that's the trouble."

"Who is Tarboe exactly?"

Shalson looked slightly surprised. "Thought you'd know that. He was a colonel in the war, in charge of a home security section after he lost an eye helping the Resistance."

"Home security. Do you mean counter-espionage?"

"Call it that if you like. Security, espionage, counter-espionage, they all merged into each other. What Tarboe does nowadays I don't know, but I should guess it's more of the same."

"Why were you following me?"

Shalson puffed deliberately at his pipe. "Now, look, young fellow, I may be able to help you with some information, but before I do I've got to know where I stand. What's your interest in Bogue?"

The train rattled into a station. A man walked up and down shouting: "Ham Street, Ham Street." The train started up again on its slow journey through the Marsh. Fields and sheep could still be seen in the gathering dusk. It seemed to Applegate that this man knew too much to be deceived by the tale he had told Tarboe.

"You know about Eddie Martin's death?" Shalson nodded. "And Montague?" Another nod. "I got mixed up in all that and became interested in it. Afterwards I might have left it alone, but I was threatened by some of Bogue's old friends – "

"Eileen and Craigen?"

"And Jenks."

"Is he in with them now? He's a real character, that one, always gets the dirty end of the stick. And?"

"That's about all. I want to know what it's all about, why I'm being threatened, what the gathering of the clans is for." He saw no reason why he should tell Shalson about Bogue's fortune.

"Ah. Tarboe told you I was with Bogue on that trip to Madrid?"

"Yes. He said all the others – pilot, co-pilot and Bogue – had parachutes that failed to open. Remarkable coincidence."

"Um." Shalson eyed him over the pipe. "What did you think of that?"

"I thought it was very much like murder."

"Would you say so now? Fact is, Tarboe spared your feelings a bit. Bogue was clever, I don't have to tell you that. He suspected something might be wrong, I don't know why, something to do with the way Tarboe shut down on his drug-running game perhaps. He told you about that?"

"Yes."

"Well, Johnny always looked out for number one. He had his equipment checked at the last minute, discovered the parachute was dud and had it changed. He told me that as we left the airfield. 'In case you've any doubts about it, Skid, I've got a substitute pack on,' he said. 'Accidents will happen, I know, but I don't want one to happen to me. My life's too infinitely precious to be lost through any kind of accident.' I was always called Skid then. He must have seen something queer about the way I looked, because he began to talk about making my fortune."

"How?"

"That's what he didn't say, not precisely. But he told me he could do it. He said he had all the money in the world and there was enough for both of us to share." Shalson looked a little sideways. "You know anything about that?"

"Tarboe didn't say anything," Applegate replied truthfully. "And then?"

"Then the port engine caught fire, as arranged. Bogue looked at me and saw I had expected it. 'Come on, Skid, we'll jump for it,' he said. And he got the hatch open. I knew his parachute was all right." Shalson sucked deliberately at his pipe. "So I did what I had to do. I shot him twice. Through the head."

149

It was quite dark. The train ran into Lydd station. One or two doors banged, footsteps sounded on the platform. Applegate felt for some reason desolate, as if a familiar landmark had been removed, or he had heard of the death of an acquaintance once well known but not seen for years. This was the end of a quest, the end of his paper chase, the trail inevitably led nowhere, it ended abruptly in an aeroplane. In the aeroplane had ended a life of many twists and turns, the life of a man engaged desperately in a struggle to outsmart the world. But none of us outsmarts the world, Applegate thought, not the slickest crook nor the most innocent player of the stock market. Life had its plan for every individual, and any escape from it was illusory. At the end of one escape road there waited the unexpected bullet in the aeroplane, and another was suddenly revealed as a *cul-de-sac* from which there was no honourable return, no recourse but the revolver placed in the mouth. Every variety of escape is an illusion, Applegate thought, and the part of a wise man is to conform, to accept everything. Accept the bowler hat and the striped trousers, accept strap-hanging and head crouched over office desk, take out insurance policies on a non-existent future, accept cancer, tubercle, wasted kidney, cirrhotic liver, that lead to death called natural.

These somewhat cheerless thoughts were perhaps reflected in his expression. Shalson said gently, and it seemed irrelevantly: "I'm a Jew, you know."

"What?"

"A Jew, a German Jew. That's partly why I had it in for Bogue."

"I don't understand. I thought that Bogue helped Jews to escape from Germany, from the Nazis." Covertly he studied Shalson's face and – so great is the power knowledge exerts on us – the features that had seemed obviously those of a Kentish native now took on a Jewish cast. He observed the wide, fleshy nose, a little curved perhaps, and seemed to discover something Semitic in the hand gesture with which Shalson greeted his remark.

"He helped them, oh, yes. He helped them as a man helps somebody away from a firing squad and drops them into a sewer where they choke to death. Have you never heard of the deal the Nazis made with the Jews, to get them out of Germany?"

"No."

"You are very innocent. In 1938 there were still many Jews left in Germany who had not been accommodated in the concentration camps. There was a Jewish organisation called Mossad le Aliyah Bet, the Committee for Illegal Immigration, which helped Jews to get away from Germany, and also arranged their illegal immigration into Palestine. The Mossad leaders made a direct deal with the Nazis. The Nazis wanted the Jews out of Germany. They knew that those smuggled into Palestine could be relied on to cause trouble. Eichmann, head of the German Central Bureau, set up facilities in Germany for the emigration of Jews, but he told Mossad that the actual transportation must be left to the Jews themselves and also to private enterprise. Bogue was part of the private enterprise."

"How do you mean?"

"By the end of 1938 the Gestapo was insisting that Jews should leave Germany at the rate of 400 a week, and at the same time they organised a travel bureau through which all emigration activities had to be arranged. The Nazi officials, Eichmann and others, took so much per head for transporting Jews into ships which weren't seaworthy. These ships could not be German, you understand, or there would have been immediate protests from other countries, Britain in particular. Some of them were provided by a half-German Greek ship owner. Others were bought by or through Mossad. Others were registered in the name of a Greek called Koudopoulos. They were the rottenest, filthiest, least

151

seaworthy boats that the people who bought them could lay hands on. The boats sailed from a dozen different ports – and they were packed with Jews, most of whom had paid all the money they possessed to sail in them. The people who went in those boats were pushed together like cattle. They had little food or drink. Sometimes the journey took weeks, especially after the war started and British Intelligence tightened its grip, and the boats were held up in one port or another. You remember how the *Fede* was held in La Spezia and those on board threatened to blow up the ship as soon as a British soldier set foot on it? No, you were too young. But that was only one case. Sometimes the boats were too rotten, and sank."

"And the Jewish underground agreed to all that? They let Jews sail in those boats?"

"What choice had they got? What other way was there of getting Jews out of German-occupied Europe?"

"And Bogue?" But Applegate almost knew the answer.

"Bogue was the English contact behind Koudopoulos. He was one of four Fascist sympathisers – respectable ones, not directly connected with the party – who helped to arrange sailings. Bogue dealt with the Mossad, he also dealt with Koudopoulos, and of course also with the Germans. Some of the money he got went to the Germans, no doubt, but he must have kept a packet for himself. Money is a curse," Shalson said with a passionate bitterness, a kind of terrible zest. "Filth. Destruction. Touch it and you're done for."

"So the way Bogue helped the Jews was by helping to get them on those boats?"

"Yes. I sailed on one of Bogue's boats, the *Zaline*, which sailed from a little port in Bulgaria called Mancic, early in 1940. My mother and father were on it. My father owned a small chain of clothing stores. He knew all the right people, used to be invited to Goebbels' dinner parties. Thought they would never touch him, his connections were so good. When his windows were smashed and clothes looted he went to Goebbels in person. The little doctor laughed at him, told him he had better get out while he had a whole skin. My father talked to Goebbels about principle, perhaps he should have talked about money. For money a man will do anything.

"There were six hundred and twenty of us on the *Zaline*, on a boat meant for perhaps fifty people. It was twenty-five yards long, its engines were no good, it leaked. There were no maps, no navigator. Not that it mattered, because the *Zaline* sank in the Black Sea. Of old age, you might say."

"And your father and mother?"

"There were just three lifeboats, and I was able to get them into one. Myself I am a strong swimmer, I took my chance in the water."

"You had a lifebelt?"

Shalson's laugh was like a bark. "Lifebelts, what do you think it was, the *Queen Elizabeth*? There were no lifebelts. I was picked up after an hour, by a British cargo boat. My mother and father were drowned. Their boat was hopelessly overcrowded. I was lucky. I got a job, and it was not in the Pioneer Corps, but with Tarboe. And I found out about the *Zaline*, and Bogue's connection with it. As the war went on I found out a lot about Bogue. Tarboe knew what he was doing when he picked me as Bogue's escort."

"How well did you know him, Bogue, I mean?"

"I saw him twenty times, perhaps."

"Was he as persuasive as people say?"

Shalson knocked out his pipe and put it in his pocket. The burst of passion had gone, and again he looked simply solid and reliable. "I'll tell you the thing about Bogue. You listened to him with two parts of yourself. One part knew that he was simply a liar and a cheat, and that everything he said was some kind of a trick. The other part just heard and believed. I don't know why. Because it wanted to believe, I suppose. I just know that's the way it was."

"For you as well?"

"For everybody. While you were listening to him."

The train stopped with an expiring puff. They were just outside Bramley. Applegate put his head out of the window into a cold, starless night, and withdrew it suddenly as a train whistled by him, a snake whose dark coils were broken by small patches of light. They started again with a jolt. He remembered something.

"One more thing. There's somebody else involved, a man who has the lobe of his left ear missing. Do you know anything about him?"

"I think so." Shalson's hand went up to his left ear and pulled. The lower part of the ear came away, revealing jagged flesh and an old scar. "This is plastic. Pretty good match, don't you agree? I haven't worried about wearing it for a long time, but when I learned that Eileen and Barney Craigen were down here I thought it might be useful."

Applegate stared at him, obscurely troubled. The train ran into Bramley Station.

Chapter Twenty-two

"I'm staying at the Bramley Arms," Shalson said. Applegate looked round for Hedda's old car, but it was not in the yard. They walked up the slope into the country road.

"What's your interest in all this?" Applegate asked abruptly. "Tarboe said you'd retired."

A beam of light directed from the opposite side of the road played deliberately first on Shalson, then on Applegate. "*Down,*" Shalson shouted, and flung himself towards the hedge beside which they were walking. Applegate dived the other way and found himself in a shallow and, fortunately, fairly dry ditch. There were two sharp cracks. Then the torch beam played again over the part of the road where they had been walking. Applegate wriggled a little farther along the ditch and looked for a gap in the hedge. Now came an answering crack from his own side. That would be Shalson. The torch went out.

Silence. And, behind the silence, uncustomary night sounds, a body moving cautiously but clumsily on the other side of the road. Then four shots. Applegate, head poked up just above his ditch, saw the spurts of flame. Wild firing. From his own side two shots and a yelp, quickly cut off. A body crashing along, elephantine. The sound of a car starting, farther up the road. Encounters that can mean death are rarely more personal than this, spurts of flame in the dark.

155

Applegate heard a whistle behind him on two notes, high and low. He whistled back. Shalson's voice said: "Here." They met on the road.

"Winged him," Shalson said. His voice was as calm as if their conversation in the train had gone uninterrupted.

"Who was it?"

"Barney, I should guess. He was always a fool with a gun."

"You use one yourself, I see."

"Haven't had occasion to use it for years." With no perceptible change of tone he said: "Take a little advice. If you're not on business, leave this thing alone. People are going to get hurt before it's finished."

Hedda's car was approaching along the road. Applegate would not have thought it possible that he could be so glad to recognise its characteristic sound, something between a furious knock and an asthmatic wheeze. It came thundering on them and shrieked to a stop as Applegate shouted: "Hedda."

She leaned out of the car. "Sorry I'm late."

"We've been shot at. This is Mr Shalson. He hit whoever it was and they went off in a car. Did you pass one a couple of minutes ago?"

"Yes, going pretty fast. Didn't see who was in it. Good shooting, Mr Shalson."

"We were never in much danger if it was Barney," Shalson said. "Can you give me a lift to the Bramley Arms?"

At the pub they rejected his suggestion that they should come in for a drink. He lingered with his hand on the door. "You don't carry a gun, Applegate?"

"No."

"They're professionals, you know, Barney and Eileen, even if they're not very good ones. You're an amateur."

"I'm in this too," Hedda said.

"With all respect, another amateur. But it's your affair I suppose." Shalson appeared under the pub lantern, burly and mild. "Good night."

He disappeared, leaving half a dozen unanswered questions chasing each other in Applegate's mind.

Chapter Twenty-three

The answers to these questions, and even the exact nature of the questions themselves, remained unresolved at breakfast the next morning. Applegate stuffed scrambled egg into his mouth and brooded upon the exact purposes of all the people involved, and the nature of Johnny Bogue and his fortune. Hedda appeared from the kitchen, wearing a ridiculously small black and white check apron. She carried a saucepan. "More scrambled egg?"

"I've had enough," Applegate said absently. He held out his plate for more, and at once began eating it. Maureen Gardner, across the table from him, giggled.

"I say, you are scoffing it. Hedda's a smashing cook, isn't she?"

"Smashing."

Deverell sat at the top of the long table. "Miss Pont is a lady of many accomplishments," he said politely.

Applegate frowned. "What do you mean?"

"She is an accomplished cook. Also a singer." He held up a finger and from the kitchen they heard her singing "See the pretty lady up on the tree."

Applegate frowned again. "You're moving out today, aren't you?"

"To the Bramley Arms. It is all part of my education, no doubt." About Deverell's speech, smooth and classless, there was something un-English.

"And when are you off to the Anarchists?"

"At the end of the week, I hope," Maureen said. "I've written to Enid Klug, she really runs the Community. Of course I could just go."

"That would be the Anarchist thing to do," Applegate agreed. "And if I'd been you I wouldn't have stuck a stamp on the letter, because buying stamps means supporting the state. Then if I'd been Enid Klug I wouldn't have accepted the letter because of the fivepence to pay on it."

Maureen said severely: "Anarchists have got manners. That's why I've written to Enid Klug. And they don't make feeble jokes like yours, either."

Hedda came in with a tray piled high with scrambled egg and toast. "I'm ravenous. Thank God to get away from Brooker-Timla. And shall I tell you something else? This is shop bread, not our filthy homemade stuff." She sat down and began to eat greedily.

"Good morning, good morning." Pont appeared, beaming. He looked no longer the frantic creature of two nights earlier, but the Jeremy Pont originally seen by Applegate, pink-skinned and clear-eyed, wrapped in his euphoric dream. If he had heard Hedda's last words, if he disapproved of the scrambled egg rapidly disappearing into her mouth, he gave no sign of it. The bright beam of his glance, radiating almost tangible warmth, moved from one to another of them and settled on Applegate, who was dazzled by his smile.

"Charles, my dear Charles. Don't let me interrupt, but when you are finished might I have a word?"

"I've finished now."

"Are you sure? A little more... " His radiant eye swept the table in search presumably of Brooker-Timla food, but failed to find it. "Shall we have our word then, my dear fellow?" An arm was placed round Applegate's shoulders as they made their way to Pont's office.

159

"Let me be frank," Pont said when Applegate was seated in a chair overlooking the neglected garden. "For the last day or two I have not been myself. I am like other children of nature, I need freedom in which to stretch my wings. Lowering skies, the fury of tempests, these have more effect on me perhaps than upon those less finely constituted. However that may be, I have not been myself. I admit it and apologise."

"Really, that's not at all necessary." Applegate was embarrassed. "The circumstances – enough to upset anybody – "

"Not at all," Pont beamed. "They did not upset *you*. I may not have shown it, but I have been impressed, in the highest degree impressed, by your imperturbable calm. Too often I have found fine-grained assistants who flinched from the hard facts of life. Frankly, I often felt they should have been pupils rather than teachers. Your own emotional balance has been wonderful."

"Thank you."

"Now we must look to the future." The light in his blue eye was martial. "You have seen enough to know that a great educational experiment is being conducted here. Must it end because of one unhappy incident? Never! I will not permit it. Janine will not permit it." At mention of his wife he looked thoughtful for a moment, then brightened again. "Last night I received a telephone call from Leo Gaggleswick, secretary of the Jacob Reitz Foundation. You know the Foundation, of course."

"No."

For a moment Pont looked mildly shocked. Then euphoria regained control. "A wonderful organisation. Devoted to the cause of experiment in education. They have a large sum of money donated by Reitz, the armaments manufacturer, for that purpose. If at times in the past I have seemed to criticise them… " He left that sentence where it was, and began a new one. "Gaggleswick had read all about the – ah – Montague incident in the papers. He wanted to know where we stood. I told him without equivocation. 'Gaggleswick,' I said. 'An experiment in freedom is ending, in freedom under law. I have given fifty years of my life to the cause of…' " Perhaps Pont perceived a certain restlessness in Applegate, for he gave up this sentence too. "So Gaggleswick has promised support, substantial support. Janine and I are going up to London this morning for a meeting with him. There is only one condition which, apparently, has to be observed under the administration of the Fund. A certain sum has to be put down by – ah – by… "

Applegate began to see the conversation's drift. "By you."

"Or by somebody connected with me." Pont put his head slightly on one side and looked at Applegate. "I have the very highest opinion of your practical abilities."

"Thank you."

"And it seems to me there is a bond of sympathy between us. I could offer you a partnership."

"I'm afraid – "

"The sum required would not be large. A mere thousand pounds."

"A thousand pounds."

"And you would have the privilege of playing a leading rôle in something that is no longer an experiment, but has behind it…"

The door opened. Maureen Gardner put her head inside. Applegate had never been more pleased to see anybody. "Telephone for you," she said to him. "In the hall."

" – a great tradition," Pont finished rather lamely.

"There's nothing I should like more," Applegate said insincerely. "But I just haven't the money."

Pont began to deflate slowly. "Come now, my dear Charles. You can't have taken this job for the money attached to it." He laughed feebly. "You must be a man of substance."

"I wish I were. That isn't the case at all, I'm afraid."
Applegate edged towards the door.

The old face sagged, the bright eyes dulled. "If you were
able to give a guarantee, even, it might be acceptable."

"Absolutely impossible." His fingers were on the handle.
"I deeply appreciate the honour. Sure you will find many
more worthy who are eager to… " Applegate left a sentence
of his own unfinished as he closed the door on Pont's
stricken face. Just like an old baby, he told himself angrily,
building up a whole fantasy out of a casual conversation.
When he reached the telephone he shouted a "Hallo" into it.

"Hallo, Charles. This is Henry."

The agelessness and sexlessness of the voice baffled him.
"Henry who?"

"Henry Jenks." The voice was reproachful now. "Surely
you haven't forgotten?"

He responded with a short sea-lionish bark. "Is that
likely? After one of your pet thugs shot at me last night."

"Dear, oh, dear. That was a most regrettable mistake."

"It might have been if he'd been able to shoot straight."

"Barney is hasty. And foolish." The voice now had a slight
nasal whine. "If I were in control of affairs I would have
nothing to do with him. He is not a gentleman." This seemed
too self-evident to need reply. "I hoped you would be free to
have lunch with me today. At the hotel. I do feel that we
should have a little talk together to clear things up."

"Our last little talk didn't seem to help."

"That was Eileen. She is really impossible."

"I'm fairly impossible too. I don't see that we have much
to talk about. Will Arthur be there?"

The voice said meekly: "Not if you don't wish it. I hope
you will bring your Egeria with you."

"My Egeria?"

"Miss Pont. It would be a great pleasure to meet her."

162

After all, he thought, what have we got to lose? At least it shouldn't be dull. "All right. But we shall leave a note of where we've gone, and in whose company. No funny business."

"Of course not." Jenks sounded quite shocked. "You really have got, what shall I say, the wrong impression. Can you and Miss Pont meet me in the cocktail bar at a quarter to one? I shall look forward to it very greatly."

Chapter Twenty-four

Their departure from Bramley was not wholly without incident. Getting Janine off in time to catch the London train occupied some time. It was always difficult, Hedda said, to get Janine out of the house before midday, and so it proved. For some time she could not be found, and when finally discovered she proved to be in a state of curious excitement, and was unwilling to accompany her husband. Her excitement baffled both Hedda and Applegate, for it was plainly unconnected with intoxication. She was simply unwilling to leave Bramley.

Since Gaggleswick had particularly asked for Mrs Pont to accompany her husband, however, Hedda was firm. On the railway platform Jeremy discovered that he had no money, and Applegate lent him four pounds. The depressive interview between them was forgotten, and mania evidently again in the ascendant, as he waved furiously from the train window. Opposite him Janine, an impressive statue, wig perfectly in place, sat with closed eyes.

Deverell had moved out to the Bramley Arms, but Maureen followed them around. She complained indignantly that she would be left alone for lunch, and that anyway there was nothing to eat. She refused to be taken in to Murdstone with them, stating her intention of walking five miles over to Thirlwell, where there were some much-decayed fortifications built against the threat of Napoleonic invasion to be seen. She was quite happy when allowed to make some enormously thick corned beef sandwiches. Corned beef, forbidden by Brooker-Timla but occasionally smuggled in by Hedda from the village shop, was apparently her favourite food. She stood beside the iron-studded door waving a fat hand as they drove away.

They had plenty of time to get into Murdstone, but when they were halfway there the engine hiccuped and died. While Applegate stood by helplessly, Hedda fiddled angrily with the engine, snapping words over her shoulder. "Screwdriver. Smaller one. Not that, stupid. One with the black handle."

Her temper was not improved by the fact that it was Applegate who discovered the cause of the stoppage when, ashamed of his inactivity, he looked at the petrol gauge and saw that it was below zero. Fortunately, Hedda carried a spare can, but the fact that he had made the discovery infuriated her nevertheless. She drove into Murdstone with furious disregard of road rules, and at a bend they had to swerve violently to avoid a green lorry.

"That's funny."

"What?" Her voice was grim.

"I'm almost sure Barney Craigen was driving that lorry. And Arthur was with him."

Hedda merely grunted. The car drew up, smelling slightly of burning rubber, before the Grand Marine Hotel at ten minutes to one, and Hedda went away to wash. As she came into MERICAN AR afterwards, Applegate, seeing her for the first time in a skirt, saw with regret that she had very thick legs. Ignoring the legs, however, if you could ignore the legs, the green coat and skirt suited her excellently. Above it her blue eyes shone with their customary bright yet vacant light. The brightness was perhaps enhanced at sight of the whisky sour waiting for her.

She took her place on one of the high, uncomfortable red-leather stools and said to the barman: "What's new?"

"Very little down here, and that's a fact." He held up the glass he was polishing.

"Mr Jenks been in?" Applegate asked. "Tall, thin – "

"I know Mr Jenks. And his friend who only drinks tonic because gin might go to his head. Often in, but not this morning. Staying to lunch?"

"Yes."

"Leave the rump steak alone. Tough as old boots. And don't touch the stewed beef, it's horse. Try the lobster. Not much they can do to lobster. I mean, either it is or it isn't."

"You're right there," Hedda said. "Have a drink."

"Just one little snort before lunch, I don't mind if I do. A drop of gin and pep to settle the old t-u-m. Here's how."

Hedda said thoughtfully: "Here's how. Seen anything of another friend of ours, very big man, gold teeth, was in here a night or two ago?"

"Barney, you mean. Have I not seen him? Without Barney this bar might as well shut up. Set your watch by him. On the doorstep every day at opening time. Had his right arm in a sling today, said he sprained his elbow last night. 'Well, Barney,' I said, 'as long as you've got just one arm that can raise a glass you're all right.' You've missed him by – oh, quarter of an hour. Wasn't quite himself today."

Applegate glanced at Hedda. It had been Barney with the gun. "Does he come in alone?"

"Sometimes he's with Miss Delaney, lives up at the water tower. Sometimes with Mr Jenks' side-kick, you know, the soda-pop kid."

"Arthur."

"Arthur, that's right. Very thick, Barney and Arthur. Don't know that Mr Jenks is best pleased. Takes all sorts to make a world, I always say." The barman rolled his eyes. "Good morning, sir. What'll it be?"

Jenks came hurrying towards them, his mincing walk almost a trot. "I've been caught up in a conference. So nice to see you again, Charles. Miss Pont, do pray accept my apologies, and have a drink."

Jenks was positively gushing. While they had a drink with him he talked in a manner that Applegate remembered as uncharacteristic. The anxious expression was still there, horizontal bars of worry still marked his forehead, but the total impression was of a distracted gaiety. And his subject matter, the weather, the quietness of Murdstone out of the season, the pleasure he would feel in getting away when his business here was done, was hardly inspiring. Applegate began to think that they might, after all, be in for a very dull lunch.

When they were at the table, in a great cold empty room overlooking the sea, he said: "Does business include the attack on me last night?"

Jenks' eyelids fluttered. "That was a complete misunderstanding."

"You mean it was Shalson they were after. How is Barney today, by the way? I hear he's got his arm in a sling."

"He had a little accident. These things will happen." A very old waiter tottered towards them. With relief Jenks said: "Shall we order? What do you recommend today?"

"What's that, sir?" The waiter put hand to ear.

"I said what do you recommend, what is good?" Jenks' voice, though raised, was still precise.

"Oh, yes, all good, all very good. The steak's very good."

"Lobster," said Hedda and Applegate together. Jenks looked slightly surprised. "I shall have the steak," he said.

The old man nodded, grinning foolishly, and was tottering away when Jenks said to them without enthusiasm: "A bottle of something, or is it too early in the day?"

"Not at all," Applegate said firmly. "Waiter," he shouted. The old man clapped hand to ear and turned with an appalled face. "The wine list," Applegate roared. Hedda looked at him admiringly.

"Immediately, sir. There's no need to shout."

Jenks looked at the wine list unhappily. "Will you leave it to me? A bottle of – ah – number twenty-seven."

"Thirty-seven, sir?"

"*Twenty-seven*," Jenks said, alarmed. Thirty-seven, obviously, was expensive.

"With steak, sir," the waiter said reproachfully.

"White wine with steak."

"I abominate drinking at midday," Jenks said passionately. "For myself, of course. My stomach."

"Why do you want Shalson out of the way?" Applegate asked. "What harm can he do you?"

Jenks crumbled a roll with his long fingers and made it into neat pellets. "Charles is so direct, isn't he, don't you find that?"

"I'm pretty direct myself," Hedda said. "So it doesn't worry me."

"Those of us accustomed to the – ah, niceties of diplomacy – "

"Come on now," Applegate said. "You weren't all that diplomatic when you were poking a gun into my back. Why are you all so worried about Shalson?"

"Shalson is really not a nice man. You might go so far as to say that he is ruthless. I shouldn't get mixed up with Shalson, if I were you." He looked at his wristwatch and then out through the window at the slate-grey sea. Two distant puffs of smoke indicated ships. Delicate spears of rain slanted down at the pavements. It occurred to Applegate that Jenks was nervous. The waiter brought three plates of thick brown cornflour soup.

"Shalson told Charles a good many interesting things," Hedda said. "We understand the situation pretty clearly now."

Jenks looked from one to the other of them with his anxious eyes. "What did he tell you?"

Applegate tipped some of the soup into his mouth. It tasted slightly like brown glue. "You were passing on information during the war to a German agent named Holmstetter. I thought you told me you had nothing to do with Bogue after the thirties."

"You lied about that," Hedda said flatly.

Jenks smiled wanly. "I am a devotee of truth, my dear young lady, but sometimes it is foolish to tell the complete truth."

"He told us – Charles – about Bogue's fortune," Hedda said boldly.

"What did he tell you?" Jenks pushed aside his soup. One hand crept up to the red spot on his cheek.

" Where it was."

"And what it was," Applegate improvised.

"Did he now?" Jenks' tone was almost playful. "That was very kind of Shalson. Perhaps you'd tell me. Where is it, and what is it?" They were silent. "No, no, my children, I'm not sheep enough to have that kind of wool pulled over my eyes. I doubt if Shalson knows enough himself to be able to tell you anything important. Shalson is *not* reliable."

"You told me yourself that what you wanted was your share of Bogue's fortune," Applegate said.

"Perfectly true, my dear Charles." Almost kittenishly he added: "I didn't say what or where the fortune was."

The waiter moved slowly towards them. "Mr Jinks, Mr Jinks," he quavered, looking round the room under the apparent impression that there were other people in it.

Jenks, half out of his chair, was dabbing at his lips with his napkin. "Yes, yes."

The old man looked at him with dim surprise.

"The telephone."

Placing one foot daintily before another, yet manifestly hurrying, Jenks crossed the room. While he was away Hedda exhorted Applegate to some kind of action.

169

"You don't get *at* him. Really say something to him where it hurts. What is he but an old queen, after all? Slug Monahan would have run him ragged by this time."

"I'm not Slug Monahan."

"That's obvious."

"Was he your boxer friend? The one who used you as a punching-bag?"

She nodded. There was a wistful look on her face. "Sometimes I regret him. With Slug you saw life."

"I'm sorry you don't think you're seeing it with me. I'll arrange for you to be shot at next time." Stepping daintily, wriggling sinuously, Jenks recrossed the room. He gave them a shy, sly smile. "Awfully sorry. An old friend who is coming into town. Someone I've been expecting. A little business matter, you know. He will be here in half an hour."

"I thought it might be Arthur," Hedda said. "I'd been longing to meet Arthur. I only saw him that night in here, but I thought he was cute with his little razor. He *is* cute, isn't he?" Jenks looked down his long nose. "Tell me, have you made provision for Arthur when you get your share of the money?"

"I love Arthur like a son," Jenks said smugly.

"But then you loved Montague like a brother," Applegate pointed out.

"Poor Frankie." Jenks looked out to sea and smirked slightly. There was silence while they attacked the food. Attack was indeed the word. The barman's remark that there was little you could do to lobster had made no allowance for the fact that you can freeze it. Reposing in their shells the lobsters looked attractive enough. This appearance was deceptive. They resisted easily the first gentle approach with fish knife and fork, and Applegate was driven to digging his fork in and pulling savagely at the flesh. Thus torn from its moorings the lobster revenged itself by proving absolutely tasteless. It was with some pleasure that he saw Jenks sawing

170

away vainly at the edges of his steak. The wine, by some accident, was quite drinkable. Applegate used it to wash down strings of lobster.

"What did you really bring us here for?" Hedda asked abruptly.

Jenks choked slightly on a piece of steak. "What?"

"You said you wanted to have a talk. What about? So far you haven't told us anything."

"Really, you're awfully direct too. Such a pair."

"If you've got a proposition to make, let's hear it."

"Not exactly a proposition." Jenks wriggled, and looked at his wristwatch again. His anxious eyes stared seawards. "Eileen was really cross with this young man. She was quite in favour of some strong action being taken. I was able to dissuade her."

"Being shot at is quite strong enough action for me."

"I told Eileen you were not unfriendly, only curious. I like curiosity, I am curious myself. But just at the moment your curiosity cannot be allowed. It is a nuisance to us and a danger to yourselves."

Hedda began to hum "Tell me the Old, Old Story." Upon Jenks' pale cheeks there showed a touch of pink. "No more than a nuisance, believe that, since you are far from realising the true position. We have been waiting, some of us, years for this time, and we shall not be stopped by a couple of children still, as the vulgar saying goes, wet behind the ears."

"Has Shalson?" Applegate asked.

"What?"

"Has Shalson been waiting years for this time too?"

"We shall look after him when the time comes. But what you two need is a few days' holiday. You are not needed any longer at the school. Take a week off. Fly to Italy, Venice, Rome, Florence. The masterpieces of art, what an opportunity to see them. And then you will have each other. Or to Paris if you like. Paris in the spring, ah, me. What wouldn't I give to be your ages again." Jenks kissed the tips of his long fingers. "And not a penny to pay. We will look after everything, Eileen and I. We are not rich, but you will find us generous. Just for a week. Then you will return, we shall have gone, our very existence will seem a mere dream. What do you say?"

"Really, you're a most immoral old man," Hedda said. "It's not the things you say, it's the way you say them."

"Even if we were to accept your offer it's very doubtful whether we should be allowed to leave the country," Applegate commented. "The Inspector in charge of the case is very interested in our activities, Hedda's and mine."

"He thinks you killed Frankie." Jenks cut off a giggle.

"I doubt that, but he said we were both in trouble up to the neck, and might be in danger."

By this time they were drinking coffee in the lounge where Applegate had first met Jenks. Now the door of this lounge opened and a burly, tanned figure walked quickly across to them. "They told me I should find you in here, Jenks. How are you?"

The newcomer was a man perhaps in his early fifties. He was rather noticeably dressed in a suit patterned in a small black and white check, with white shirt, red and grey tie and very shiny black shoes. There was a pearl stickpin in the tie, and more pearls gleamed in his cuffs.

Jenks' manner as he rose to his feet was obsequious. "How nice to see you, Mr Mallory."

Mr Mallory gave Applegate and Hedda a cursory glance, then drew Jenks aside and whispered to him.

"I'll be ready in five minutes," Jenks said.

"Right. My car's outside." With a nod to them all Mr Mallory left the room.

"A snappy dresser," Hedda said. "Who is he?"

The anxious look, which for a few moments had been absent from Jenks' eyes, returned to them. "It was Mr

Mallory who telephoned. He is a very important man, a friend of mine. In the way of business, you understand. Now, if you will excuse me."

"Thank you for lunch," Applegate said. "And for the offer. Handsome, I'm sure."

"The offer. Yes, yes. It was nice to see you." He was plainly anxious for them to be gone. Applegate waited five minutes in the front hall for Hedda.

"I looked at the reception book," she said. "Mr Earl Mallory from São Paulo, Brazil. What does a nut from Brazil want with Queenie Jenks?"

"That must be his car." They both looked at the enormous Buick with a left-hand drive that stood in the hotel car park. Applegate peered through the window. "It's got the name of a car hire firm inside. A London one, so presumably he drove down."

They walked along towards Hedda's car. The rain had stopped and a sad sun shone over the sea. Almost on the horizon the ships still trailed their spires of grey.

"Has the purpose of that lunch occurred to you?" Hedda asked.

"What do you mean?"

"Jenks didn't really expect us to fall for that suggestion of his about a holiday. He didn't want anything at all."

"I don't understand you."

"He wanted to get us away from Bramley, that's all." She revved up the engine, let out the clutch, and they bounced and bucketed away. They went, however, no farther than round the next corner, where they jerked to a stop. Applegate looked at her in surprise.

"What's wrong this time? No petrol?"

"We ought to find out something more about this Mallory who puts Jenks in such a flutter, don't you agree?"

"I don't know. If Jenks wanted to get us away from Bramley, wouldn't it be a good thing to get back there?"

"Use your loaf," Hedda said with some irritation. "Jenks doesn't mind what we do any more, otherwise he wouldn't have left us alone. Let's have a look at Mallory's room." She stepped briskly out of the car and slammed the door. Applegate followed her with a slightly sickish feeling. As they walked along Hedda spoke out of the side of her mouth, like a girl in an American film. "Should be easy. Room number's thirty. Hardly ever anyone on the reception desk. Just nip in and take the key."

"I don't think – "

"Then stay outside."

Addressed thus peremptorily, Applegate felt he had no course but to follow her into the hotel. There was nobody at the reception desk, but Hedda clucked with annoyance. "No key. Hasn't got a trusting nature." She made for the stairs.

"What are you going to do now?"

"Get into his room. Slug used to do little jobs like this when he couldn't get any fights."

"Why couldn't he get any fights?" Applegate was momentarily diverted.

"Lost half a dozen fights in the first couple of rounds, and in the last one he lay down before the other man actually hit him. Feeling tired. Watch up that end, will you?"

Applegate nervously patrolled the end of the corridor while Hedda dropped to her knees beside a door near the other end, took from her handbag something that looked like a small screwdriver with several prongs on it, and fiddled with the lock. Applegate was so absorbed in watching her that he quite failed to hear a door open just by his side. He jumped with surprise to find himself addressed by an old lady dressed all in black, with a scarf apparently made of mauve towelling wrapped round her head. "Young man, has lunch been served?"

"Oh, yes, I think so. It's rather late for lunch now, I think."

"Then I shall have a bath." She crossed smoothly, as though on wheels, to the door opposite, opened it and disappeared. Hedda had disappeared also. Applegate walked up the corridor, opened the door numbered 30, and found her going through the contents of a case with several foreign labels on it.

"Here." Hedda threw over to him a small book. It was a Brazilian passport, made out in the name of Max Eckberger. His address was given as 28 Calle Simon Bolivar, São Paulo, and his profession as banker. Eckberger had travelled a good deal recently, chiefly in South America. The passport was stamped for Venezuela, Chile, Peru, Colombia and the Argentine. In Europe he had visited Switzerland, France, Italy, Denmark, Greece and Great Britain during the past year. The portrait on the passport was that of the man who called himself Earl Mallory.

"A banker." Applegate was astonished. "What can a banker want with Jenks?"

"Here's the name of his bank." She was now going through papers in a black briefcase. "Banco Grando Metropolitano di Brasil. President, Max Eckberger. And a lot of letters about credit facilities, long-term loans available, that kind of thing. Don't look at me, keep an eye on the corridor. Here are some more letters. It's a new bank apparently. Listen. 'The Banco Grando Metropolitano di Brasil has been approved by the Brazilian Government. It can offer facilities equal in all respects to any other bank in Brazil. Its President, Mr Max Eckberger, has been associated for years with many of the most important commercial enterprises in South America, including Tin Mines of Bolivia, Limited, Grand Brazilian Loan Corporation, Associated Venezuela Petroleum, South American Import-Export Company, etc.' What do you think of that?"

"Anything else?"

"Silk shirts, silk pyjamas slightly gaudy. Assorted cuff links, very pretty diamonds in one pair. He certainly is a snappy dresser. Letters of introduction from people in Brazil to a lot of firms here."

"Hurry up."

"Don't fluster me. Here's another suitcase, empty. Suits in it probably. Yes, here they are hanging up. He looks after his clothes, Maxie or Earl or whatever his name is. Hung these up before he began to look for Jenks. Afraid they would get creased." Applegate, watching the corridor, heard the sound of a cupboard and drawers opening. "Yes, just look at this green double-breasted suit, my it's sharp. And green and white snakeskin shoes as well. Toilet things all of the best, all tortoiseshell." Applegate glanced round to see her fiddling with the handle of a glass. "No sign of secret compartments, handles screwing off or anything like that. Not that one would expect it, with an eminent banker."

"Nothing personal?"

"Nothing. Let's get out. Fingerprints, I think, we don't worry about." She brushed back a lock of hair from her forehead and looked frowningly round the room. "Pretty straight, but I dare say he'll know we've been here. I'm not an expert."

"You seem to me to have a dangerously high degree of accomplishment."

"You'd be surprised." As they walked out of the hotel she said: "What did you make of that?"

"I don't make anything of it, unless this man's masquerading as Eckberger. Even then it doesn't seem to make much sense."

She started the car and they shot away. "Seems to me I am just beginning to see a glimmer of sense somewhere," she said.

Chapter Twenty-five

It began to rain again, large drops from a dark sky, as they got to Bramley village, and by the time they had reached the weed-grown drive of the Hall the sky was almost black and the downpour torrential. Rain drove through gaps in the canvas hood, and Applegate huddled into his sports jacket. They ran for the iron-studded door together.

When they were inside the house Hedda began sniffing anxiously. He caught her shoulders, swung her round and kissed her. The response he obtained was adequate but not enthusiastic. "Someone's been here."

"How do you know?"

"Tobacco smoke. Wasn't here when we left." She began to poke about uncertainly. He went into the modern addition, walked through it and came back to her. Rain beat against casement windows of deserted classrooms. The whole place was extremely melancholy.

"Nothing," he said to her.

"Try upstairs." They went through the bedrooms, Hedda sniffing everywhere in a way that after a time seemed to him purely comic.

"Lost the scent, dear bitch?" he asked.

She glared at him, ran downstairs again and turned left into the dining-hall and to the kitchen quarters beyond. She had gone back to the dining-hall when he heard the mewing, a faint thin sound.

"Do you keep a cat here?" She shook her head. "Then listen."

The sound seemed to come from the kitchen quarters, but they could see nothing there to account for it. Applegate began to go round pulling cupboard doors open. Then he exclaimed: "Of course. The cellars."

In the cupboard that led down to the cellars they found Maureen Gardner, gagged, bound and dirty, with a bruise on her cheek. She had managed to work the gag a little loose, and the mewing sounds they heard had been her cries. Her clothes were torn. Tear stains made furrows down her face.

They untied her, patted her shoulder, gave her a small shot of whisky and listened to her story.

"I started to walk to Thirlwell, but it began to rain and I came back. I've just begun to read Proudhon, and I thought really that was more important than going for a walk in the country. Property is theft, he says, and – "

"Yes, yes," Applegate said hurriedly.

"So I got back here just after one o'clock. There was a lorry in the courtyard."

"A green lorry?"

"That's right, do you know who it was?" She wiped her nose with a dirty handkerchief. "So I came inside and listened and I heard a noise down in the cellar. I went down to see what was happening. There were two men, a big one with a thick neck and a young one. I asked them what they were doing."

"That was brave." Applegate patted her shoulder again.

"I just wanted to know. Well, they caught me and tied me up. When they did that I hit my face." Her finger touched the bruise. "The young one kept showing me a knife and grinning, but I wasn't frightened."

"What were they doing?" Hedda asked.

"When I got there they were fiddling about with that ring, you know, the iron ring on the wall. I couldn't see just what

178

they were doing with it. Then they tied me up and put me up here, so I couldn't see but I could hear. There was a sort of clang and a lot of noise, as if they were turning over old bottles or something, or perhaps it might have been tins. The big one said: 'Christ, it isn't here.' The young one said it was no good looking any more. The other one said: 'But it's got to be here. It was here a couple of days ago. The old girl won't half give us the bird if we go back without it.' The young one said – you know what – about the old girl. They seemed to search around some more and the big one said it must be you. 'That bloody interfering school teacher and the bit who goes round with him have found it,' he said."

"Fancy being called a bit." Hedda bridled with pleasure.

"Whatever it was they were looking for they didn't find it. They talked about what to do with me. The young one wanted to kill me, he said: 'We ought to do her now,' but the big one said they'd been told no trouble, and I couldn't tell anything important… " Maureen Gardner's shoulders began to shiver, and she gave a loud sob.

"Cheer up," Hedda said. "After all, you haven't suffered death, or anything worse than. Have a drop more whisky."

She drank the whisky, hiccuped and stopped shivering. "I must look awful. I'd better go and wash. What were they looking for?"

"I wish we knew," Applegate said.

While Maureen washed he followed Hedda down the cellar steps. They looked at the iron ring, apparently set immovably in the wall, and tugged at it.

"There must be some spring we haven't discovered." His fingers searched unsuccessfully for a wedge or projection. "But I suppose it doesn't matter all that much now, since whatever it was has gone."

"Charles." Her fingers were digging into his shoulder. He turned to face her.

"What's the matter?"

Her arm quickly coiled itself round his neck. His head was brought down to meet her in a jarring, bruising kiss. "Don't you realise what this means, Charles. They'll think you've taken this thing, whatever it is. They'll be after you. Remember what happened to Montague and Martin."

He disengaged himself with some difficulty. "If they really think that, they won't kill me. Or at least not before they find out where I've put the thing."

"If that's any consolation. I should imagine Arthur would be pretty good at thinking of nasty things to do to people."

"You'd be in trouble too. After all, you're in it with me."

"I'm only the bit who goes along with you. But you're in real trouble, Charles. Look after yourself."

"Would it worry you if I didn't?"

But she had broken away from him now and was going up the steps again, mockingly singing the words he had heard before:

"See the pretty lady up on the tree,
　The higher up the sweeter she grows.
　Picking fruit you've got to be
　Up on your toes."

Chapter Twenty-six

At five o'clock Hedda drove in to collect the Ponts from Bramley station. As she swept into the courtyard and jolted to a stop, Janine emerged from the car, statuesque and in a way magnificent. Behind her came a small, crumpled man hardly recognisable as the enthusiastic Jeremy who had waved from the train window. He sank down into a chair in the dining-hall and stared straight ahead of him, plump hands tightly clasped. Applegate raised interrogative eyebrows at Hedda, who turned down her thumbs.

Suddenly Jeremy spoke – or rather, it was less that he spoke than that some impersonal oracle uttered, ambiguous as oracles often are, but impressive in its dull monotone. "Deceit and trickery. Folly and lies. Theft and murder. And a lifetime's work ruined. Nothing more. This is the end."

"Gaggleswick turned you down?"

"Gaggleswick!" The voice was raised indignantly for a moment, then dropped again to the monotone. "Gaggleswick knew nothing. A joke."

Applegate understood. "To get you away from here. So Gaggleswick knew nothing. Was he pleasant?"

"He was *pleasant* enough. But to be compelled to ask such a thing, to make such a journey, and to find out that it was a *joke…* " Jeremy began to laugh, in uncomfortable loud hiccups.

"Hedda, the whisky," Applegate said, his tone perhaps resembling that in which, long ago, Holmes asked Watson for the hypodermic.

Jeremy drank some whisky and stopped laughing. He hardly listened, however, to Applegate's explanation that the telephone call was undoubtedly part of a plot to get everybody out of Bramley Hall. The plump hand was slightly raised, then lowered, more words were murmured. "A plot, the vilest plot that man could hatch." It was a bad sign, Applegate thought, that the old man should drop into blank verse.

"What are we going to do with him?" he murmured to Hedda, who shook her head. Maureen Gardner, who clung to them both as if they were firm poles in a shifting world, watched silently. The question was resolved by the reappearance of Janine, who entered the dining-hall walking slowly but without her stick, and tapped her husband on the shoulder.

There was some change in Janine, an exaggeration of the change they had noticed that morning. She seemed to be in a state of suppressed excitement that had nothing to do with intoxication. After the rigours of the day she was almost incredibly cheerful.

The little man looked up and caught at her large white hand. "Freedom," he said. "Freedom within the rule of law. The self and the non-self. A helpmeet in a million."

Slowly, as if magnetised by her hand, he rose to his feet. "Tomorrow is another day," she said as she led him upstairs.

Applegate was just remembering that it was time for tea when the telephone rang. He heard Jenks' voice, whining a little.

"Charles, I would never have believed you were such a deceiver."

"I don't know what you mean."

"Listening to my little plans for you as though you didn't know all the time."

"Know what?"

"What it's all about," Jenks said archly. "But myself, I altogether welcome it. I've always said we should co-operate, you and I. *Other people*, of course, may not be so pleased, but we shan't worry about that."

"Including Arthur."

"Oh, Arthur." Jenks dismissed Arthur. "But now we're really right out in the open we just must have another meeting. A round-table conference."

"Cards on the round table."

"Yes. After all, there may still be a *few* things you don't know."

"About Max Eckberger, you mean, alias Earl Mallory? It wasn't quite cards on the table when you introduced us, was it?"

"Ah, but we didn't know you were so clever then, although I always said to Eileen that you were a clever young man. But that wasn't all I meant. Can you come along this evening?"

"Where to?"

"A convenient meeting place for various reasons would be the Rivoli Concert Hall. Do you know it?"

"Barnacle Bill and the Limpets."

"That's right. It's a concert party worth looking at," Jenks said enthusiastically. "If you could be there just before the end of the show, about eight o'clock, say."

"All right."

"By the way," Jenks said, too casually, "you'll bring everything along with you, I suppose."

"I hardly think you could expect that, under the circumstances."

183

"Perhaps not. Anyway, remember that from now on, Charles, you and I are partners." His voice was liquid with sentiment.

"I'll remember. Goodbye."

Chapter Twenty-seven

At half past seven that evening a curious little party left Bramley Hall. Hedda, wearing a blue jersey and black slacks and looking more than usually determined, crouched over the wheel of the old car. Applegate sat next to her, thinly cloaking by a masquerade of self-possession a particular nervousness about his mission and a general nervousness about her driving. In the back Maureen Gardner contentedly ate the congress tarts and doughnuts which she had bought earlier in the day at the village shop.

The reason for this tripartite mission was Hedda's immediately expressed conviction that he was walking into a trap. She was eloquent upon the subject. Her blue eyes blazed as she talked about it, and Applegate found her arguments the more difficult to resist because privately he agreed with them. He was less convinced that the situation would be improved if she accompanied him, but about this again she was so insistent that he gave way. Feebly he mentioned the police, a little shame-faced when he heard her mocking laughter.

"The police, indeed. What are you going to tell them? That a gang of crooks think you've stolen some immensely valuable thing they're after, whereas really you're perfectly innocent but want to bring them to justice. Can you imagine what Inspector Murray would say to that?"

Maureen, who had been listening in silence, suddenly said: "Who did steal it? This thing, I mean, whatever it is."

"Obvious," Hedda said promptly. "Shalson. That's a kind of a friend of Charles' who was once a secret service agent and is still very handy with a gun."

"I'm not quite sure... " Applegate said slowly.

She snapped her fingers in irritation. "Simple enough, surely. Jenks and his lot haven't got it. We haven't got it. There's nobody left but Shalson."

It seemed to Applegate that there was a flaw in this logic, but he was unable to formulate precisely his objection to it. "All right. I suppose you'd better come, although I can't think what use it will be for two of us to walk into a trap rather than one."

Smiling like an amiable tigress, she assured him that in her company his strength would be as the strength of ten.

"I want to come." They had forgotten Maureen. "I don't want to be left alone here. Those men might come back. Besides, it's – it's eerie. Please take me with you."

Applegate and Hedda looked at each other. "You'd be better off with Enid Klug."

"Who's Enid Klug?" Hedda asked.

"She's found the ideal life in Essex. A hundred acres in Essex with madrigals, hand crafts and Morris dancing."

"He's being facetious," Maureen said without heat. "It's the Anarchist Country Community, you remember I told you about it. I'm going there in a few days. I don't want to be murdered before I go, if you know what I mean."

"We shall have to take her," Hedda said. "After all, she did see Barney and Arthur. She's a witness."

"And three heads are better than two, particularly when one of them is mine," Maureen said complacently.

Applegate said nothing. It seemed to him that he was sunk beneath an immense wave of feminine self-esteem.

Hedda's driving into Murdstone was even more erratic than usual. Applegate felt impelled to protest when she pulled out behind a lorry and almost shaved the wheels of an oncoming charabanc.

"Don't take so many chances," he said.

"What?" The noise as the car rattled along was tremendous. "I can get seventy out of her. Hold on to your seat." The noise increased, the needle crept up to sixty-five, in the back seat Maureen gave a delighted small scream. The car swayed like a ship in a storm. They rounded a corner. In front of them a large car was parked, another car came towards them rapidly on the other side of the road. Applegate closed his eyes and awaited the inevitable. When he opened his eyes again after an agonised screaming of brakes they were some six inches behind the large car, and Hedda was smiling like a cat who has lapped cream.

"Phew! You do drive well," Maureen said from the back.

"Don't I," Hedda delightedly agreed.

They reached the Rivoli in time for the last ten minutes of the show, and stood at the back of the hall. The audience seemed to be composed of the same, or almost exactly similar, figures, and Applegate could not see anyone he knew. Suddenly he was touched on the arm, and turned to meet Jenks' apologetic smile. Barney and Arthur were a yard or two behind him. "So glad you could come," Jenks whispered. His smile became almost a grimace as he saw Hedda.

"There they are," Maureen said loudly. "The men who attacked me."

The boy Arthur put his hand in his pocket. Barney looked at Jenks, who wriggled unhappily.

"Shall I get the police?" Maureen took a step towards the exit. Barney and Arthur moved between her and the door.

"Be quiet, little girl," Jenks furiously whispered. "You shall have an ice cream when this is over."

"Yes, be quiet, Maureen," Hedda said. Maureen subsided. Applegate turned his attention momentarily to the stage. In spite of what had been promised, the turn now was one he had seen before. The stringy blonde climbed the steps in her dirty nightdress and Barnacle Bill staggered on from the other side of the stage, croaking:

> " 'It's only me from over the sea,'
> Cried Barnacle Bill the sailor.
> 'I'm all lit up like a Christmas tree,'
> Cried Barnacle Bill the sailor."

To Applegate's surprise he saw that Jenks also was looking with marked attention, first at the stage and then at him. There was something wrong, or at least something strange. What was it?

"I'll carm dahn and let you in, I'll carm dahn and let you in," sang the stringy blonde. Barnacle Bill huffed and puffed about the stage, took a swig from the bottle, took off his false nose to use his handkerchief (that was a new bit of business, Applegate remembered), and roared:

> " 'Then hurry before I bust in the door,'
> Cried Barnacle Bill the sailor."

There was one other new turn, in which Barnacle Bill sang alone, with enormous gusto, an unintelligible song rather reminiscent of one sung by Charlie Chaplin, which in his case was accompanied by vigorous gestures, apparently of defiance. This was received coldly, and about the whole performance there seemed, indeed, to be something wrong. Applegate was still wondering what it was when the curtain came down and Barnacle Bill and the Limpets stepped out to take their share of genteel hand clapping. It was when Barnacle Bill stepped forward that Applegate noticed that his hair was not grey streaked with black dye, but genuine dark hair. The concert party disappeared and Murdstone's octogenarians, with a sprinkling of fifty-year-old youngsters, began to move towards the exits.

"Come along now, there's somebody I want you to meet." Jenks went to the right.

Applegate hesitated. "What about my friends?"

"Oh, they must come along, by all means. We're all friends here, I hope."

Applegate jerked a thumb at Hedda, and they pushed their way against the stream in a line of which the tail was brought up by the watchful Arthur. Jenks opened a door which led into a small passage, and the passage took them back-stage. Then he opened another little door. They walked by a small room where the Limpets, chattering like sparrows, could be glimpsed putting on shabby street clothes. Jenks paid them no attention, but knocked on a door at the end of this passage. Not until a deep and pleasant voice called, "Come in," did he turn the handle and stand aside, with a certain obsequious flourish, while they made their entrance.

Inside the room a man stood in shirt and trousers, his braces patterned with dancing girls. The man was rubbing grease paint off his face and looking into a cracked glass on the wall. "What do they give the boss himself but a piece of mirror the size of a postage stamp?" he grumbled cheerfully. "It's a scandal. Remind me to put down a question about it in the House, Henry, will you?"

Then the man turned round, holding a towel in one hand, and saw them – or perhaps he had seen them all the time. "Mr Applegate, I presume," he said. "Mr Applegate and party. Make yourselves at home."

The man was stocky, almost fat. His thick curly hair was abundant, and it was hardly streaked with grey. The head was well shaped but jowly, and about the body too there was more than a suggestion of flabbiness. The eyes were remarkable. In colour they were a slaty blue-grey. They were large and fringed by dark, thick lashes. But the remarkable thing about them was that these beautiful eyes lacked all the warmth and friendliness that was in the man's voice. They were cold, assessing eyes, and Applegate saw them move quickly, consideringly, from him to Hedda, on to Maureen, and then back to him. Then he said the simple words that he had never expected to say, words that ended a quest.

"You're Johnny Bogue."

Like all quests fulfilled, he thought as he stood there in the crowded little room, this one ended in disappointment. Here was the enigmatic Johnny Bogue, marvellously alive, the Johnny Bogue who had occupied so many of his thoughts over these last days, the invisible hare of the paper chase, the seducer, shyster, confidence trickster, whose personality had seemed to present an insoluble problem. Now here was the figure about whom he had woven fantasies, a chunky little man running to fat, and what was there complex about him, after all? One of nature's vulgarians, evidently – consider the dancing girls, the jocose greeting, the slight clownishness for which Applegate had been unprepared. An insignificant little man, even, except for those hard eyes. And it was very possible that he was indulging a fantasy even about the eyes. He remembered Tarboe's words. "You are too romantic, Mr Applegate."

Hedda put a hand to her mouth, startled for once out of her usual coolness. "I thought he was dead."

"Everybody thinks I'm dead. They've thought so for so long that I'd resigned myself to being a permanent corpse above ground. But circumstances said no. You're Miss Pont." The blue-grey eyes made a bold appraisement of her, an appraisement, Applegate realised, which held a sexual quality missing when the same eyes had looked at him. It was a commonplace enough look, a vulgarian look, yet beneath it Hedda flinched as if she had been slightly scorched.

"And what's your name, young lady? I don't believe I've heard of you."

Maureen eyed him with undisguised interest and admiration. "I'm Maureen Gardner. I'm at the school, was rather, until it finished."

"What are you going to do now?"

"I'm leaving at the end of the week to join the Anarchist Country Community at Shovels End in Essex."

"Are you now?" Bogue turned round to the cracked section of glass and talked while he knotted his tie. "I used to be very interested in Anarchism when I was a young man. In fact, I'll tell you a secret, I spoke on Anarchist platforms in Glasgow just after the war, that was the First War, you know. I was a red-hot revolutionary then, hot as you are now, I expect. Trouble with Anarchism, I found, was it's against human nature. In a small group, yes, providing you're all idealists, Anarchism's fine, answers all the problems. In a feudal society – well, yes, it's still got some kind of answer. But once you get labour-saving machines, motor cars, aeroplanes, not to mention all the bombs we're inventing to save civilisation, what can Anarchists do but settle down in country communities at Shovels End?" Bogue turned round and appealed to her, his arms spread wide, his face serious.

Maureen goggled at him. She had been won over, Applegate saw, won over as only a girl could be who had perhaps never been taken seriously before. "You think I shouldn't go?"

"Not at all." Bogue thrust his arms into jacket sleeves. "We learn from our mistakes, if we ever learn. But the important thing is to have the capacity for making mistakes. To anyone of your age, faced with a choice, I'd say just this. Do the daring thing, the unusual thing, don't do the commonplace thing."

"Yes." Maureen expelled what Applegate unhappily felt to be an almost reverent sigh.

"That's what I've just been doing, turning up here as Barnacle Bill the Sailor. Was I good? All right, don't answer that, but you'll agree it was unexpected."

Jenks was fidgeting. "I don't want to hurry you, Johnny, but… "

The glance Bogue gave Jenks was different again in quality, the easy contemptuous look of a man sure of his own superiority. "Don't get St. Vitus' Dance, Henry. You know Henry," he appealed to Applegate.

"I know Henry."

"I've known a lot of Henrys," Bogue said meditatively. "And you could roll them all up into one, a Henry who's a little bit shifty and very, very nervous and is always hoping to fiddle something for himself on the side, but never has the guts to do it successfully. And that's Henry Caution here to a T. My old Dutch, he is, faithful unto death. Never let him tell you anything else. Has he told you anything else?" Bogue looked at him now with such quizzical roguishness that Applegate could not help laughing.

"He may have done."

"Don't let him kid you. Henry loves me, don't you, Henry? He thinks I'm a genius." Jenks smiled unhappily as Bogue put an arm round his shoulders.

"Shall we go? There's a lot to talk over."

"Suppose we don't want to go," Hedda said.

Bogue dropped his arm from Jenks' shoulders, looked surprised. "If you don't want to come, you don't want to talk, all right. I can't make you."

With her thumb Hedda gestured at Barney and Arthur by the door.

Bogue laughed. "What those boys have been up to before I got here I don't know, but while Johnny Bogue's here there'll be no rough stuff. Stand away from that door, boys."

Reluctantly they moved a couple of steps away from the door. Bogue shook a cigarette from a packet, lighted it, stared at Hedda. "If you want to go, Miss Pont, nobody's stopping you. If you want to stay and hear a few explanations... " He held out the packet of cigarettes.

Hedda looked at the door, then at Applegate, and took a cigarette. It was, he felt, somehow a gesture of capitulation.

Chapter Twenty-eight

Barney drove the car. Hedda sat with him in the front, and Bogue was by her side. The other four sat in the back. When they reached the water tower Bogue jumped out and walked quickly round to the little side door, which opened before he could ring the bell. The rest of them followed at leisure.

"Johnny," Eileen Delaney said, "was it all right, Johnny?"

"Of course it was all right. They loved me, isn't that so?" He appealed to the others.

"It was a mad thing to do, but if you're sure it was all right, nobody noticed – "

"Don't fuss, Del. You know I don't like to be fussed. Is Max back yet?"

"He rang up from London. He should be here in half an hour. You shouldn't have done it, Johnny, it was crazy." Down the parrot nose two tears slowly rolled.

"I like to be crazy, didn't you know? Del, we've got guests. Applegate, here, you know, and I know him too." He jerked a thumb. "You saw me when I was looking out of an upper window like a character in the *Prisoner of Zenda* or something. But now, do you know Miss Pont and Miss Gardner?" He made this introduction with a formal gravity that obviously delighted Maureen. Was Hedda similarly impressed by it? Applegate could not be sure.

Eileen Delaney was still expressing her ladylike pleasure at meeting Hedda and Maureen when a key turned in the door. It opened and Deverell came in. He stood for a moment stock-still, expressionless. Bogue said: "You know him, but I don't think you know who he is. My son, Geoffrey."

Now that he saw the two together, Applegate wondered how he could have failed to recognise Deverell's likeness to the snap of Bogue, a likeness not of particular features but of general aspect. Bogue was speaking again.

"Geoffrey's been what you might call masquerading for a day or two at my old home." Old home, Applegate thought with a slight shock of surprise, of course it was Bogue's old home.

"You killed Montague," Applegate said. He spoke with certainty.

"He ran into a little trouble, but nothing that can't be straightened out," Bogue said. Deverell said nothing, but looked at Applegate thoughtfully. "Now, Del, my dear, aren't we going to be a little bit crowded for our conference? I don't want to say I prefer anybody's room to his company, but Barney and this boy here, what's his name – ?"

"Arthur," said Arthur.

"You make Miss Gardner nervous and perhaps you make Miss Pont nervous. I'm not sure you don't make me nervous, so just take a walk round the houses, will you."

Arthur looked at Jenks. "I don't think – "

"You don't think and you'll never learn to think, so why not button your mouth," Bogue said lightly. "You're talking to me, not Henry. Don't mix me up with Henry. I'm not like Henry in any way at all."

"Should we go and have a hand of nap upstairs, chief?" Barney asked in his hoarse voice.

"Nap, draw poker or blind man's buff as long as you get out of here." When they had gone up the stone staircase Bogue pulled at his tie and threw it off, then turned a chair round and sat with his arms round the top of it, smiling at them. Remember what he is, Applegate said to himself, he's a cheat, a blackmailer, a man who traded on the misery of Jews. Yet even while he told himself these things he felt the waves of Bogue's easy charm washing over him. He shook his head like a man trying to disperse the early fumes of alcohol, and looked at Hedda to see if she was similarly affected. She was staring at her shoes.

"Let's talk." Bogue waved a hand at Applegate. "Will you begin or shall I? What do I call you, Charles, Mr Applegate, it's up to you? But you'd better call me Johnny. Everybody else does."

"Call me what you like." Applegate found it necessary to clear his throat. "You begin. Tell us why you're here at all, and why everybody thinks you're dead. A man named Shalson told me he'd shot you twice."

"Did Skid tell you that?" Bogue laughed. "He was always a bit of a romancer. You shouldn't believe everything Skid says. You want a proof he didn't shoot me – well, here I am. But you'll only get mixed up, listening to a romancer like Skid. Would you like me to tell you the story now, straight up, just the way it was? All right. Let's begin in 1943, when I said goodbye to England, home and beauty. Things were rather awkward then."

"They found out you were acting as a double agent, and decided you were expendable." Applegate quoted from Colonel Tarboe.

"Is that what they told you? Then let it go," Bogue's voice did not lose any of its warmth and richness, but Applegate thought he saw a momentary flash of something like anger in the blue-grey eyes. He tried to press home what seemed in some way to be a tactical advantage.

"And you were just going to become the richest man in the world."

"Yes. You know all about that." Why should he assume that, Applegate wondered? "Counter espionage decided to murder me, it doesn't sound so pretty when you put it like that, does it? Skid was told to do the job, but changed his mind at the last moment. Where is Skid, by the way?"

The boy who now had to be thought of as Geoffrey said in his soft voice: "He left the Bramley Arms this morning and took a train to London."

Bogue pulled at his jowl and frowned. "Skid's not a fool. I wonder." He dismissed whatever it was he wondered. "So Skid and I jumped together. We parted company soon after we landed. The plane crashed and the death of Johnny Bogue was announced. I must say he didn't seem to be greatly lamented. It's rather a shock to read your obituary notices, but it's better than being dead."

"That was more than ten years ago."

"So it's a life history you're wanting, is it? Here's my card." Applegate took it and read: *Norman P Gambal.* In the bottom right-hand corner of the card was printed: *Gambal United Enterprises, 133 Calle Getulio Vargas, São Paulo.*

"Mr Mallory-Eckberger comes from São Paulo too."

"It's a great city," Bogue said enthusiastically. "Second city in Brazil, shooting up faster than Los Angeles, and full of opportunities for a commercial genius like me. You ought to come out to São Paulo, Charles. Organise the cultural side of life there, it's a bit lacking in culture."

"Drinks and sandwiches." Eileen Delaney reappeared from behind a curtain that must lead into a tiny kitchen.

"This is real hospitality," said Bogue. "Have some whisky, Hedda. You look like a girl who'd drink whisky."

"Do I?" As Bogue handed her the glass their fingers touched. Applegate was surprised to feel in himself a twinge of jealousy.

"Ham sandwich? Del's own cutting, but she won't mind me saying it's not like what we had at Bramley in the old days. They were real parties we gave then, you'd have enjoyed them, Hedda."

"I'm sure I would." Now Hedda turned on Bogue the full light of her blazing eyes.

"Did Nella Fish enjoy them too?" Applegate asked.

He had been hoping to disconcert Bogue, but perhaps that was impossible. The plump little man put down the half-eaten sandwich and stared at him thoughtfully, then said with what was surely a deceptive mildness: "That was such a long time ago. I've forgotten. Don't ride me too hard, Charles, or we shan't be able to do business, and that would be a pity."

"What were you doing in the concert party?" Applegate heard Maureen's voice almost with a shock.

"Do you know, I'm almost ashamed to tell you, it's so silly." Bogue smiled shyly, disarmingly. "And Charles here will never believe anything I say anyway, because he's been listening to the gossip of too many old women. The fact is, a boat dropped me off here a couple of days ago, and since then I've been waiting for Max. I got bored, and I found out that Barnacle Bill used to be an old chum of mine. I did a lot of amateur theatricals when I was at Bramley Hall, did you know that? I thought it would be fun to take his place just for one performance. So Barney slipped him a tenner, didn't mention my name of course, and he stepped out for one performance. Does it sound like fun, Maureen?"

"Oh, yes."

"It was madness, Johnny, and you know it," Eileen Delaney said.

Bogue pushed away his chair, walked over to a window and stood beside it, gesticulating excitedly. "All right, all right, it was madness, you say. I say it was the kind of thing a man like me has to do every so often if he's going to stay alive. Do you know what was out there, Del? A lot of old crows and fossils who wouldn't have anything to do with Johnny Bogue when he was in his prime. Can't let that man Bogue have the Town Hall for a speech, he's a Fascist. Don't go to Bogue's parties, he's a vulgar fellow. Can't accept the money he's given towards the new school, it might be tainted." Bogue's voice was high, almost out of control. His hands were shaking. "They had a genius here and they didn't know it. They had a genius in this country, and first they put him in prison, then they give instructions he should be knocked off. Do you know what's wrong with them all, politicians and soldiers and security boys and all? They're jealous. They were jealous of Johnny Bogue, afraid he would show them up for what they were, mediocrities and lickspittles. That goes for them all, from Ramsay Mac onwards and downwards. They put their foot on Johnny and pressed hard. But Johnny Bogue was too smart for them. You have to wake up early in the morning to be smarter than Johnny. Did you understand that song I sang them, any of you? Of course you didn't, you're too polite. It was in back slang and it went: 'You sons of bitches, you can kiss my – ' "

"Johnny," Eileen Delaney said sharply.

He stopped. My God, Applegate thought in fascinated horror, he believes all that, it's real to him, the man really is a bit mad. All that stuff about injustice and mediocrities, part of him believes it. Slowly Bogue's face lost its mottled, purplish look and he regained control of his hands. In his usual rich, warm voice he said: "That's the answer to your question, Maureen. It was the Anarchist in me coming out."

Maureen's "Yes" was a whisper.

"Now, let's get down to it. I'm dealing with you, Charles, is that right?"

"You're dealing with me," Applegate said.

"All right. You've got the stuff through a bit of luck. When Geoffrey went to look a couple of days ago it was still there, packed up. Now it's gone. But having the stuff doesn't mean you can do anything with it. I can do something with it, but I haven't got it. Now, where is it?"

"You don't expect me to tell you that."

"All right, you've tucked it away somewhere. What's your proposition?"

"I don't see why I should make any proposition."

"Really, Charles, all this fencing," Jenks said reproachfully. "I shouldn't have expected it from a *direct* sort of person like you."

"You won't make a proposition, all right. Here's mine." Bogue was talking quickly and sharply now, partly to confuse him, Applegate thought, partly to obliterate the recollection of that outburst. "A five per cent cut of the proceeds. That's after deducting expenses."

"Five per cent." He was genuinely surprised. "That seems very little."

"My dear Charles, have you any idea of how much we shall clear on this deal? With any luck at all it will be half a million pounds. Net."

Applegate pursed his lips for whistling, but made no sound. He looked at the other faces. Hedda, lips slightly parted, was looking at Bogue. Eileen Delaney leaned back in her chair, one thin veiny hand tapping on the other. Jenks snickered suddenly, cut the sound off. Deverell (to give him the name that seemed to come most easily) stared at Bogue with painful concentration. Tension increased in the room, quite tangibly, as if a switch had been turned on that rarefied the atmosphere. From this tension only Maureen Gardner, sitting back on a sofa, seemed immune.

Bogue went on. "That makes your share twenty-five thousand. Is that too bad for a lucky discovery? Bearing in mind that you'll keep right out of the picture, taking none of the risk."

Applegate found it necessary to touch his own lips with his tongue. "I didn't know it was as much as that."

"For a lucky dip like yours, I should say it was pretty good."

"How do you make out that we're taking none of the risk?" Hedda asked. "You're going to Brazil, right?"

"We're going to Brazil," Bogue agreed.

"You're leaving an unsolved murder behind you. The police won't like to leave it that way."

"Well?"

"Do I have to spell out every word? Charles is linked with the murder, and so am I. If we're to be clear, arrangements will have to be made to hand over" – she looked hard at Bogue – "the guilty party."

"You don't miss a trick, do you? It's a point you've got there, but I'd sooner talk about the cash side of it first. When we've come to an agreement on that – "

"No." Hedda said it decisively. "First of all we've got to know we're safe."

Bogue stared at her hard for a minute, then burst out laughing. "That's some girl you've got there, Charles."

"He hasn't got me, nobody's got me. Are we going to talk about that or shall we go?"

Bogue laughed again, laughed until he had to wipe his eyes. From his rumpled jacket he produced a case with cigars in it, and offered them round. Some not very obscure compulsion made Applegate, who rarely smoked them, accept one of the fat, formidable cylinders. A great deal of puffing and flaring went on while the cigars were lighted. Jenks, Eileen Delaney, Deverell and Hedda lighted cigarettes. Blue smoke rose into the air, producing, curiously, a relaxation of the tension in the room. Bogue waved his cigar at Hedda. "You have the floor, my dear. Tell us what you want." He sat down in a chair, leaned back and closed his eyes. His cigar pointed upwards.

"First we ought to get it clear what did happen," Hedda said in her hard voice. "There's a lot Charles and I don't know, we admit it. Eddie Martin was killed by Barney because he wanted to play it alone, is that right?"

Eileen Delaney croaked an answer. "Six weeks ago now Johnny got in touch and told us what he'd been able to arrange with Max. Without Max it was no good, you understand that?"

Hedda nodded. Did they know that, Applegate wondered, and how?

"That was the first we heard of Johnny, the first we knew he was alive. He didn't trouble to get in touch until he wanted something. That's Johnny's kind of faithfulness, years of silence until he wants you. You want to remember that."

Bogue opened his eyes, looked at her. "Just get on with it, Del. They don't want to hear your private grief."

"Eddie was just coming out of prison, and Johnny wanted him to handle it. You know about Eddie?"

"My chief of staff," Bogue murmured.

"We know about Eddie," Applegate confirmed. The fumes of the cigar made his eyes smart.

"But Eddie was half-smart. When I told him the set-up the first thing he did was to get a false passport, stamped for Brazil. Then he got in touch with Max, to fix a deal with him, and Max told Johnny. Eddie was told to work with me, but he came down here alone. I sent Barney down after him."

"And Barney killed him." The little woman said nothing, but stubbed out her cigarette.

"Then Montague. Do you want to talk about Montague, or shall I?" She looked at Deverell.

Of them all, Applegate thought, Deverell behind his calm exterior showed the most sign of strain. Now he jumped to his feet and words spattered from him like confetti. "For God's sake let's get this over and talk about something serious. Montague was a little rat. When I saw him he suggested we should work together, said he was an agent of Henry's." Deverell's voice was scornful. "Told me Eileen wasn't to be trusted. Then he said something about you, Dad, and I – "

"All right." Bogue took the cigar from his lips, spoke emphatically. "Don't say any more, Geoffrey. You got into a scrape, but it's nothing to worry about."

"At that time you didn't know Mr Bogue was alive," Hedda said to Jenks.

"No. It came as a shock to me. A pleasant one, of course."

"We decided to let Henry in to avoid any more trouble," Eileen Delaney explained.

"That covers everything," Hedda said briskly. Bogue opened one eye to look at her and then closed it again. "Now all we have to decide is what to do about it. As far as Charles and I are concerned, we shall be quite content if Craigen and Deverell are handed over to the police. Is everybody agreeable to that?"

There was a moment of appalled silence. Then Bogue sat up straight in his chair, put down his cigar, and laughed again. He leaned over and pinched Hedda on the thigh. "You're a girl after my own heart, Hedda, you really are. Catch you out in a bluff and you try another bluff. The answer is no. I can safely say that nobody on my side is agreeable to the suggestion, and you know it."

"Outrageous," Eileen Delaney croaked. Deverell looked angrily at Hedda.

Bogue put his hands together. "At the same time, let's admit it, you've made a point. We've got to hand over somebody. Who is it to be? I don't think it need be two people, Eddie's death was suicide in the book."

Applegate took the cigar out of his mouth. His tongue seemed to be made of leather. "The police are not satisfied. They're liable at any time to link it up with Montague."

"I see two possibilities," Bogue went on, as if he had not spoken. "All of us here are ruled out, for one reason or another. But – " He jerked his thumb upwards.

Eileen and Jenks were both moved to protest. Jenks' hand went up to the pimple, his voice squeaked. "No. I won't hear of it."

The woman croaked. "Johnny, you're joking."

Bogue spread his hands in a gesture placatory, negligent, amused. "All right, I'm joking. Let's forget it. Let's talk about money, I'm willing."

Hedda said: "No."

There could be no doubt now of the amusement in Bogue's voice. "You say no. All right, argue it out with her, Del, Henry too. Settle it how you like, I'll still be happy."

"Leaving out everybody in this room," Applegate said.

"That's right. Leaving out everybody in this room."

Jenks and Eileen both began talking at once. Then Jenks gobbled in his throat, and she spoke:

"You're losing your grip, Johnny. You don't want to let this bitch dictate terms. It's not like you. After all, we've got them here."

Now Jenks came in, bustling with grievance. "I really quite agree. I'm very fond of Charles, but – "

"We were going to be partners," Applegate said. "Remember that."

"But here they are, after all."

"And here they might as well stay," Bogue added. "Is that your meaning, Henry?"

"Well." Jenks wriggled uncertainly. "I mean to say, after all, it's not up to them to dictate terms to us. We negotiate, if I may say so, from strength."

"You always were a fool, Henry," Bogue said, with weary contempt. "Tell him, somebody. You, Hedda."

"You might be able to get things out of us, but you can't afford to have any more trouble down here. Is that right?"

Bogue sighed and stretched luxuriously. There were damp patches under his armpits. "Of course. We have them, sure.

THE PAPER CHASE

They have us. In a different way, but they've got us just the same."

"But I don't see… " Jenks was pulling at his long blue chin. He looked petulant.

"You never did see, Henry. You were born without sight, and you'll die blind. We let Barney and your boyfriend get information out of them by their little tricks."

"I wasn't suggesting – "

"Stop your cant, that's what it comes down to. Maybe they get it easily, maybe they have to kill one of them. But even if it's easy, what happens afterwards?"

"We could shut them up until we're out of the country." Jenks' voice faltered. He looked down at the ground.

"And then they get out, and they know enough about what goes on to stop the whole thing. What it comes down to is this, we've got to get rid of them or they've got to come in. Now, my conscience isn't clear enough to stand a weight like getting rid of them. I don't know about you. Don't worry, Maureen, I'm only talking about something that isn't going to happen."

Applegate saw that Hedda was holding Maureen's hand. Jenks muttered something.

"Barney and your boy are different. They don't know B from a bull's foot. Barney's handy with a knuckleduster, and I don't doubt the boy's good with a knife, but what have they got up top? You could spread their grey matter thin and still get it on a sixpence."

"Arthur's a good boy," Jenks said indignantly. "Just because he never finished his education there's no need for you to be mean about him."

" – his education," Bogue said pleasantly. "You're getting on my wick, Henry. What do you say, Del?"

"I couldn't let you turn Barney over. He's not very bright, but he'd never do that to you or to me."

205

"All right, all right." Bogue spoke to Hedda. "There's your answer then, my dear. You can't have either of them. We must leave the police to make their own conjectures."

"Come on, Maureen." Hedda and Maureen stood up. Applegate put down the butt of his cigar and stood up too.

"Johnny, you're not going to let them go," Jenks squeaked alarmedly. "Johnny."

Bogue was tilted back in his chair, eyes closed. "It's no use, Henry. What Hedda wants is reasonable enough but you say she can't have it. Let them go."

Deverell, very pale, had moved between Hedda and the door. "Let them go, Geoffrey." Eyes closed, plump face lifted so that double chin was eradicated, Bogue gave an impression of indifferent sweet reasonableness. In this reasonableness there must be a trick, for the man was made up of nothing but tricks. Yet, looking at the relaxed figure stretched in the armchair, short legs comfortably folded, it was hard to believe in a trick.

Eileen Delaney took another cigarette and tapped it on her thumbnail. Her beady eyes looked at Jenks.

Deverell stood aside. Hedda reached the door, grasped the handle. In his chair Jenks, long and thin, wriggled like a worm under torture. The words he spoke were hardly audible. "...what you like."

Bogue did not speak or move. It was Eileen who rasped: "What did you say?"

"I said do what you like." Jenks pulled a white handkerchief from his pocket and blew his nose.

Still without opening his eyes, Bogue said gently: "It's not what I like, it's what *you* like. We throw Arthur to the lions, do we?"

"Do what you like, do what you like." Now Jenks' voice was almost a shriek. Unmistakable tears ran down his narrow cheeks. His phrases came confusedly. "I should have known better…mixed up with again…always destroyed my happiness…hateful sadistic beast."

Bogue sat up, pulled down his creased waistcoat, smiled brightly and boyishly. "Once a Henry always a Henry. All right. Take your hand off the door handle, Hedda, and sit down again. It's Arthur."

"But can we be sure he'll do it?"

"Where Henry is concerned money comes first, everything else is a bad second. Now, Arthur shouldn't present too many difficulties. Get him picked up on an assault charge, flashing that Boy Scout knife of his. Did Arthur know Montague, Henry?" Jenks nodded miserably. "Good. Plant some letters from Montague on him strongly suggesting that their relationship was what you might call compromising. Have you got any letters from Montague that begin just straight, without 'Dearest Henry' on top?"

"Frank wasn't like that." Jenks' voice was miserable.

"That's not important. Have you got anything that might do?"

"I expect so, yes."

"Then that will save the trouble of tracing and copying. Not that the police will ask too many questions when Arthur is delivered into their laps and we've disappeared. Not if I know the police. And I do know the police." Bogue's smile was positively impish. "Now, if everybody's happy, let's get back to what we were talking about. We've wasted enough time on Arthur."

Applegate looked at his watch. The time was twenty minutes past nine.

Chapter Twenty-nine

The lights were too bright, the room was too full of smoke, his eyes were smarting and blinking with it.

"Can we have the window open a little?" he asked. Deverell moved behind a curtain, and a window screamed slightly. There was no perceptible thinning of the atmosphere. A chair scraped above them, feet clattered, Barney's great body appeared.

"Heard a noise," he said. "You want me?"

Eileen answered: "No, Barney."

"Can we come down now? The kid and I are getting browned off up there."

"Aren't you playing nap?"

"Nap!" the big man was scornful. "He don't play nap. All he does is read kid magazines, Westerns. How long you going to be?"

"Not long." She spoke soothingly, as if to a child. "You just lie down and have a rest."

Barney clattered upstairs again. Bogue was talking about percentages and expenses. Applegate deliberately abstracted half his mind from what was being said and tried to work out exactly what it was that could be worth half a million pounds. It must, he thought, be the proceeds of some great robbery, and Eckberger was for some reason excellently placed to act as fence. A jewel robbery, a bank robbery?

Impossible to know. He must confine what he said to remarks about stolen goods, without particularising.

He was suddenly aware that he had missed something. "What was that?"

"It's a terrible thing to get old. You can't hold an audience any more." Bogue's well-shaped mouth was smiling, but the eyes were hard.

"I'm sorry. It's hot in here. May I take off my jacket?"

"We've got a gentleman here at last," Eileen cackled. "I like you, Charlie. Take it off, you won't shock me."

Applegate folded his jacket carefully and hung it over the back of his chair. "I'm listening now."

The look Bogue gave him had about it something puzzled. "I was telling you the way in which the money was split. Henry gets five per cent and thinks himself lucky he was let in on it. Del gets ten per cent for old times' sake and pays Barney out of it. You and Hedda get five per cent, out of which you can set up Maureen in her own Anarchist community if you want to. The rest belongs to Max and to me."

"Eighty per cent." Applegate whistled. "You don't do badly out of it, I must say."

"It was our idea, it's our risk, we pay the expenses. What can you do without us? Nothing."

Hedda said coldly: "It's just as true that you can do nothing without us. I think we should split equally, the three of us, after reckoning out Jenks' and Miss Delaney's shares."

"I don't like this," Bogue said. He looked from one to the other of them with a stare so coldly impersonal that Applegate felt a shiver down his back, the kind of shiver he did not associate with fear, but with the cold touch of a barber's clippers on his neck.

Eileen was frowning. "They're asking too much."

209

"I don't mean that," Bogue said slowly. "I mean they shouldn't be asking at all."

"My God, Johnny, they want to get the most they can out of it, which of us doesn't?"

"Not these two. You remember what you said about Applegate, he's a gentleman. He shouldn't be dickering about so many per cent. And he's not bothering. He's not really listening to what I'm saying, even. Or the girl either. Shut that window, Henry. And Geoffrey, you'd better stand by the door."

Hedda said: "If this is a trick to get us to take five per cent, it won't work."

Bogue glared at her. "Something tells me I'm not the one who's playing tricks round here. Now, Applegate, where's the stuff?"

The icy clippers stretched farther down Applegate's back. With outward calm he said: "Where you can't get at it."

"After we've melted it down, what do you think Max is going to do with it?"

"Why, sell it, of course."

"In what form? How can we use the gold after it's been melted down?"

"That's something for you and Max to decide." He knew as he said this that it was disastrously wrong. They were all on their feet. Jenks had taken out his small revolver with the mother-of-pearl handle, Deverell at the door was holding a larger revolver that gleamed blue in the light, Eileen Delaney was shrieking something unintelligible at Hedda. Maureen cowered in a corner of the room, with her hands to her mouth.

In all this movement only Bogue was still. His plump fingers moved on the chair arm. He said quietly: "What makes you think we're dealing with gold, Charles? You haven't a notion of what we are dealing with, have you?"

Applegate was speechless. Hedda said: "Because we try a little bluff… "

"Don't tell me this was any kind of bluff, Hedda. You're speaking to an expert. You don't know anything, either of you, nothing important. You've never seen the stuff."

"We haven't had a chance to look at it," Applegate began.

Bogue cut him short. "Be quiet. You've caused us, as well as yourselves, enough trouble already."

"Come over here, Charles. I want you." There was a note of appeal in Hedda's voice. He got up and moved slowly over to the sofa, his body pierced by inimical glances. Hedda pulled him down to her and pressed her body against his in what seemed a desperate kiss. Jenks sucked in his breath, and Eileen whistled coarsely.

Hedda broke from the kiss and nibbled sharply at his ear. Was the situation, then, so desperate, was this a farewell bite? Words were murmured, as it seemed miraculously, into his ear: "Gun in my hip pocket. Distract attention." Was it conceivable that those words had been spoken by the Hedda who now gripped his hand convulsively?

"It's a funny time to choose for canoodling, but there's no accounting for tastes," Eileen Delaney said.

"That – er – arrangement about Arthur is no longer good. I want you to understand that, Johnny." It was Jenks. "I made it only under extreme pressure."

"Shut up," Bogue said without heat. He looked at the three of them, a little fat man intent and gloomy where a few minutes ago he had been so gay. He spoke slowly, weightily, as he must often have spoken in the House of Commons. "Perhaps I am wrong and one of you really does know something. If that is so, I appeal to you, here and now, to say so. It will be in your own interests, even more than in mine."

Silence. Hedda's grip on Applegate's hand tightened. Bogue sighed. "I was afraid of it. I'm sorry, but we can't let you go."

"Shall I tell Barney and Arthur to come down?" Jenks asked, with a little anticipatory wriggle.

How does one create a diversion, Applegate wondered? At that moment two were created for him. At Jenks' words Maureen Gardner screamed, and screamed again, with the full power of her lungs. And at the door there was a discreet tapping – three taps, then one, then three and one again.

"Stop it, you little devil," Jenks cried. He ran across and put his hand over Maureen's mouth, yelped with surprise and anger as she bit it. Eileen Delaney came across to help him. Deverell had turned to the front door. This, if ever, was the moment. Applegate ignored the struggling three on his right, ignored Bogue who stood placidly by his chair, and flung himself across the room in a flying tackle on Deverell.

The boy's back was to him, and there was no difficulty in bringing him down, but then they were on the floor together, and Deverell was as slippery as a cat. Their bodies strained together in a parody of the way in which he had clasped Hedda on the sofa. Two feet away, no more, Deverell's revolver gleamed bluely on the floor. Applegate, while shifting his hold on Deverell in an attempt to get some kind of scissors lock on him, was afforded a view of several pairs of legs. Striped trouser legs and thin stick-like affairs in expensive stockings, were mixed with puppy-fattish immature legs, stocking-less. Down you go, striped trousers seemed to be saying, bent forward at knee joints. Applegate grasped firmly a head of hair, edged body towards the blue thing unattainable, no more than two or three hands' distance away. Beyond that little forest of legs, toppling now as if blown over by wind, others could be glimpsed occasionally, black pipe stems and shapeless brown trousers.

What could Hedda be doing with her gun? The black pipe stems disappeared, air blew on his face, agonising pain came to his groin. His grip on Deverell's hair was, it seemed automatically, released.

Bogue's voice said: "All right. Joke over." The current of air on his face was cut off. He moved, and the pain in his groin increased so that he gasped. A pair of brown suède shoes with well-creased trousers above them was beside him, a new entrant on the scene. One of the shoes moved in his direction and he felt a prod, hardly a kick yet not gentle. He sat up, feeling slightly sick.

The room was as crowded as one in a Marx Brothers film. Maureen Gardner wept face down into the sofa, her skirt up to reveal an expanse of fat thigh. Jenks stood by her side looking smug. Eileen Delaney was looking with a glass at a scratch on her cheek. Craigen and Arthur, a pair of Marxian gangsters, gazed at the scene in astonishment from the staircase. Deverell was combing his hair. Mallory-Eckberger, wearing a suit of more conservative style than the black and white check, but still adorned with the pearl stickpin and cuff links, looked down on him from what seemed to be an immense distance. And Hedda, self-designed as the authoress of salvation? Hers, surely, was the most Marxian spot in the whole tableau. Hedda lay face down on the floor, looking gloomily at him. Bogue, with an irresistibly mock-modest air, stood with one foot on her buttocks, like a tiger-killer beside his prize. In spite of the pain he felt, Applegate began to laugh. He recognised, in this ability of Bogue's to turn almost anything to comedy, one facet of his charm.

"Hallo, Max," Bogue said now, with a chuckle. "The old man's out of condition, but still able to practise judo on little girls."

"Some kind of party?" Eckberger looked round, frowning.

"It's over. They're going upstairs."

Maureen Gardner raised a dirty tear-stained face. "Father," she said unemotionally.

"My dear Maureen, I'm not your – "

"Not you. Him." She pointed at Eckberger. "You're Roger Gardner. I'd know your profile anywhere."

"Thank you," Eckberger said. The profile, Applegate saw now, was a kind of wreck of the one Maureen had shown him in the photograph.

Bogue laughed. "A case of mistaken identity. When did you last see your father, Maureen?"

"I'm not mistaken. I *know*."

"What's the use, Johnny, she does know. I knew it was stupid to come back here." Eckberger stood looking at Maureen, then walked over and patted her head.

"You never wrote to me, I didn't know whether you were alive or dead."

"There were difficulties." Eckberger continued to pat her head.

"I used to think that one day you'd send for me, if you were alive. You never did. Now you've come, will you take me away with you?"

"To Brazil?"

"Wherever you live."

"Perhaps. I'll have to talk to Johnny about it. And I'll have to get used to the idea of a daughter." Eckberger smiled down at her, a smile of such vulpine falsity that Applegate almost shuddered to see it. "Will you go upstairs now. I've got to talk to Johnny."

"Shall I see you again soon?"

"I promise that," Eckberger said, with another smile of the same kind.

"First floor. Barney and Arthur, you look after them," Bogue said briskly. Applegate and Hedda scrambled to their feet. "We shall have to decide what to do with you. About that I've got my own ideas. But I have colleagues, and they'll have to be consulted."

"What ideas?"

"You're looking run down. A sea voyage would be good for your health. Hedda could learn the elements of judo. Maureen could be reunited with her loving father. We shall see."

Chapter Thirty

The spiral staircase had only an elementary handrail. With Barney in front of them, Arthur behind, they went into the first-floor room, which in size was almost a replica of that below. Cards lay face upwards on a table covered with a dirty cloth. There were crumbs on the floor, an untidy bed in a corner. Barney stood by the door and waved a hand.

"Make yourselves at home. Not very posh, but it's the best we can do." He dusted a kitchen chair with his handkerchief.

Hedda and Maureen sat on the chairs pulled up at the table, Applegate on the bed.

"Got a great sense of humour Johnny has," Barney continued. "All that stuff about a sea voyage."

"You mean we're not going on one?" Applegate asked.

"Sure you are. Question is, will you get to the other end of it? Dangerous things, boats. Then we get on a plane, and of course you never know what may happen in a plane."

"Where do we get on the plane? France, Africa?"

"That would be telling." Barney gave Applegate a glance heavy with suspicion.

"Smoke, Barney?" Hedda took a cigarette from a pack and threw it to the big man, who struck a match on his heel. "Junior's too young to smoke. I'll tell you something. You want to ask how many seats there are on that plane."

Barney's brow was furrowed. "Don't get what you mean."

"Count us out. There's still a lot of you left. Johnny, for one. Then Max, or whatever you call him. Then Henry, Eileen, you and junior here. That makes six. What sort of plane is it he's got?"

"What's it to you?"

"From the conversation downstairs it might be a four-seater."

"What conversation?" the boy asked. He stood by the door playing with his knife.

"They were agreeing who they should fix for Montague getting killed. They settled on you."

Barney turned his bull head from one to the other of them. The boy stopped playing with his knife. "Henry would never shop me."

"Henry loves you like a son. But then he loved Montague like a brother. Remember what happened to him? Henry cried into his handkerchief about you, but he said, yes."

The boy said something. It was not clear whether it was meant to apply to Jenks or to Hedda or to life in general.

"Honestly now, do you think they're going to let you trail along with them all the way? You know yourself you talk too much, Barney. Suppose you got talking out there? They'll ditch you both somewhere on the route."

Barney swallowed and said nothing. Hedda continued. "Why don't you go down now and ask Henry what he had in mind for Arthur?"

Head thrust forward and shoulders down, Barney looked round him, bullishly bewildered. He roared with anger, shook his head, and then bewilderment found relief in action. A great hand swung up and struck Hedda across the face so hard that she was almost knocked from her chair. A cry came into Applegate's throat, he was on his feet, he had hold of Barney's trunk-like arms, he was trying desperately to establish some kind of grip that would move this man mountain, he was being lifted bodily and shaken, not gently.

But there was something else happening. In the moment when he was moved, as though by a suddenly released spring, into that hopeless assault on Barney, he had seen something in the passage outside the door against which Arthur leaned. What was that something? Darkness where light should be, a shadow falling on the stairway from above when, surely, there was nobody upstairs. Then, as he was thrown violently on to the bed, he was aware that something had happened in the doorway. Arthur was being pushed forward into the room and a rough, warm, countryman's kind of voice was saying: "At it again, Barney. Pity you can't find someone your own size, but then there aren't many big enough, are there?"

Shalson. Barney turned round. Arthur turned too, turned and ducked and raised his knife all in one movement. Applegate could never be quite sure what happened afterwards, it was all so quick. Arthur closed with Shalson, the knife's glint bright in his hand. Then he seemed to be spinning round, there was a sharp *crack*, and he dropped to the floor. Shalson, in the pepper and salt suit he had worn in the train, stood smiling at them. He smiled, but one hand was in his pocket, and in his manner there was nothing suggesting amusement.

On the floor Arthur did not move.

"You've killed 'im," Barney Craigen said, in shocked disbelief.

"It's called self-defence. You all saw the knife."

"But how did you – ?" Applegate found the question hard to frame.

"If you choose the right place on a man's neck and hit it, he falls down and doesn't get up again. And this wasn't even a man, just a gutter rat. Now, Barney, I know you can't shoot, but at this distance – just feel him, will you?"

Applegate patted Barney in the right places. He had no revolver.

"Relying on your two fists and your native wit, Barney," Shalson said. "They never were enough."

" 'Ow did you get in?" Barney's aitches suffered under the stress of emotion.

"I climbed up to the second floor. It wasn't very difficult. I did much harder things in the war."

"Do you really mean he's dead?" Hedda was staring at Arthur.

"His neck's broken." Applegate, too, looked down at the body on the floor, while a line from an epitaph, *Who was alive and is dead*, moved in his mind. Death can be violent yet casual, the affair of a moment merely. Arthur now would have no more need of his shabby-smart suit, the bright knife he had used as protection against the world would gather rust, the few small thoughts in his head had stopped. *Who was alive and is dead.* Applegate looked at the thing on the floor, and thought about his father and mother.

"They're all downstairs, I suppose," Shalson asked. "And they put these watchdogs in charge of you. Don't shout, Barney. You've stayed alive a long while for a stupid man, and if you're lucky you might live a few years longer yet. Tell me what's been happening."

They told him. "So you don't even know what the stuff is," Shalson said. "You'll soon learn. Which of them have got guns?"

"Deverell, Jenks, Eckberger perhaps. And I suppose Bogue took yours," he said to Hedda. She nodded.

"Four. Now, Barney, you go downstairs. When you're two from the bottom call out that the girl is giving trouble. I'll be right behind you."

Barney went out of the room, clumped heavily downstairs. The rest of them moved in Shalson's wake. They heard Barney call out hoarsely: "That girl's giving trouble. We want a bit of help."

A chair shifted in the room below, Bogue's face looked up at them. Dextrously Shalson pushed Barney to one side so that he was covering both of them. Slowly, saying nothing, they moved into the downstairs room as in a kind of ritual dance. At the doorway Shalson spoke. "If you don't want Johnny to get it, throw your guns into the middle of the room. Applegate, Hedda, come out and make sure they throw them down."

"Be careful," Hedda said. "He practises judo."

"You don't have to tell me. Johnny and I know all each other's little tricks."

The revolvers were thrown to the floor. Applegate had not expected that they would be, but there was something in Shalson's manner that compelled belief in his seriousness. There were four of them, including the one Bogue had taken from Hedda. Applegate took two, and gave Hedda's gun back to her. Shalson held the fourth loosely in his left hand.

"Get on the other side of the room, all of you. Standing up."

Now they were all over there, the little lobby leading to the front door behind them. Bogue said composedly: "This is ridiculous, Skid. You're letting your taste for melodrama run away with you. You've got the stuff, that's right, isn't it? All right, then, let's talk about it."

"First of all, I want to tell a little story, for the benefit of my friends over here, who aren't sure what's going on."

"Where's Arthur?" Jenks asked in a high voice.

"Having a rest."

Barney Craigen said: "A good long rest. You won't see your boy again. That bastard's killed him."

Jenks came at Shalson, hands outstretched like claws, screaming. Shalson stepped away and it was Applegate who hit Jenks, and felt the tall man's nails rake his cheek. Jenks went down, but he was up again in a moment. This time

Applegate tapped him gently on the head with the gun-butt. Jenks fell down and lay moaning.

"So much for love," Shalson said. "Now the little story. Have you heard of the wartime currency forgeries put out by the Germans? They were an attempt, and in their limited way a successful one, to undermine Britain's economic position. The forgeries were organised by the German Government, they were carried out in a special section of Oranienburg concentration camp and most of the workers employed on the forgeries were camp inmates with technical skills, who never came out to tell their stories. Secrecy was well preserved, as well as it can be where a number of people are involved.

"The distribution also was ingenious. The chief distributors were two or three respectable German bankers – respectable as the Nazis counted respectability. They opened accounts with banks in neutral countries under the pretext that they had English money which they wanted to get out of Germany. Neutral banks were sympathetic, understanding. Nobody knows how much forged money passed into circulation and was accepted by the Bank of England. Nobody knows how many million pounds the scheme cost this country before the forgeries were detected. Nobody but the Bank of England, and they will never tell. The Germans realised that the forgeries were bound to be discovered eventually, and they decided to step up the pace of Operation Bernhard, as it was called. They began to employ less respectable agents. Their point of view was a peculiar one. They were not worried so much about a return on their money. Their chief concern was simply to inflate the amount of currency in circulation."

"Bogue was one of the agents," Applegate said.

"Yes. You know he was discovered to be a double agent, and as such expendable. It wasn't known at the time, but was discovered later, that Bogue was to be the chief distributor of forged notes in England. Parcels containing a million pounds in these notes had been smuggled through to him. He was to use the money principally for paying various German agents in England."

The pieces fell into place, Applegate thought. *I shall be the richest man in the world.* And in the meantime he was uncommonly short of money, because of the cutting down of his drug supplies.

"This fact was not known to the agent named Shalson who travelled in the plane with Bogue, to make quite sure that the plan for expending him was carried through." Shalson's face was no longer ruddy, but almost pale, deeply thoughtful. "Bogue had checked his parachute at the last minute and changed it, as you know. He realised what was intended for him, and from the moment that the plane left the ground he set himself to corrupt Shalson. He was doing it to preserve his own life, of course, but I think there was something beyond that. He positively enjoyed corruption, Bogue. For a long time he wasn't successful, not until he said he had all the money in the world and there was enough for both of them to share.

"Now why should that have appealed to Shalson? He was a Jew, his parents had died indirectly through Bogue, he had every reason to hate Bogue. That was partly why he had been picked for the job. Yet, when Bogue began to talk about money – not little sums of money, not a mere bribe, but money in enormous amounts, hundreds of thousands of pounds – Shalson was gripped. He listened. He knew everything bad about Bogue, yet he listened. I wonder why? Some basic sense of insecurity, awareness that when the war was over he would be a displaced person in society – "

"And Shalson was a Jew," Eckberger said. "Keen on the money-bags."

"I don't forget that." Shalson's brown eyes looked at Eckberger. "Bogue was clever in making just that approach.

He was always clever. Shalson listened to him, asked for details. Bogue told him about the million pounds that had come over. The money was useless to Bogue now, for he could never return to England. But Shalson could go back. Shalson could get the money. On Shalson's next trip out of England he would join Bogue. They would disappear into some country where war was still a distant echo – one of the South American republics say – and they would settle there for the rest of their lives. The way Bogue put it he was trusting Shalson, because Shalson would know where the money was."

"Skid, there's no point in going into this." In Bogue's voice there was almost a note of desperation. "It's ancient history."

"Ancient history interests me." It must have been an extraordinary scene, Applegate thought. The little toy moving through the air, piloted by men unaware of their doom, and shut away from their hearing a man talking, talking for his life, using his quarter-truths to convince an enemy who had no reason to trust or to forgive.

"There isn't much more to tell. Shalson listened. There was no excuse for him. He knew all about Bogue, he knew what Bogue was, a cheat and a crook, a man without loyalty of any kind to a person or a country. More than that, a man who found loyalty of any sort ridiculous. Shalson knew all that and he still listened. There is no excuse for him."

"And so?" That was Hedda, looking reflectively at Shalson.

"And so Shalson kept his revolver on his knee. Couldn't make up his mind. Waited for his mind to be made up for him, I suppose you could say. When the engine caught fire, Bogue had the hatch open in a minute. 'Come on, Skid, let's jump,' he said. 'There's a fortune down below.' He laughed. And while the revolver was still on Shalson's knee, while Shalson was still making up his mind, he jumped. Shalson jumped after him. Flanner and Grimes jumped too, but they weren't as clever as Bogue. Their parachutes didn't open."

There was sweat on Bogue's face. Shalson's gentle voice went on. "They landed in open country. Bogue's leg seemed to have been injured, he couldn't stand without help. Shalson got him up, and made the mistake of turning his back. You should never turn your back on anybody, certainly not on Johnny Bogue. Shalson was picked up twenty-four hours later. He had severe concussion from head injuries."

Bogue wiped his forehead with a handkerchief. "I never meant to kill you, Skid."

"You didn't. But I still have headaches sometimes."

"The paper chase," Applegate said. Suddenly he was unable to contain his laughter. "All of you chasing after forgeries. Murder done for them. The paper chase. Oh, dear." He rocked backwards and forwards. They stared at him uncomprehendingly.

"The plane," Hedda said. "There should have been a third body."

"Bogue had made provision for that as well as he could. The plane burned to a skeleton. In it were found some things of Bogue's, the metal buckle of a belt he wore, some fragments of a briefcase and of shoes."

"No body."

"A body could not be provided. For this Bogue relied on Shalson, who had to explain his own conduct in some way. Remember this was Portugal, wartime, there were no facilities for official inspection of the plane. Shalson said he shot Bogue through the head, and the report was never queried."

"Tarboe accepted it?"

"Tarboe accepted it. But the concussion had a lasting effect on Shalson. His powers of concentration became poor. He was retired from the service. Of course Bogue had never told him where the money was hidden. He was going to do that after they dropped."

"I don't see the point of all this," Eckberger said. "You've got the money, why don't we talk about that?"

Applegate pointed at Eckberger. "I'm not sure that I understand even now. What's he got to do with it?"

"The Bank of England are wise to these forgeries now," Shalson said. "It would be no use simply spreading them around in this country, you see that."

"Yes."

"So they were useless to Bogue until he met Max in South America, and Max was able to obtain permission for opening – what's it called?"

"The Banco Grando Metropolitano di Brasil."

"Eckberger must have some pretty influential friends in South America," Applegate said.

"Or I have, don't forget that possibility." Bogue seemed more at his ease now.

"Or you have," Shalson agreed. "Can't you guess what the bank's capital will be? A million pounds in forged currency notes."

"But when those notes get back here they'll be recognised as forgeries," Applegate said.

"Yes. The game wouldn't last long. How long do you reckon?" he asked Bogue politely.

"About six months. But three will be enough."

"Yes. Within three months, you see, they'll have converted their clients' stocks and property into perfectly good currency. Then one night the bank will close its doors, the bank's clients will find themselves a good deal poorer, and the trickle of forgeries back to the Bank of England will become a flood. By that time Messrs. Bogue and Eckberger will be somewhere else."

"And so will Skid Shalson," Bogue said.

Shalson's look was direct and guileless. "Not Skid Shalson."

"Then what do you want?"

"I've come here to do what I should have done a long time ago. I'm going to kill you, Johnny."

Bogue began to talk quickly, his eyes flickering from one to the other of them, and Applegate understood what Shalson had said about Bogue's talk. *You listened to him with two parts of yourself. One part knew that he was simply a liar and a cheat. The other part just heard and believed.* Was Shalson, part of him, hearing and believing now? Applegate hoped not, but watching the flickering eyes and the gesturing hands, listening to the rich pleading voice, he could not be sure.

"What is it you want, Skid? You want to shoot me, you want to get your own back because I played a dirty trick years ago. Here I am then, go ahead and shoot. But before you do it, think. Use your brain box. Ask if it's worth while. With what you've got hold of there's enough to make us all rich, without a lot of risk attached to it. Kill me and that's over, you're saying goodbye to a fortune. You think because I dealt them from the bottom last time I'll do it again. But ask yourself, Skid, what chance had I got? What would you have done in a plane with someone who'd been told not to let you out of it alive?"

Shalson listened to him attentively, the revolver in his right hand pointed somewhere in the region of Bogue's stomach.

Suddenly Bogue grinned, the naughty boy's grin that Applegate had seen before. "Besides, Skid, this time you've really got us by the short hairs. Last time you only had a promise. This time you've got the stuff."

"You're mistaken, Johnny," Shalson said.

"What do you mean?"

"I haven't got it."

Bogue was staring hard at Shalson. "I do believe you're telling the truth, Skid. But you know where it is."

"I haven't any idea. And I don't care. I told you what I came here for. I came to kill you, Johnny."

"In that case... " Eckberger said, and his hand dropped to his side. Applegate remembered that Eckberger hadn't been searched. He saw Maureen rush across to her father, shrieking: "No, no." He saw Bogue fling himself sideways, Deverell dive to the floor, Shalson's face change expression. All this was as though wax figures had suddenly become animated. But had he really seen all this, or was it something he imagined afterwards? He could never be sure, he was not sure of anything except that the whole room had exploded into an inferno of noise and blood.

The noise. A blaze of indistinguishable voices, shrieking, crying, groaning. *No, no...oh, don't do it.... I'm hurt... Johnny, I'm trying to...out – out, let me out...* All this was confused, was the background only to more powerful noises. The breaking of glass, for instance, a tinkle and then another tinkle. Enjoyable rather, like a small boy hitting a cricket ball through a window. But that, of course, was only a background sound too. In the foreground were the bangs, the ear-cracking bangs and the good firework smell that went with them, the bangs that came from Eckberger and from somewhere behind him that must be Shalson and Hedda perhaps, and a gun had been snatched from his own hand, there was something hot in his hand, and a tremendous *crack* as it seemed from beneath him.

There were too many people in the room and now some of them were lying down.

The windows must be open. Somebody had opened the windows and the curtains were flapping.

Within the noise the smoke, the blue firework smoke that rose confusingly into nostrils.

A door opening, a door banging.

And then the blood, the blood from nowhere. A river of blood coming from the other side of the room, from the door. Blood that he slipped in, stupidly looked down at, there by his own feet. Blood, a red much darker than he had imagined, dark certainly rather than bright. Suddenly he was very close to this blood, it was necessary to look at it more nearly, people were shouting something. *Oh, oh,* somebody kept repeating, *Oh, oh,* and that was his own voice. Then something seemed to split inside his head, the blood was very near now, he was conscious of the sweet smell of it mixed with all the other smells. And that was all.

Chapter Thirty-one

He blinked, and blinked again, at an unknown room, white walls, white ceiling, all anonymous. Then he looked at the impedimenta by his bedside, spittoon, orange juice, flowers, and knew himself in hospital. He moved and pain went through him. His body seemed tied to the bed.

It seemed only a moment later, but must, in fact, have been hours, or even days, when he looked at the world again and saw something incredible. He blinked, but it did not go away. Tarboe sat in a chair by the bed, looking with one eye at him, with the other at the wall. "Feeling better?" he asked.

"I suppose so." Applegate lifted his head from the pillow in an effort at comprehension. "Oh."

"Shouldn't do that," Tarboe said. "You stopped two of Eckberger's bullets, and one was in the shoulder, not too far from the heart. Take it easy."

"Eckberger." Recollection came back. "What happened to Eckberger?"

"Dead. Shalson shot him. Shalson's dead too. Bogue had another gun you were too careless to take off him. Pretty fair holocaust, as a matter of fact. When our chaps got in the whole place was what you might call running with blood. Bit uncertain what actually did happen, but I think you can say that little girl Maureen saved your life. She jumped at Eckberger when he was going to shoot."

"Is she – "

"She's all right, got a slight flesh wound. Gone off to some crackpot place called Shovels End."

"The Anarchist Country Community." He laughed, and stopped when it hurt. "I hope she'll be happy."

"Seemed to be. Jenks will stand trial, didn't get a scratch on him. We got Barney and Delaney too, though she was shot through the head, doubtful whether she'll live." Tarboe coughed. "We're not worrying too much about who fired all the shots, putting any hits down to Shalson. After all, Shalson's dead."

"And – "

"Bogue, of course you want to know about Bogue. He shot Shalson. Tell you something funny about Bogue, he might have got away. Doubtful, but he just had the chance, he'd got to the door. Know why he didn't? Turned back for that son of his who'd got shot in the leg, tried to get him out too."

"Who shot Deverell – Geoffrey?"

Tarboe's wandering eye glanced briefly at the ceiling, then down again. "You."

"And Bogue couldn't get him out."

"No, he waited that extra minute too long, till my men had organised outside. Saw it was no use, dragged his son upstairs and they fought it out up the spiral staircase."

"What happened?"

"Both killed," Tarboe said briefly. "Bogue tried to shield the boy. Hadn't a chance."

"What about" – he found it hard to utter the name – "Hedda?"

"Miss Pont." Tarboe's wooden features relaxed into something approaching a smile. "Not a mark on her. Take more than a little shooting match to hurt that girl."

Applegate sighed, and for the first time fully realised the implications of Tarboe's presence. "But you – you knew Bogue was alive all the time."

"Yes. We never quite accepted Shalson's story, though he didn't know that. No body, you know, there should have been a body. Never traced him in South America, didn't try very hard. But when all that activity started up round Bramley we guessed something was up, and began to take an interest. Can't let a million pounds' worth of forged notes get into circulation, wouldn't do. The local Inspector chap, Murray, was working with us. He tried to warn you off, we all tried to warn you off."

"The money." Applegate suddenly remembered. "Where was it?"

Now, there could be no doubt of it, something like a human smile melted that Red Indian impassiveness.

"It was down in the cellar. If you'd merely turned that ring instead of pulling it you'd have seen the ring hid the keyhole of a safe. The money was there for years. Then somebody moved it from that safe."

"Who?"

"Somebody who got a key to the safe when she bought the house. Somebody who wanted a hiding place for certain essential bottles. Don't you remember it was bottles that Barney and Craigen found in the safe?"

"Janine," Applegate gasped. "But what did she do with the money?"

"She thought she'd found a fortune. That's why she got so excited. She put it in the place where she'd kept her bottles. In the airing cupboard. Handed it over now of course." He looked at his watch. "I must go. Just thought I'd pass the time of day. Stick to writing detective stories in future. Goodbye."

The door had hardly closed after him when Applegate heard the voice. It was singing:

"A park at night reveals a sight most shocking,
A young man's hand upon a young girl's stocking."

The door opened. She came in. She was wearing the black jumper and red jeans that she had on when he first saw her standing by the car. Applegate was conscious of impending doom. Freedom, freedom, he thought, freedom farewell. He thought for a moment of her thick legs, then put them out of mind with the reflection that she almost always wore jeans.

"You're better," she said. "They say you'll be up tomorrow and out in a week."

"Good." They were silent. "Where are Jeremy and Janine?"

She laughed. "Didn't Tarboe tell you? They've gone with Maureen to join the Anarchist Country Community. Janine was heartbroken when she had to give up her million pounds, but I believe she's going to get some kind of small official reward. They were both delighted when Jeremy was appointed as some kind of lecturer at the Community. It was Maureen's suggestion. Janine seems quite to have given up drinking, for the moment at least. They sent their love to you."

"Good."

They were silent again. "I've thought over that proposition you made me." She approached the bed.

"What proposition?"

"Marriage. I've decided to accept." Now she was very close to him. Her lips were slightly parted, her eyes shone.

"Be careful of my shoulder," Applegate said. "I am far from well."

"I shall cure you." The lips pressed on his did seem to have some reviving effect.

"If you could move just a little more off my shoulder," he suggested.

"I've thought of a ready-made plot for your next book," she went on briskly. "A young man – as it might be you – is in some romantic place in the Far East as it might be Smyrna – "

232

"I've never been farther than the Mediterranean."

"We can go on our honeymoon. In a hotel there he meets a beautiful young woman whose husband has just disappeared. She's stranded, you see, in the hotel. And then the chief of police, a fierce figure but romantic, becomes involved – "

"Haven't I read something like this before?"

"Nonsense," she said decisively. Applegate abandoned his objections. Yes, yes, yes, he said, not listening, but simply looking at her. He knew that, in any important sense, he would never say no again.

JULIAN SYMONS

THE BROKEN PENNY

An Eastern-bloc country, shaped like a broken penny, was being torn apart by warring resistance movements. Only one man could unite the hostile factions – Professor Jacob Arbitzer. Arbitzer, smuggled into the country by Charles Garden during the Second World War, has risen to become president, only to have to be smuggled out again when the communists gained control. Under pressure from the British Government who want him reinstated, Arbitzer agreed to return on one condition – that Charles Garden again escort him. *The Broken Penny* is a thrilling spy adventure brilliantly recreating the chilling conditions of the Cold War.

'Thrills, horrors, tears and irony'
– *Times Literary Supplement*

'The most exciting, astonishing and believable spy thriller to appear in years' – *The New York Times*

Julian Symons

The Colour of Murder

John Wilkins was a gentle, mild-mannered man who lived a simple, predictable life. So when he met a beautiful, irresistible girl his world was turned upside down. Looking at his wife, and thinking of the girl, everything turned red before his eyes – the colour of murder. Later, his mind a blank, his only defence was that he loved his wife far too much to hurt her...

'A book to delight every puzzle-suspense enthusiast'
– *The New York Times*

The End of Solomon Grundy

When a girl turns up dead in a Mayfair Mews, the police want to write it off as just another murdered prostitute, but Superintendent Manners isn't quite so sure. He is convinced that the key to the crime lies in The Dell – an affluent suburban housing estate. And in The Dell lives Solomon Grundy. Could he have killed the girl? So Superintendent Manners thinks.

JULIAN SYMONS

A MAN CALLED JONES

The office party was in full swing so no one heard the shot – fired at close range through the back of Lionel Hargreaves, elder son of the founder of Hargreaves Advertising Agency. The killer left only one clue – a pair of yellow gloves – but it looked almost as if he had wanted them to be found. As Inspector Bland sets out to solve the murder, he encounters a deadly trail of deception, suspense – and two more dead bodies.

THE PLAYERS AND THE GAME

'Count Dracula meets Bonnie Parker. What will they do together? The vampire you'd hate to love, sinister and debonair, sinks those eye teeth into Bonnie's succulent throat.'

Is this the beginning of a sadistic relationship or simply an extract from a psychopath's diary? Either way it marks the beginning of a dangerous game that is destined to end in chilling terror and bloody murder.

'Unusual, ingenious and fascinating as a poisonous snake'
– *Sunday Telegraph*

Julian Symons

The Plot Against Roger Rider

Roger Rider and Geoffrey Paradine had known each other since childhood. Roger was the intelligent, good-looking, successful one and Geoffrey was the one everyone else picked on. When years of suppressed anger, jealousy and frustration finally surfaced, Geoffrey took his revenge by sleeping with Roger's beautiful wife. Was this price enough for all those miserable years of putdowns? When Roger turned up dead the police certainly didn't think so.

'[Symons] is in diabolical top form' – *Washington Post*

OTHER TITLES BY JULIAN SYMONS AVAILABLE DIRECT
FROM HOUSE OF STRATUS

Quantity		£	$(US)	$(CAN)	€
CRIME/SUSPENSE					
	THE 31ST OF FEBRUARY	6.99	11.50	15.99	11.50
	THE BELTING INHERITANCE	6.99	11.50	15.99	11.50
	BLAND BEGINNING	6.99	11.50	15.99	11.50
	THE BROKEN PENNY	6.99	11.50	15.99	11.50
	THE COLOUR OF MURDER	6.99	11.50	15.99	11.50
	THE END OF SOLOMON GRUNDY	6.99	11.50	15.99	11.50
	THE GIGANTIC SHADOW	6.99	11.50	15.99	11.50
	THE IMMATERIAL MURDER CASE	6.99	11.50	15.99	11.50
	THE KILLING OF FRANCIE LAKE	6.99	11.50	15.99	11.50
	A MAN CALLED JONES	6.99	11.50	15.99	11.50
	THE MAN WHO KILLED HIMSELF	6.99	11.50	15.99	11.50
	THE MAN WHO LOST HIS WIFE	6.99	11.50	15.99	11.50
	THE MAN WHOSE DREAMS CAME TRUE	6.99	11.50	15.99	11.50
	THE NARROWING CIRCLE	6.99	11.50	15.99	11.50

ALL HOUSE OF STRATUS BOOKS ARE AVAILABLE FROM GOOD BOOKSHOPS
OR DIRECT FROM THE PUBLISHER:

Internet: www.houseofstratus.com including author interviews, reviews, features.

Email: sales@houseofstratus.com please quote author, title and credit card details.

OTHER TITLES BY JULIAN SYMONS AVAILABLE DIRECT
FROM HOUSE OF STRATUS

Quantity	£	$(US)	$(CAN)	€
THE PLAYERS AND THE GAME	6.99	11.50	15.99	11.50
THE PLOT AGAINST ROGER RIDER	6.99	11.50	15.99	11.50
THE PROGRESS OF A CRIME	6.99	11.50	15.99	11.50
A THREE-PIPE PROBLEM	6.99	11.50	15.99	11.50
HISTORY/CRITICISM				
BULLER'S CAMPAIGN	8.99	14.99	22.50	15.00
THE TELL-TALE HEART: THE LIFE AND WORKS OF EDGAR ALLEN POE	8.99	14.99	22.50	15.00
ENGLAND'S PRIDE	8.99	14.99	22.50	15.00
THE GENERAL STRIKE	8.99	14.99	22.50	15.00
HORATIO BOTTOMLEY	8.99	14.99	22.50	15.00
THE THIRTIES	8.99	14.99	22.50	15.00
THOMAS CARLYLE	8.99	14.99	22.50	15.00

ALL HOUSE OF STRATUS BOOKS ARE AVAILABLE FROM GOOD BOOKSHOPS
OR DIRECT FROM THE PUBLISHER:

Hotline: UK ONLY: **0800 169 1780**, please quote author, title and credit card details.
INTERNATIONAL: **+44 (0) 20 7494 6400**, please quote author, title and credit card details.

Send to: House of Stratus Sales Department
24c Old Burlington Street
London
W1X 1RL
UK

Please allow for postage costs charged per order plus an amount per book as set out in the tables below:

	£(Sterling)	$(US)	$(CAN)	€(Euros)
Cost per order				
UK	1.50	2.25	3.50	2.50
Europe	3.00	4.50	6.75	5.00
North America	3.00	4.50	6.75	5.00
Rest of World	3.00	4.50	6.75	5.00
Additional cost per book				
UK	0.50	0.75	1.15	0.85
Europe	1.00	1.50	2.30	1.70
North America	2.00	3.00	4.60	3.40
Rest of World	2.50	3.75	5.75	4.25

PLEASE SEND CHEQUE, POSTAL ORDER (STERLING ONLY), EUROCHEQUE, OR INTERNATIONAL MONEY ORDER (PLEASE CIRCLE METHOD OF PAYMENT YOU WISH TO USE)
MAKE PAYABLE TO: STRATUS HOLDINGS plc

Cost of book(s):————————— Example: 3 x books at £6.99 each: £20.97

Cost of order:————————— Example: £2.00 (Delivery to UK address)

Additional cost per book:————— Example: 3 x £0.50: £1.50

Order total including postage:———— Example: £24.47

Please tick currency you wish to use and add total amount of order:

☐ £ (Sterling)　☐ $ (US)　☐ $ (CAN)　☐ € (EUROS)

VISA, MASTERCARD, SWITCH, AMEX, SOLO, JCB:

☐☐☐☐☐☐☐☐☐☐☐☐☐☐☐☐☐☐☐☐

Issue number (Switch only):

☐☐☐

Start Date:　　　　　　　**Expiry Date:**

☐☐/☐☐　　　　　　　☐☐/☐☐

Signature: _____

NAME: _____

ADDRESS: _____

_____

POSTCODE: _____

Please allow 28 days for delivery.

Prices subject to change without notice.
Please tick box if you do not wish to receive any additional information. ☐

House of Stratus publishes many other titles in this genre; please check our website (**www.houseofstratus.com**) for more details.